C000233667

PENITENT

Mark Leggatt

PENITENT
Mark Leggatt

© Mark Leggatt 2023

The author asserts the moral right to be identified
as the author of the work in accordance with the
Copyright, Designs and Patents Act, 1988

All characters appearing in this work are fictitious.
Any resemblance to real persons, living or dead,
is purely coincidental.

All rights reserved.

No part of this publication may be reproduced, stored in a retrieval
system or transmitted in any form or by any means, electronic,
mechanical, photocopying, recording or otherwise, without the prior
permission of:
Fledgling Press Ltd, 1 Milton Road West, Edinburgh, EH15 1LA

Published by:
Fledgling Press Ltd,
1 Milton Road West,
Edinburgh,
EH15 1LA

Cover design by Graeme Clarke
www.graemeclarke.com

www.fledglingpress.co.uk

ISBN: 9781912280629
Printed and bound by:

Print-on-Demand-Worldwide, Peterborough

For Claude Renard

Those who were seen dancing were thought to be insane by those who could not hear the music.
—Nietzsche

Chapter I

Friday, 13th of December.

The stone in Edinburgh is never truly warm. The soft
sandstone is dug from the hills around the town,
emerging golden and pink. Even in the height of the
short summer, if you press your fingernails into the
grey, sun-baked stone it will powder, and the damp and
cold of centuries of winters and northern rain will chill
your skin and seep through to your heart. And yet she
reels and dances in her grubby finery, in carved stone
of crowns and spires stretching into the sky above the
monuments of church and state. But you can smell it on
your hands, the reek of filth that once lined her streets
and seeped into the sooty, rain-sodden stone, and hangs
there like a sickness in an old whore.

In the midnight darkness of my room, the blue lights
pulsating three floors below, I had not looked out the
window. But in the morning as I hurried out the door
to the street, the dark smear showed where blood had
soaked into the stone. The DNA of the building had
changed, and the rain would be too late. I ran from the
scene and up the hill towards the Old Town, nauseous at
the thought of all the blood that had leached into the soft
stone of Edinburgh over the centuries.

Once across Princes Street, the freezing wind pushed me up the Mound towards the Old Town, my legs shaking, and I stamped my feet in a rhythm to force an order and establish control. At the High Court on the corner, the Royal Mile ran left and right on the wide spine of rock that stretched behind the Castle, all the way to the Palace at the foot of the Mile. As on every working day, I paused and placed a hand against the stone of the High Court, imagining the beat of the Old Town's black heart, then looked up and around at the high walls and gothic spires that seemed to pierce the low, shifting clouds. The only way for builders to clean Edinburgh stone was to remove a layer. Sometimes they had to go deep to scour out the blackness, from the centuries of smoke and soot suffocating the town under a black pall. Despite their efforts, it looked like the whole town had been wiped by a dirty cloth. Across the road were buildings of medieval stone, some of which remained untouched, and where the thick filth seemed slathered on, smothering the golden stone.

It was 07:30 and the nausea returned. I had stood in this spot every working day for the past twenty-two years, at 08:30. But Lord Campbell had asked me to attend an hour early. This had never happened before. He did not say why, or who else would be there. My vision swam and I flattened my back against the stone for support. There would be a good reason, no doubt. It could be any form of urgent legal investigation or enquiry, although there was nothing in the news, and no rumours in legal circles or on social media. My case files contained only contract disputes. Lord Campbell's chambers were a few hundred yards away down the Mile, and I vowed to slip out and return to touch the stone at 08:30. These are habits that I hold dear and close to my heart. They give me an acute, tactile sense of control and order.

Sometimes, when my anxiety rises screaming from within, I retreat to the very bowels of the chambers, the dank medieval rooms below the basement that are too damp for habitation, and then stand alone in the dark until the fear of drowning in panic dissipates.

Swallowing hard, I pushed myself from the wall and stepped onto the Royal Mile, hurrying past St. Giles, then turned into the narrow entrance of the Advocates Close. It reeked of urine from the previous night's revellers, as it had done for five hundred years when the ancestors of Lord Campbell had first established their legal chambers. On the wall the metal gate to the steps was unlocked and pinned open.

I climbed the short flight of steps to the old wooden door studded with iron and turned the handle. At the end of a low, narrow corridor, Lord Campbell's door stood open. The metal-tipped heels of my brogues clicked against the uneven flagstones. Portraits of lawyers lined the walls, the paint blackened and stained with age, their faces almost indecipherable, but each resembling the other, in a dynasty that stretched to Lord Campbell's door. The doors to the other offices were open, and showed the same low, medieval ceilings, flagstone floors and small, square windows. Computer cables ran up the wall and along the windows, or under ornate Persian rugs, some threadbare near the door. I could hear the crackling of the fire and smell the wood smoke, and strode forward to stand in the doorway.

Lord Campbell sat in his shiny suit, high on a cushion, like a child sitting in his father's chair, leaning over his desk, his head bowed, engrossed in a sheaf of papers. The fire behind him spat sparks up the chimney. I always found him a vacuous poseur, and his position owing to his name, rather than any proficiency in law. He valued my work, although solely for its efficacy. He laughs with the others, treating me as an idiot savant, but that does not concern me. He's just another noise outside my office. I care only for those things that matter. And Lord Campbell, for all his finery and frippery, does not matter. Above the fireplace was a picture of his father, the late Lord Advocate, a great man who had served every Conservative government since the Sixties. I despised them both and the line of swine that preceded them.

His head jerked up. "Ah, Lawless."

My voice was hoarse. "Good morning."

"Come in, Lawless. Please, sit down."

Shoving the door closed, I sat opposite him on an ancient, upright wooden chair that creaked at every joint.

Campbell sat back and placed his hands in his lap. "Firstly, thank you, Lawless, for coming in so early. I know you're a man of habit, and I admire that. But the gravity of this issue requires a different and more confidential approach."

I clasped my hands to stop them shaking as a welcome anger warmed my stomach. If this sleekit gype had called me here for a private chat away from the others, it would not warrant such a self-important, clandestine approach. He simply had to close his bloody door. "If there is any issue with my work, then I see no need for…"

"What? No…" He leaned forward. "Lawless, you

are the most diligent and dedicated lawyer I have ever worked with. Your attention to detail is obsess... No, it's..."

"It is obsessive. It is a gift and a curse. I am well aware of my approach to matters of law."

"Well, it's a blessing to me."

I did not reply. I hoped my indifference would be audible.

"Lawless, we have not always seen eye to eye and there are occasions when I could have been a more considerate and supportive employer. But, you must know, I value your work a great deal more than any other member of these chambers, and that should have been made clear. You plough through the most complex case law faster than any other lawyer in Scotland. It is an extraordinary gift. I fully understand that you like to stay under the radar and not indulge in the usual showbiz antics of our brother lawyers. Others have come and gone over the years, but you are the bedrock of this firm. I see you happy and content in your work. Is that simply my comfortable illusion?"

A wet log hissed on the fire. I am happy and content if I step out of these chambers intact every evening and make it back to the safe harbour of my flat. "No. I'm fine."

"You're a man of strict habits. And in all your time here I've never seen you indulge in office romances or petty political battles, or even tittle tattle. You rise above it all. I have always admired that."

Others would describe me differently. The young lawyers upsetting the line of pencils on my desk to annoy me, and then laughing as I rearranged them with a ruler. They murmur about me being autistic, and their ignorance and insensitivity around such a condition infuriates me. I am nothing of the sort. I simply desire order and I am more than aware of my obsession, and the compulsion. It is who I am.

Campbell sat back in his chair and had to stick his elbows out to reach the armrests. "Hector, you're here because you are the only lawyer I can absolutely trust. You are the only person in whom I can confide with complete candour."

Shifting my weight in my chair, the creaking made me fear it would collapse under me. I had no idea how to reply.

"Are you still involved with King George's School," said Campbell, "our old alma mater?"

"Yes, I taught marksmanship to the Army Cadets last year. We use the Army's firing range at Castlelaw in the Pentland Hills. They now have an Army instructor. I was no longer required." If I had levelled a rifle at him, the muzzle would touch his forehead.

"Those schooldays at the range were always grand fun," said Campbell. "But the army was never for me, so I've no idea why my father sent me to King George's."

The lie stunned me into silence. It was well known that was he expelled from Heriots for some salacious transgression. King George's was usually for sons of the military, a boarder school while officers and NCOs were overseas on service. My father had taught English there, and teachers' children were allocated a place.

"There have been..." Campbell closed his eyes for a moment, "some reports. Very disturbing reports." He stood and looked out the narrow window onto the Royal Mile. He made to push his chair back, but it was too heavy for him to move. "What I'm about to tell you is in the strictest confidence. It is no exaggeration when I say that this is akin to a state secret. And many powerful men would go to any lengths to ensure that it stays a secret." He looked directly at me. "I am not one of those men, Hector. I will not bow down." He lifted his chin. "What is carved in stone above the close we enter every day?"

My eyes were usually squeezed shut against the smell to bother reading it. "*Fiat justitia ruat caelum.*" Let justice be done though the heavens fall. "It originated in the Roman Senate."

Campbell sat down. "I am in possession of a signed statement by a young man. It describes a paedophile ring operating at King George's School. It identifies a man and details his abuse. Another man is yet to be identified."

The blood rushed to my neck and face. For a moment the thought of grabbing him and pushing him face first into the fire flashed through my mind. "Is this why I'm here? You suspect me of…?"

He held up his hands. "Hector, please, I hold your integrity in the highest regard. There is no doubt that if you had any knowledge of these terrible crimes you would have informed myself or the police. That's why you are here. You are the last person on earth to be involved in such horror."

The blood pounded in my ears. A shiver ran through me and my face twitched. "Two men?"

"Yes. Now, you have excellent skills in legal investigation, you know the school and how it operates. You have talked to the boys in the normal course of your association with the Cadets, no?"

"Yes, on occasion, although they have said nothing."

"The abusers operate within a small group of boys. The most vulnerable and those they can threaten and manipulate. They are most likely not in the Cadets. What I want you to do, Hector, is use your skills to compile the evidence against these men."

"My skills?" So, this was it. My skill in building a criminal case. My attention to detail that had made me the enemy of many grandiose defence lawyers. I relaxed in the chair, but it creaked once more and I sat forward. "Does anyone else know of this?"

"No. And we can trust no one. King George's is a cradle of politicians and top brass. If news of an investigation got out, MI5 and Police Scotland would close it down. And possibly close these chambers. And you. So, think carefully. You can walk away and I will accept your word that you will tell no one. If you choose not to help me, then the abuse will continue. This task requires levels of dedication, guile and strength not found in ordinary men. Nevertheless, you have my complete assurance, Hector, that I understand."

We sat in silence. There was no doubt. I lifted my head and sat up straight, then grabbed the edge of chair as it groaned and threatened to collapse. "I'll do it."

Campbell reached over and shook my hand. "Thank you. Thank you, Hector." He lifted a folder on his desk and took out a piece of lined paper. It was torn from a school jotter.

He handed it towards me. A name. The bile rose high in my throat.

"They say a problem shared is a problem halved," said Campbell. "But that is really not the case here." He held out a hand for the paper, folded it once then placed it on the fire.

The childish scrawl in pencil, of the name Mungo Hastings, flared and turned to silver ash.

"Such is the influence and power of Mungo Hastings, that Westminster will not allow any scandal to emerge. It will bring down the Government. And I know from personal experience the lies and duplicity of Mungo Hastings."

I said nothing.

"But then you probably knew such gossip," said Campbell. "When I was young, we were close friends. We were never seen apart. Then he assaulted a boy at school. I got the blame and was expelled. His family were members of the school board. And he went on to be Head Boy. He was a liar and a pervert then, as he is now."

"I had heard… Something of that story."

"I'm sure. But this is not revenge. A man in my position has no need of such tawdry desires."

And Mungo Hastings would wipe the floor with you in court, I thought. A mouse against a lion of the law.

"No, my personal revenge pales into insignificance compared to the abuse of a child. It has taken all these years, but at last the beast has shown his true colours. We cannot let him continue." His hands shook when he took them from the arm of the chair, and he rubbed them against his face, wiping his eyes.

I had never seen him so affected.

Campbell cleared his throat and thrust his chin into the air, his eyes blinking. "At least at King George's I was away from his malign influence. God knows what would have happened to me if I stayed."

He sat in silence. Pressing my palms together, I

slowed my breathing for a moment until I was ready. "You said two men?"

"Yes. One remains unidentified. And I'm sure you can see why we cannot give this case to any of our regular legal investigators. Ex-policemen are part of a network that may be entirely compromised in this instance. I want you to gather the evidence on these two men. Please, do not talk to the boys. We cannot place them in any danger. Gather all the evidence you can. Try and find the second man, but Hector…"

My hands gripped the chair.

"If there is any suspicion of our activities, we will lose everything. And all the evidence will be destroyed." Campbell opened a drawer in his desk and lifted out a large camera and lens. "I dabble in photography in my spare time. This is a 35mm SLR that uses rolls of film. A relic from before the digital age. Do you know how to use it?"

"Yes, sir, I have something similar at home and have used it in the past." The cold nights on the roof of my building, hidden from view, and trying to catch the Northern Lights or the storms coming over from Norway.

"Good." He handed over several rolls of film. "I have a darkroom at home. When a roll is complete, deliver it here at this time."

"I'm sure I can…"

"I will hide the rolls and only develop them when we are ready to go public. It's easier to hide rolls of film than stacks of photographs."

"But a digital camera and memory card will be safer."

"No, we must keep everything offline. Analogue and old school. Do not store any evidence in electronic form, it would be vulnerable to being hacked, stolen or destroyed. We must not underestimate the abilities of the Security Services."

I shoved the rolls of film in the pockets of my jacket. "Understood."

"You have little time to prepare, I'm afraid, although I know you will do what you can." He turned to where the paper that had held the name was a thin film of ash. "Hastings returns to Edinburgh late tonight."

The thoughts raced in my head, but none that made sense. I needed order. I needed away from here.

"Now, I'm giving you two weeks' holiday. Your work will be delegated to others with an explanation that you have a medical condition that requires rest and that you are not to be contacted."

"But…"

"Don't worry, you have far more important things to deal with. Go home and prepare for your investigations and remember, nothing digital or online. If you have to contact me, then we shall meet here, at this time. Any questions?"

"You said you had a statement from a young man, detailing the abuse. Would that not be sufficient testimony? Should we not search for corroboration as a priority?"

Campbell face tightened and he sat back in his chair. "You would have found out in your investigations, so it makes sense to tell you." He half-turned towards the window. "A young man came to me last week. An ex-pupil of King George's. His behaviour at the school had become so disturbed that he was expelled three months ago. His father is overseas on operation. Social services soon lost track of the boy. He refused any help and took

17

to the streets. His life descended into the gutter, into drugs and prostitution. It was he who told me of the abuse by Hastings. He was terrified." Campbell's voice shook. "But when I heard his story, I promised him I would protect him, and sat with him as he wrote his statement. The page was wet with his tears. The next day he was found dead. By his own hand." Campbell looked down at the desk. "His name was Alex Gillan." He pushed himself off the chair. "You must go. Others will arrive soon."

I stood and turned towards the door.

"Though the heavens fall, Hector."

Chapter II

I know who I am. My shoulder brushed the wall as I weaved down the corridor towards Advocates Close. *I know why he chose me.* At the end of the corridor is a mirror for those adjusting their wigs and robes before going to court. *There are no mirrors in my house. I know what I look like.*

The bitter wind had picked up and funnelled down the narrow entrance to the close, cleansing the stink. To the left lay the steep steps descending towards Cockburn Street and then out to Waverley station, but I had to touch the High Court stone once more.

The wind lessened once past the corner of the High Court and I stood with my back to the wall, one hand flat against the cold stone and the other pretending to check my phone. It took a few moments to get it out of my pocket, my freezing fingers slipping on the plastic. Staring at the blank screen, a faint sense of order tingled through my hand pressed against the stone. This time, the black heart would beat for me.

Campbell might protest that his actions were not born out of petty revenge, and I had no doubt that any decent man would hold the justice of the children above all, but he would not deny himself that pleasure when the time came. He would dance alone in his chambers, in a childish jig of retribution.

I know why he chose me. I am no fool. I am deniable. If MI5 found me then Campbell could deny everything and save his skin, and his chambers. And if it came to it, he would. His new found love for my work didn't fool me. But he trusted me, the only one he could tell. The only one in that office with a shred of dignity or common decency. And they would not look away as I was torn apart.

My legs weakened and I knelt to stop myself from falling and placed a hand on my shoelaces, keeping my head low. I had to establish order. My anger rose at this public display of weakness, at having been put in this position and my blood coursed and the skin on my neck warmed, despite the chill. I tested the strength in my legs then stood, my hand on the stone one last time and turned away, down towards the Mound and Princes Street.

Below me, from the top of the Mound, lay the roofs of the New Town and I wanted to be home. The panic started in my chest and surged through me and tears welled up in my eyes, and I was almost overcome with a desire to simply stop and lie down in the street. In front was a bench beside a bus stop. No, people would pass on the way to the office. Across the road an alley led up to the Writer's Museum, and in the corner to the left, a heavy wooden table sat in the courtyard of a café. I stumbled across the road and sat on the bench, my collar zipped up until it was under my nose.

My legs were clamped together, arms folded tight across my chest, my torso rocking back and forth. There's something different with me. What others would call wrong. But it's not wrong to me, it is my suit of armour. It gives me power and control and makes me happy. From my pocket I took out five one pound coins, counting them and passing them from one hand to the other and spoke out loud, my voice masked by the wind whipping around my face and hair. *One, two, three, four, five.*

My colleagues laugh and mock me behind my back, but I do not care. I do not care for their opinions. They are nothing to me. I treat them with kindness and respect even when it is often undeserved, because it pleases me, and because it is the right thing to do. And my indifference is my retaliation. Many can stand insults, few can stomach being ignored.

One, two, three, four, five. My rules and habits have always held me together. A warm calm returned to my chest as my grip slackened to hold the coins in my palm.

A picture of the name on the schoolbook paper was fixed in my mind. Mungo Hastings. Secretary of State for Scotland, and a Westminster cabinet minister. My head snapped back and I squeezed the coins tight and slowly passed them from one hand to the other until the tremors stopped. I had attended the trial of a man accused of child abuse. Mungo Hastings had given his personal witness and assurance under oath that the accused was with him and nowhere near the orphanage where the abuse had taken place. The case fell apart. The two victims took their own lives. And the accused man that walked free was now the Prime Minister.

It didn't take a lawyer to work out what would happen when Mungo Hastings was found guilty.

Hastings would face me in the dock, listening to

my evidence and to the words that would bring down a Prime Minister and a government.

Leaning over, I placed my forehead onto my cold fists and thought of the boys laying on the ground and pointing their rifles down the range. Had any of them been abused? Their faces appeared, looking back at me, but they did not talk or smile. They had no voice. They could not stand up in court. They would be torn to shreds. As would their lives.

Even if they came for me, it must be done. The name of Hector Lawless would be on the lips of every news organisation across the globe. My life would be picked apart on news shows and social media. And a few hundred yards behind me, my papers and my evidence would be recorded and stored in the annals of Scottish history, in the vaults of the National Library of Scotland.

Looking north, the clouds seemed to reach down to touch the skyline of the New Town as if to smother the truth, but everyone would know the name of Hector Lawless. The boys would have a voice through me. And the thought of what came after and the hounds of the press made my head twist hard to the side. Although for once, it did not seem to matter. It truly did not seem to matter. I stood and leaned on the table and found my strength. I held on tight to the coins for a moment then placed them back in my pocket, took a few deep breaths of the freezing air and stepped down onto the Mound towards Princes Street.

There would be no return to this life once the truth was told. I would disappear. Sell the flat and take off somewhere warm, somewhere quiet, where no one could find me. This dream that often came to me in the night. Now, the idea made me smile. Because my work would be done. There could be no greater work than this. A career of contract disputes and defending wealthy capitalist criminals would be forgotten, as all the ghosts of the men and women who had sat at my desk for five hundred years before me were forgotten. The boys would be believed and helped, and those that followed would be saved. I would save them.

Taking longer strides, I pulled down the zip of my jacket and let the wind blow around my neck and face. The cold gave me a power. Campbell could not trust any other legal investigator, or those retired policemen playing at being private eyes. They could not do what needed to be done. They have their masters. They will always have masters. Campbell had asked me to simply gather evidence. But he knew that if Hector Lawless gathered evidence it would be detailed and comprehensive. I am, after all, a details man. He knows the depth of my planning, my passion for the finer points of law that infuriates those around me. It would be more than a few photos. He was expecting a report that would nail a defence lawyer to the deck before he even opened his mouth. Picking up speed, I let my arms swing at my sides, feeling the coins jangle in my pocket as I turned onto Princes Street. Campbell was right, none of this evidence could be kept online. Any suspicion of an investigation and they would close ranks and MI5 would destroy any evidence. The entire combined forces of the establishment would rise against me.

I turned towards George Street, striding to the top of the hill, my jacket open and the gusting wind spurred me on. Across the River Forth the hills of the Kingdom of Fife were still in darkness under coal-black clouds.

The wind turned and came from behind, pushing me

down the hill. Campbell said he wanted everything on film. But if Campbell's office or home were raided then everything would be gone. And all my evidence.

The entrance to my street was crowded with parked cars and lined on both sides with Georgian terraced houses, four storeys high. It always reminded me of Downing Street in its simplicity, which hid grand Georgian ballrooms and light-filled drawing rooms, even though most of these mansions had been divided up into flats. My own flat was on the top floor. If they came for me, there was no escape other than over the rooftops, the secret playground of my youth.

At the corner of the building was a gap in the terrace, where a cobbled lane led through an arch to a row of mews cottages behind the building, used as garages. The lane under the arch was dark and damp, but I was nearly home, and soon emerged into a courtyard. The rear of the terraced houses lacked the style and finely worked sandstone of the front and were covered in cast-iron pipes and heating vents. My garage door opened into semi-darkness, then locked behind me. Above the workbench was pinned a Polaroid of my father and me, bent over the engine bay of a Morris Minor. I was wearing my King George's school kilt. Anger made my head fly back and my shoulders twist around, one leg giving way, but I held on to the workbench and slowly forced myself down until the scent of old oil in the wood, that had fallen from my father's hand, calmed and strengthened me.

Campbell might prosecute the case and demand the full penalty of the law, but while the evidence was gathered, I would be outside their world, which made me almost laugh out loud.

Outlaw.

If they came for me, I would lose everything. *Both preparations and sacrifices must be made.*

Chapter III

The door closed behind me. At the end of the short passage lay the square hall at the centre of my flat, and where my bedroom door lay open. My bed was unmade. A shock stabbed through me, thinking I had disturbed a burglar, then realising the covers lay where I had thrown them back early in the morning. I strode down the hall and made a vow that this would never happen again. From now on, whatever happened, order and routine would be paramount, for there was no moment in my life where it had been more important. This is what happened when my daily habits were disturbed. It was unacceptable.

Pulling the bed clothes tight around the edge of the mattress, I leaned over and picked up her pillow, which lay untouched next to mine.

I held her pillow in my hands. It would be twenty years this summer. She had left early in the morning before I woke. She had loved me. She had told me so the night before, in my arms. In the morning, all that was left was the depression in the pillow where her head had been. It was silly and sentimental to keep it all these years, but it's all I had of her. It is truly all I had. For she had come to say goodbye.

By the time the winter sun shone through my

bedroom window and woken me, she would have been on a train with her parents, on the journey that would take them to Australia. There was no question of her staying behind. We were so young.

And from that night she carried our child. She did not know. In the days before such things were possible, I did not know her final destination, other than the ship docked in Sydney. I placed her pillow next to mine.

I am told I am not an unattractive man. I have enough vanity to be pleased by this, but it has no relevance to my work. There has been occasion where young ladies have been especially kind to me, although they are soon dissuaded. I no longer have the skills to engage in a relationship and do not know if I would value such a thing.

I turned out of the bedroom and stood in the middle of the hall, the doors leading off to the other rooms. My flat was much the same as all the other flats in the building. They were alike in the size of the rooms, the bedrooms and box rooms. But the layout was always different where the smaller rooms had been arranged to fit into the larger, older layout and much grander rooms of the original mansion house, with vast drawing rooms, music rooms and ballrooms. In the years after 1800 when the building was completed, staff numbers had slowly declined as the factories grew, and over the years the political and social power of the aristocracy and haute bourgeoisie had melted away. From the Crimean War to the Second World War, each grand building in the New Town had been subdivided and sold off. Grand fireplaces still stood in the entrance halls, black and empty, and the wide, winding staircases remained, leading to every level, lit by a central cupola during daylight hours. But now the high doors on each floor led off to narrow corridors and to much smaller rooms. It was not uncommon to see a fragment of an ornate cornice appear high on the wall of a windowless box room that had once been the corner of a ballroom and lit by high Georgian windows and candelabra.

My front door opened onto the original grand staircase. I had grown up in this flat and knew every inch of the building and every noise made by its ancient wooden skeleton, clothed by soot-flecked sandstone. Above me was the hatch to the attic and in front, the door of a small, windowless box room. I opened the door. Shelves lined one side and were filled with my collection of stationery. On one shelf was a thick plastic ring binder. I picked it up and turned to the other side of the box room, lined with cardboard storage boxes, then laid the folder on a box and blew dust from the cover. It was not marked with a name. I know her name.

And if the storm comes, she must never be found.

She became a teacher. Years later, when such things were possible and information appeared online, it was evident that she had moved with her parents to Queensland. As online access increased so did the picture of her life and a little of what had happened since that day. Over the years I gathered more information and on occasion very much enjoyed looking through the folder, perhaps at Christmas or New Year, wondering what might have been. Like me, she had little time for social media, but as a teacher, her photograph appeared on the school website. She was so beautiful. And so was her daughter. My daughter.

The shock of discovery has never left me. I saw a young girl in her arms and assumed a happy union with her husband. He was tall and seemed kind and affectionate, and in the photographs they had together she looked so young, yet happy and content, and it made me happy. This was, in fact, akin to an act of voyeurism, though there was no malice in my intent.

For a long time, I told myself to be satisfied with my findings, that she had taken a profession, started a family, and from accounts she seemed happy and content. But, I am a details man. On discovering the date of the young girl's birth, it was a simple task to trace back to the day her mother had left Edinburgh. For years this kept me awake when sleep was all I desired. My daughter grew, proud and happy, but the joy in my heart was to see the face of her mother once again.

That day I placed the folder in the box room and for ten years it was never opened. Then, on the anniversary of the day she left, I wanted to see her face, her beautiful face because it would make me happy even though it had been so long ago, and to see how they had grown. I found my daughter's social media page.

There was no happiness. Only a message saying that after a short illness her mother had died and her family loved her and missed her so much. That day the folder was closed and stored in the box room once more, and I did not believe I would ever be happy again. But after this morning, there was a light, shining and warming in my soul, if you believe such a thing exists.

It was not happiness, it was something much greater.

I held the folder tight to my chest and carried it into the hall. Even if she had escaped the storm yet to come, the jackals of the press would be there to feast on her memory.

Chapter IV

I never thought I'd grow old here. I never pictured myself, back bent, shuffling from room to room, and I've never known why. Standing in the hall, the doors led off to each room. The door to the box room stood open, the boxes neatly stacked against the wall. Whatever happened from this day on, everything would change.

My mouth dried and an anger arose in me, flaring through my chest and down to the tips of my fingers which gripped the folder. What would happen to those men in prison would not be enough, yet such was the law. This was how it should be, how it had to be. The alternative was chaos and butchery. My heart slowed as the anger passed. But it would return. Because I knew myself, and knew it was time to leave.

For good or bad, when I stood in the dock to give evidence, my name would be on the lips of every newsreader or screaming headline of the vacuous, vicious print media. They would tell of my behaviour, my dedication to my job, but they would titillate their readers with tales from former colleagues, and turn a simple desire for order and neatness into a freak show. I am no fool. I know how they sell their news. Give the readers what they want. Scandal, treachery and filth.

Feed their fears and soothe them just enough to let the terror return each day, so they buy another daily edition to get their fix. Facts don't sell advertising.

My head fell back and I closed my eyes to rid myself of these thoughts. What would happen could not be stopped, although precautions could be taken to protect myself.

The folder was heavy in my hands. Nothing must be allowed to taint her memory or identify our daughter. And when she held her newborn, did she think of me? And when she was dying, was my name on her lips, unspoken?

Did she remember my name?

It was of no matter. No one would find any connection to her. The only connection was here, in this folder.

In the sitting room, the morning was grey through the windows. And for all the brown, heavy Victorian furniture that my parents had left me, all still in the same place, the room seemed irrelevant and ethereal, then cold and empty and it was comforting to me.

At first, it was a pinprick of light in the darkness of my mind, but it grew. Faint yet strong. It was exciting in a small way, then it made me shiver with fear, or pleasure. A heat rose in my throat against the cold around me, then on my face and hands, and through the coldness of everything in my life it felt like the end of a season. Winter would end, and I had the unyielding sense that this was my leaving. I would shuffle off this chill skin and find somewhere by a warm sea. My Spring, which would come. It felt natural and true. And it could not be stopped.

But I must leave before the storm broke. When I had finished compiling my evidence against Mungo

Hastings, then the verdict would be next and then the heavens would fall.

The flat would have to be abandoned and everything in it. Except my yellow bowl in the kitchen. This did not make me pause. Around, above and below me was just wood and stone. I was proud of not being emotionally attached, then I held the folder tight against my chest. Such is the way and the weakness of human nature. Yet it would not be a threat to me. Preparations would be made, in detail. Avoiding the press before a trial would be straightforward. My passport was up to date and a taxi would take me to a container port down the coast rather than an airport, and the next day would see me in the Netherlands with the European continent open before me. Money would not be an issue. My parents had moved their wealth offshore many years before they passed away. It was not a fortune, but would enable me to live comfortably. And since my youth, perhaps I had always wanted to leave.

And there was so much to leave behind, but nothing that mattered. Nothing other than what was in my hands, her pillow and the bowl in the kitchen. I crossed the room to the fireplace, where the logs were stacked ready to light, and knelt and placed the folder on the floor.

I did not need this paper and ink. Her face was clear in my mind, every detail, lit by candlelight on our last night. I struck a match to light the kindling under the logs, which burned fast with a yellow flame, blackening the logs on top. To the left of the fireplace was a basket with more kindling, but the flames died. The chimney was cold and might fill the room with smoke. That would not matter. It would burn, and that was all that was needed. The leaving could not truly begin until this step, this offering, this cleansing.

To the right of the fireplace was an Edinburgh press, a tall cupboard that looked like a doorway to another room. I opened the door to the shallow shelves, only six inches deep, and took out a box of firelighters.

Crumbling the firelighters over the kindling, I stared into the fire, behind the logs to the blackened bricks, then stood and placed both hands on the wall while the fire smoked beneath me. What if Campbell inadvertently destroyed the evidence when processing the roll of film? Or MI5 got to him before he presented the case to the world?

Behind the stone of the chimney breast was the box room. One copy of the evidence was not enough, and the windowless box room would make an excellent darkroom for processing. After all, I thought, I am a details man.

The logs began to smoke and smoulder.

Shops would be opening soon. Hardware and DIY stores in Stockbridge or on the outskirts of town would have the photography equipment I required to construct a darkroom, and all the chemicals required for film processing. I turned away from the fire and hurried to the box room, and took down three fresh notebooks and three boxes of new pencils, then returned to the sitting room and sat at my table. I headed the first notebook 'Facts and Assumptions' and began to list the known details of the case. In the other two books, I would list the equipment that could be bought locally and that which could be bought online and delivered.

The fire had caught now, and yellow flames rolled around the logs.

Lord Campbell said that Hastings would return tonight. That did not give me much time. The darkroom aside, there were many things required. The Shipping Forecast during my morning bath had said that there was a storm coming in from the Atlantic. The words of my father came back to me, as we stood before a wide Highland glen, the mountains lost in mist, and the wind buffeting the heather around us.

There is no such thing as bad weather, laddie. Only the wrong clothes.

I decided to add some waterproofs to the list. Preparation is everything. I worked methodically, moving between notebooks as the thoughts filled my head, listing every requirement and their priority, every eventuality and its likelihood. Then I wrote each list out again and placed them in front of me on the table, and read them once more, making relevant annotations. Once finished, I felt the calm return. The simple, peaceful pleasure of working in a logical manner gave me joy. The fire was burning evenly and well across the neatly stacked logs, and that pleased me very much. It was time.

I knelt before the fire and turned the folder over and opened it at the last page, to hide her face. Her memory would leave this place. We would leave together. I fed the first photograph face down into the fire.

Her name was Elspeth.

Chapter V

It had taken most of the day and several trips in my car, mostly stuck in rush hour traffic under a darkening sky, but the last of my photographic purchases lay in the hall, and as the stack of boxes became higher, the unease began, followed by the clamour behind my eyes. I knew how it would end, and that it must not happen. It had to be stopped before the new things engulfed me.

Unopened boxes surrounded me on each side and in a moment my mouth was dry and my vision blurred with tears. All these things had been selected and paid for, yet I had not yet touched them. I had to touch them for them to be mine.

I grabbed a box cutter and slashed each box in turn, hacking through the plastic and packing to touch the contents with at least two fingers. A folding table, trays, lamp stands, bottles of chemical and others things I couldn't recall; I pushed the boxes aside as each object became mine.

When finished, I stood still among the ugly chaos, but now they were mine and would be dealt with alphabetically and in good order. I did not like strange objects in my flat. I do not like unfamiliarity. Although everything was now mine until it was released due to breakage or redundancy. All that remained was to empty each box, cut and sort the cardboard and packing into similar sizes, bind them with tape and stack them for disposal. There were so many different sized boxes. The last vestiges of panic swirled in my head and flickered in my chest, then grew like anger and my head flicked back.

My eyes squeezed shut for a moment as the horror grew, but this time I knew what to do. I can stop this, I thought. I am home, in my flat, this is mine, all this is now mine. Order and prioritise.

Hearing the words in my head warmed me. My head flicked again, this time not so hard, and holding the box cutter high above me, I began breathing slowly. I was in control. Everything could wait another few moments. Everything here, everything around me was mine, and entirely at my disposal.

A tremor under my feet told me my neighbours had arrived home, slamming their ill-fitting door. In the first days after the death of my parents this had continually annoyed me, but as I became truly alone and found my peace, I understood I could hold my calm as if in my palm, and the noise outside my world soon became irrelevant. It was all just detritus around me.

I turned to the biggest box, cutting straight slow lines to cut the cardboard into equal sizes and stacked each item against the opposite wall. The physical movement and the smooth action of the blade calmed me as it harvested each box in a clockwise direction, until they were emptied, cut and stacked.

Happy with my work, I walked through to the sitting room and sat at the table in front of my lists, checking off each item. The other purchases would arrive tomorrow via several delivery services. This thought brought back a distant flare of panic, of continual strange faces at my door and more boxes. I tried to ignore the tightening of my throat and read each list twice out loud. When my voice stopped shaking, I stood and took slow, measured steps through to the kitchen, each step in time with my breathing.

In the middle of the table was my yellow pear bowl. I lowered myself into a chair, then reached out and held the bowl in my hands. Despite the season, the yellow ceramic was never cold to the touch, and the burning sunshine colour filled me with warmth and joy. It was the colour of the sun when you look at it just before it blinds you. But this colour, I could stare at for hours. This colour healed me.

It was a school project, the first thing I ever made, and the slight imperfection of the shape made it warm and welcoming. It was me, and it was mine. Once, my mother had filled it with green and yellow pears, and the combination of colours held me in rapture. I had sat in the kitchen, pretending to read a book, and sneaking glimpses when my mother was at the stove. I had gone back to see it in the night, and sat for hours, for I could not sleep without looking at it once more.

In the morning, the shine of the fruit had faded. Over the years I have tried to buy fruit that might bring back that sensation, but never succeeded. Nothing shone like that summer day, except the bowl.

I filled the kettle and switched on my iPad then stood, eyes closed until the kettle had boiled, added two bags to the pot and counted three minutes exactly on my watch, before removing the bags. I poured the tea and carried it to the table then propped up the iPad. It was set to one page only. The Shipping Forecast.

The *'Sailing By'* theme tune played, then the sea areas and forecasts were read out. The rhythm and the words, the tone and timbre, delighted and soothed me. This simple joy always centres me and locates me in the chaos of the world. Each sea area is a reference point; I would know where I am, set against the other little maritime worlds around this island, each with their own life and existence and each indifferent to the little worlds of clamour and filth that closer surround me.

I turned to the north east, pictured the sea map of the North Atlantic and Norwegian Sea, and each area as it was read out, imagining the weather: the frigid gossamer thin white tips of waves rising high on steel grey seas, others eggshell blue, cold and becalmed, some full of storms and thrashing maelstroms, or showers skimming over the horizon into blissful, endless banks of fog where you could hide forever.

Sometimes, when sleep would evade me, I take my mind to an old wooden boat in a silver haar under a summer sun, far out to sea, nearer Denmark than Scotland, the sail hanging limp above me while I am curled up under a thin blanket. I can sleep for days on the warm wood, and the summer northern nights are silver, yet never dark.

I took more tea and felt my strength return, then scolded myself. If the arrival and organisation of all the new objects had been properly planned there would not have been such a reaction. Planning is everything. My method had lacked detail. It would not happen again. Later, my lists and notebooks would be examined once more to check the assumptions, then updated accordingly.

Order was required. I examined the sea grid map on

the screen, locating the weather as it was being read out, and mouthed the words which calmed my soul. *North Utsire, South Utsire, Viking, Forties and Fisher.*

I needed both hands to lift the pot to refill my cup. But there was no fear. No, I thought, I am a details man. I stretched my arms out to the side for a moment, then brought my hands together slowly as if in prayer and held them under my chin, then felt a pang of hunger, for in the excitement I had not eaten all day. I decided to make a *gratin*, a favourite dish, and from the cupboard I took three potatoes of similar size, hard cheese and a grater, then pulled out a large kitchen knife and held it in my hand. It was two weeks into the knife's sharpening cycle, but all would be fine.

It was a question of time intervals and efficient, planned actions. I glanced at my watch. One minute to seven.

I bared my teeth in a scream and ran from the kitchen, knocking over a stack of cardboard in the hall, and down the corridor. I lunged for the front door, unlocking the snib and smacking my head off the doorframe. I took several stairs at a time, grabbing the banister and pulling myself down and around, before my slippers slapped onto the marble hall leading to the street door and stumbled down the wet stone steps, the rain hitting my face. I turned and ran.

I didn't even think of the blood on the stone.

My vision was blurred but at the corner of my street the iron thistle on the top of the railings appeared.

Puddles of filthy water splashed up my legs and I ran with my hand outstretched, past the parked cars and stone steps to each house. In my right hand I held a kitchen knife and I stopped at the end of the street. Why was I carrying a knife? My watch read three seconds to go. Mother of God, I had just run… Two seconds… Who had seen…? One second.

I grabbed the thistle as my watch hit seven pm exactly and held on tight for a moment then let go and lifted my shirt to hide the knife. My head twisted left and right. There was no one on the street. I stood, staring along my street and felt the rain hit my teeth. My slippers were soaking and my trousers stuck to my legs. My shirt was now sodden and opaque. I kept my arm pressed close to my chest to hide the knife and started to walk home, water oozing between my toes. The thought of meeting a neighbour and attempting a smile at getting caught in the rain without a coat flashed through my mind, yet there was nothing to do but walk in the rain and hope.

No use looking behind me, that would make me seem an idiot. I fixed my eyes on the steps ahead and ran through the open door and made for the stairs. If my neighbours… There was nothing to be done. I ran up the stairs to my door. It was wide open. I threw myself inside and kicked it shut then shuffled into the hall and dropped to my knees until my head touched the floor, and the rainwater ran down my cheeks and into my eyes.

A keening sound rose from deep within my chest and echoed around the walls. *This had to stop. This was not order. This was chaos. And entirely of my own making.* I thumped my head three times off the floor until the noise faded. My coins were in my pocket but they would be wet. It would not be right. From the kitchen I could hear the iPad and focused on the words until I could feel them echoing and controlling my body. *Sole, Lundy, Fastnet, Irish Sea. Westerly backing Southerly, three or four, good.*

My breathing slowed and I sat back on my heels. It had been twenty-five years since the last attack. My beautiful order and my habits, my rhythm and rules had kept me tightly bound and held me close all these years and kept me safe. Yet sometimes the bonds wear thin, or are broken by others to drag me into their hell. I dreamt of visiting my own hell on those who do, but would not weaken myself to do so. It is not advisable for my health. If necessary, there were drugs in the kitchen and these would be used without hesitation. I am no fool.

I dropped the kitchen knife then stood, peeling off my shirt, then my trousers, socks and underwear and gathered them into a bundle and placed them on top of the cardboard stack. Stepping back into the centre of the hall, I stood with my eyes closed, arms outstretched, my palms upwards, and thought of the sea. Peace will return, I thought. Be patient.

My eyes flickered open. My front door had been left open all this time. It was closed now, but it was too late.

I knelt and grabbed the knife, thought about my trousers, and realised I would have to put the knife down to pull them on. And I liked holding the knife.

Squeezing between the boxes, I pulled hard on the cord for the bathroom light – there was no movement inside as the light flickered. I grabbed a towel and held it in front of me in one hand, the knife raised in the other, and edged towards the kitchen like an absurd *retiarius* gladiator from the Colosseum, with a trident and a net.

I am not without humour but this really was not the time. I moved through the flat, checking each room, under every bed and in all the cupboards, and then returned to the hall.

My legs still shook, so I replaced the towel in the

bathroom and looked down at the bath. There was my panacea and my medicine. I turned the taps to the correct position then picked up my clothes from the hall and stepped into the kitchen. This was, I realised, the first time I had been naked in my kitchen. I let the blind drop in the window then draped my clothes on the radiator, and returned the knife to its drawer.

Habits must adapt to fit the order, and a replacement was required for my iron thistle. I loved my thistle. I loved its darkness and smoothness. It had signalled the end of my working day for all these years. But the order had changed, and such a marker needed to be updated and relocated.

What was required was control and planning at a level of detail never before attempted. At that moment my heart thudded hard in my chest at the enormity and joy of such a task.

I stepped into the bath and slid down, lying still until the water rose and lapped my lips, then let my head fall back against the edge. The first few breaths trembled in my chest, but then I found my rhythm, and let my arms float and dreamed of sunlight.

Pulling the dressing gown around me, I sat at the table in front of my notebooks. There was no need to remind myself of the consequences of lack of planning, my damp slippers served that purpose.

The notebook dedicated to Mungo Hastings was open, showing his address. A New Town resident like myself, his family had bought their property over two hundred years ago. I was interested to know if he still owned his entire building, but Hastings was on his way home. That was the only information required at the moment.

His address was familiar. I had often walked those streets on early Sunday mornings in the high summer, when the nights never truly came, and in the warming air the sun climbed bright and glorious by four o'clock, when Edinburgh seemed capable of redemption.

At the end of his terraced street was a private garden for residents, and a small bank of trees and bushes with a clear view of the road and his home. In the dark, it would be an ideal observation point.

The rain spattered against the window of my sitting room. The forecast for inshore waters was quite specific. Tonight would be wild, wet and cold. But I must be silent and unseen.

I pulled out a cardboard box from the box room and carried it through to my bedroom. It had been over twenty years since the box was sealed, on my last day as an Army Officer Cadet at Edinburgh University. The uniform had been returned, but we had all bought our own pieces to supplement old kit, or to have something to wear while our clothes dried after exercises in foul weather. I placed it on the bed then pulled back the tape. The musty, sweet smell of Army waterproofing and that of every Quartermaster store in the country filled my mouth and nose. On top were my combat jacket and trousers, Both were from a pattern issued in the late sixties, that had just made it into my era in the OTC, and were very well-made and warm. Below was the thin, woollen one-piece thermal suit I had used for winter exercises, and below that, a thick green pullover. The boots lay at the bottom, and they would be stiff and require to be broken in once more. My walking boots would be comfortable, though wellington boots would be more practical. I took off my dressing gown and pulled on the thermal suit. The memories of sitting in a trench for hours on end came back to me, the Highland forests and wilderness, the snow gathering on the shoulders and arms of our jackets and tam o' shanters, and I decided to wear everything I had. Those lessons had not been forgotten. The pullover and trousers first, then the combat jacket and trousers. I could feel the warmth already. At the bottom of the box were two webbing belts, one fixed with ammunition and ration pouches, stained and faded with use, a balaclava, a half-squeezed tube of camouflage face paint and a combat knife.

The leather scabbard was cracked, but the long, broad knife slipped out easily, with its aromatic scent of gun oil used to protect the blade. The edge was marked where it had cut firewood or been used to clear a low scrape to hide in the heather on the hills, although it was still sharp and felt good in my hand.

The face paint would not be required if I pulled down the balaclava. It had probably dried over the years, but I tucked it into my pocket regardless. A handful of spit would bring it back to life. I pulled a webbing belt around my waist then rolled up the balaclava to make a hat and returned to the hall. On top of the boxes was a waterproof camera pouch. I fixed it to my webbing belt then pulled on my trench coat and wellington boots. It was dark outside and the trenchcoat and wellingtons would almost hide my combats.

The knife hung heavy at my side. It gave me comfort, and I deserved it.

Chapter VI

When I was young, I had an extraordinary friend. But no one could see him. No one else knew of him. His name was Harry, and when I wanted to stay in my room and read, Harry would want to sneak into the attic and out the skylight, to play on the roofs over the grand terraced houses in my street.

Of course, we were never seen together. Harry left it to me to plan this in detail. We wore exactly the same clothes. We shared the same big bed. I planned our every move, and was so happy with the trust Harry placed in me. And when something brave had to be done, like going to a sports day at my school or a university party, Harry would take my place.

The thing we loved most was our secret world on the rooftops of the New Town, running between the stony peaks, through dark forests, chasing dragons with a sword. I was always scared, but it was okay because Harry was with me. And sometimes when I became too frightened to move, Harry would close my eyes and hold me tight until it passed, and then lead me into the mountains for adventure. That was Harry. He would go to school for me if I had to do a talk in front of the class. And while I went to school, Harry would be in the Highlands, hunting and skiing. Of course, if anyone asked, Harry would say his name was Hector. We dressed the same so no one would know. Harry was brave and polite and could talk to people. But he wasn't good at school, so I would go instead, and tell him all about it later. He admired me for passing exams and he told me so, marvelling at my mathematic and algebraic equations. Harry would try to understand, but he was much better at running and fighting, charging into battle across the rooftops and killing bad guys. I liked Harry very much. But sometimes he was away and couldn't come. And I couldn't find him. Those were bad times. Yet he always returned with a story to lift me up.

Harry joined the Army Reserves at university, and loved the tough exercises, carrying ammunition and a heavy pack and rifle across the mountains and through freezing rivers. He would bring back the army rations that came in tins that you boiled or cooked over a fire, and saved the chocolate with Arabic wrappers and the red boiled sweeties each ration pack contained, with the camouflage cream still showing behind his ear where he had forgotten to wash.

But after university, when I went to work for Lord Campbell, and settled into the order and rhythm of my job, and there was no need to go out and meet people after work, which I hated. After that, we didn't see so much of each other. As you get older you lose your childhood friends and I often wondered what became of him. I missed him.

The drizzle flew up in my face when I stepped onto the street. A neighbour got out of his car down the street and I crossed over to avoid him, opening my stride, keeping a steady pace. With luck, he would not feel it was his duty to comment upon the weather from across the road.

I slowed, thinking this would take a few moments, but the driver and his wife began unloading children and suitcases onto the rainswept pavement. It was obvious by the look on his face he was glad the journey was over and it was also obvious to me that I could not wait in the street until they were gone. The children began to get back in the car from one side as the mother hauled them out from the other. I spun around and walked to the end of my street and turned down the hill.

Hastings' house was not too far. Perhaps fifteen minutes on foot. I pulled up my collar and headed deeper into the New Town. The wide cobbled road led down steeply to Stockbridge, lined by parked cars. It was badly lit and that suited me fine. I had seen the campaign letters complaining about the new, bright street lighting and how it cheapened the atmosphere, meaning their property prices, and how they petitioned the council. Money talked, and Victorian light levels were restored. Although the people who signed the letter were not the people who ventured out after dark and the low-lit streetlights did not threaten their fitful, guilty sleep behind their bolted windows. Their ugly, empty church stood at the foot of the hill, its monumental, soiled grey sandstone stretched into the sky, its generations of wealthy New Town patrons all dead or dying. A deep red glow came from the heart of the tower as part of an artistic light show, but only seemed to show that a darker power ruled this shuttered church, as it always had. A monument to a generation of empty, shrivelled hearts, and their prophets, the black-cloaked bigots that fed them their laudanum of false piety, and the only place where the filth seeped outwards to stain the stone.

The poor never worshipped there. They would have been thrown down the stairs.

I wished Harry was with me, but in my heart, I felt he never left; sometimes in the night I heard him laughing like when we were young. I crossed to the darkened side of the street, next to the hedge-filled, high railings of a large private garden, open exclusively to residents who had the key to the heavy chains around the gate. The cars at the kerb were jammed together and if a window was smashed no one would come. A few faces might appear, peering around curtains to check their car alarm. They would call the police and that was that.

A blast of wind came from the east, picked up the rain and threw it down the street, but then the rain came harder and faster and drummed on the car roofs, spat off the pavement. At the corner of the garden, several gutters joined together and water burst out over the cobbles, surging down the hill, pushing past cars and lapping up over the kerbs. Yet for all the heavens opened, it could never wash the filth of Edinburgh clean. It would merely cloud and stain the rainwater until it spilled into the Water of Leith, running under the Stockbridge at the bottom of the road and onwards past blackened stones to wash itself in the Firth of Forth.

The road wound down sharply, towards a squat, thick-stoned, two storey medieval house that had looked down on the Stockbridge when it was surrounded by pasture and had seen the tall buildings grow around it, and might yet see them fall. I turned left into an archway in the high wall, up a series of wet stairs that led to the street above, rainwater dripping from the roof, and was soon engulfed in darkness and soaking, stinking stone, before I emerged onto a narrow walkway lit by feeble lights outside doors, then up into the pale light of the street above.

One streetlamp was broken, but before me was the dark shape of hedges bordering a private garden, bound by high railings. At the corner, I stopped and looked across a narrow junction, halfway up a steep hill, and the end of Hastings' road. The rain was steady now and I crossed the junction, keeping to the far side of the street. His house sat in a terrace of four storey homes with a view over Stockbridge and the sea where it met the Firth of Forth, but all this was lost in the rain. On the other side was the private garden, railed off and locked, that extended for the whole of the terrace, built on steep wooded land that dropped away sharply down to the churning, mud thick Water of Leith. The thought of security cameras outside his house made me pick up the pace, and I kept hard to the railings, where thick untrimmed hedges poked through so passers-by could not see the residents' private, lonely pleasures. There were a few lights above doors, showing large nameplates and ornate brass knockers, but there were no lights in the windows. I counted the numbers and saw his door. The light above it shone brightly.

Unlike my own building, Hastings' door had one name only, evidence he still owned all four storeys of the town house. I kept going until near the end of the street, before it turned into a wide treelined square beside a six-storey mansion on the corner. The rear of his house could be seen over a high wall, but there was no access. Next to the mansion on the corner was a small bank of stunted trees and bushes, six feet wide. The wind came hard and a line of brightly lit windows shone out into the rain, fading when it reached the dark trees of the garden in the middle of the square. There was no one at the windows. I pulled the balaclava down and crouched between two cars, then stuffed the trench coat into my pack, swung it onto my shoulders and headed back towards Hastings' house.

A howl of wind came off the rooftops and burst through the trees across the square as waves of rain swept down the street. The balaclava was wet on my face but still warm. I strode past the mansion to the steep bank, then ran up and ducked behind the bushes and under the tree. It was quieter where the mansion blocked the wind, although the rain drowned out everything. Pushing the pack between my knees, I leaned back and braced my feet against the roots of a thick bush in front, then reached out and parted the bush to watch Hastings' front door.

The rain stopped and the wind dropped. Water dripped around me from the branches and spattered where it hit the wet earth. I felt rather foolish. There was nothing to achieve here except the photograph of a man arriving home late. The camera sat heavy in the pouch on my webbing belt. Even the most high-resolution and sensitive lens would produce nothing of interest. Did the abuse take place at this address when his wife was away? That seemed reckless beyond belief, though in my work no end of bizarre criminality has crossed my desk and proved that truth is so much more stranger than fiction. But Hastings was alone tonight. His family of two girls would not be in the house, having moved to the United States. Why did they move? No, I thought, I must make no assumptions unless they are based on evidence.

Perhaps nothing would happen tonight. All the boys

in the school would be in bed. Though this evening may have some use for testing my surveillance methods, even if they proved to be useless. The night vision goggles and sensitive camera lenses would arrive the next day.

Then the light above Hastings' door went out. I stared at the spot where the light had been. The front of the house was in darkness. A faulty bulb? On the very night I was watching it? No, I thought, there is no such thing as coincidence. Rainwater dripped from my balaclava into my eyes.

I sat back against the tree. The rattle of a black cab, its engine straining to climb the hill from Stockbridge, came from the end of the road. The back of my hands glistened with rain and I took the camouflage cream from my pocket and rubbed some across the wet skin.

Headlights swung around the corner and the cab stopped at the far end of the street. The glare from the headlights prevented me from seeing the occupants. I heard a door close, but saw nothing, and parked cars blocked my view of the pavement. Then a figure with a baseball cap pulled down over his face hurried towards me at the end of the street. Why get out of the cab at the end of the street then walk in the rain? He was thin, small, his shoulders hunched forward. He looked no more than a boy. He took quick, short steps, hugging the nearside of the pavement. I felt a coldness through me and slipped a hand down to my camera, then stopped – I had not tested it in the dark. If there was some automatic flash or noise, it might give me away. It should have been tested earlier. My head twitched at the thought. Besides, the cab was nowhere near Hastings' house. The figure hurried on, holding his jacket around him and I leaned forward through the gap in the bush. The cab pulled away, headlights silhouetting the figure, and I pulled my head back and closed my eyes as the beam swept over me, then opened them to see the boy turn towards Hastings' door. The door opened to darkness, and he was gone. A boy. He could only have reached halfway up the doorway. A skinny wee boy.

Rivulets of water ran past my legs and down the slope to the pavement. I had stopped breathing. I tried to exhale slowly, but it came out in bursts. Order was required and my five coins were buried beneath several layers of clothing, so I forced my palms together, pressing and releasing in time with my breathing. Any assumptions must be supported by fact. Well, the fact that a young boy... No, I had assumed it was a young boy because the figure was the height of a young boy and seemed to be wearing young person's clothes. And entering Hastings' house in the dark. Someone had switched the light off and opened the door for him. Facts would certainly support the assumption that the young man was a male prostitute. And if he was under eighteen, a child.

I held my hands hard together until cartilage popped in my wrists. Then the rain came back hard and burst across the street.

My work had given me insight to a world of criminality through traumatic witness statements, detailing depravity of every nature, though these are seen only from my desk. I am no longer shocked, having seen too much for too long, not just in my profession, but in the callous disregard, fear and greed in my neighbours, colleagues and fellow citizens. My legs began to shake although not from the cold. I opened my hands but could not hold them still. I squeezed my fists against my lips to close my jaw until my lungs ached and I sat there, rocking back and forth. Hastings and the others would be confronted with justice and punished, even if it cost me my last breath. And even if the punishment seemed hardly a deterrent, or indeed a punishment, a man like Hastings had very far to fall. The knife hung heavy at my waist. It felt good. Although such a course against those who corrupt children was not open to me. Such revenge has its attractions, that cannot be denied, nor would anyone coldheartedly deny it to those who have seen the aftermath of such evil perversion, the life crushed out of children before it had barely begun. But we have our system of justice, and though it is never perfect, it is right and balanced as it can be. And Hastings' fate would ensure that they would never be far away from a blade.

This would be my task, my vision. Mine was the only route to justice, through my evidence, then through Campbell. Facts and photographs would be my sword and my vengeance. Photographs of a child prostitute exiting the darkened home of the Secretary of State for Scotland near midnight. Campbell had no idea of the technology. His knowledge of low-light photography was obviously non-existent. A few rolls of fast film would not suffice. But this is why he chose me. He knew I would deliver. And none of the evidence given to him will be on electronic media, nor will it ever be threatened by being discovered online or through an accessible device. I would use my initiative to achieve this. I am a details man, focused and resourceful. He is relying upon my expertise in permissible, irrefutable evidence. And he would have it. And Hastings would fall. And if I have evidence, then the second man that

Campbell had mentioned would fall too, or be pulled into the pits of hell by Hastings.

And Hastings knew the law, and knew that defence lawyers can destroy a case through doubt in a juror's mind. He had switched off the lights in his house so he could never be seen, and had showed no face at the door. No light shone upon him. But it would, and it would be as bright as a thousand suns.

Yet here was I, carrying a knife that could result in five years imprisonment. That was the least of my concerns now. Not after tonight. Not after assuming what would happen behind that door. However familiar I was with the feral habits of some of Edinburgh's citizens, I had no desire to dwell on the matter to deduce any timings for such activities. The house remained in darkness. I sat back against the tree.

The rain stopped but the water surged and swelled around the stone of the gutter. An old man rounded the corner from the mansion, a battered Homburg on his head, hunched over in a dark overcoat which reached down past his knees, and a tall, thin, long dog on a short lead beside him, silhouetted by the street lamp. The man walked slowly, with short steps, as did the dog, holding its paws in the air for a moment, then placing them down to match its pace to the old man. I imagined the dog detecting my scent and growling at what was in the bushes, but when they drew close, a white muzzle showed against its short fur, and from what streetlight shone, it reflected on wet, cloudy eyes. Nothing existed for the dog, except the man.

The dog's nose twitched as it neared the bushes, and it held its head high for a moment, then looked away, moving closer to the old man, continuing past and down the street in the rain, the long curving tail slowly dipping then rising with the rhythm of its paws, raindrops falling from its tail. The old man placing one foot in front of the other, taking each careful step into the night together, until the glistening tip of its tail disappeared. I looked after them for some time.

Hastings' door was still shrouded in darkness. I did not know how long the boy would be in Hastings' house. In truth, it was immaterial and did not concern me. This was not a callous thought; a shorter period of time would not change the fate of the boy, only alleviate the longevity of his suffering. This task would require patience, and I had patience. As I grew from a boy to a man, I had learned her skill of patience, that she had shown with me, and I missed her every day.

I took the old camera and wound it on a frame, then placed it in my haversack and took a shot. There was no flash. I held it up and looked through the viewfinder, but I was quite sure that the film was not sensitive enough to catch any detail. Next time I would be prepared rather than rely on Campbell's knowledge of photography. I could still see Hastings' unlit door.

Hastings' guilt, that in truth could only be assumed, was firm in my mind. And through evidence, would become a reality. And it was evident that with my witness, and with the support of Campbell, that Hastings would fall, and the whole rotten house of state and establishment would come crumbling down. Standing in court, the world's eyes upon me, the press and public would surely be impressed by my planning and the level of detail I had gathered. In my heart, it shamed me to admit I took great pleasure at my observations and achievements. Certainly, there have been areas of planning where I've made mistakes, but those mistakes were only made once.

A roar came over the rooftops and the wind and rain swept the street again and swirled below the tree and around my neck, chilling my lips, the wet balaclava now cold on my face. Yet it was not unpleasant, and in my mind a picture formed of that day as a child where I found true peace and happiness. I could not go there now and have my soul despoiled with the filth around me. Later, when all around me was dark and warm, then I would go to the bright, freezing valley where the snow held everything close, where the fog had blocked off the horizons around me and the winter sunshine seeped through yet could not warm the robin redbreast where it sat on frost-covered branches. I could not go there now. That part of me could not be touched or heard. It was a source of endless solace and succour, but I would ration it and not deplete its power. Today was near bearable, but I had wandered too close to the edge, and if it happened again, I had a range of medicines to suit the occasion. Although they would interfere with my ability to perform these crucial tasks, to see Hastings and the others in jail, and to see them suffer. Most of the medicines I used are available without prescription, some from overseas, and no business of my doctor. Simple things like antihistamines taken after work can calm me, and allow me to slow and then control my thoughts. And they may be needed after this event.

The rattle of another black cab's diesel engine interrupted my reverie as it entered from the far end of the street and stopped on the corner, behind a parked car, a few feet from the kerb. One headlight shone along the line of parked cars and glinted off the wet cobbles.

A light went on in the cab and showed the driver reading his phone, but the passenger door did not open. I grabbed my backpack and pulled the trench coat over my shoulders, then twisted my stiff legs into a crouch. I could walk down the street and pretend I was just a late night drinker and get a better look at the boy. If the black cab was for the boy.

But it was too late. Hastings' door opened and the boy hurried out and onto the street. There was no time to move. I lifted the camera and took several shots. The boy kept his head down and my view was blocked by the parked cars, but the light came on in the rear of the cab before the door slammed shut.

The cab swung out and headed towards me. I caught a glimpse of a small white face, half hidden under a baseball cap, leaning against the window frame before the cab light went out and the face had passed me and was lost in darkness. The cab accelerated out of the corner and pulled away out of sight.

I sat staring at the empty street where it had been, then looked back to the house. The light above the door came on, shining on glistening black paint, throwing shadows on the brass knocker.

It was over. But there would be a next time. I slid down past the bushes and onto the pavement and didn't look at the door, kept my head low and hurried to the corner, pulling off my balaclava.

The rain had stopped and the air was cool and wet in my nose and throat. Through a gap between two houses the light still shone at the rear of Hastings' house then blinked off. Was that a face? Did he look at me?

I almost cried out for him to look at me, to see his nemesis, but I turned and ran.

Chapter VII

Running was a mistake. I had jeopardised my own safety and the entire operation. All I needed was a nosey policeman to find me wearing a trench coat over a combat suit and carrying an illegal knife.

The rain fell steadily and no cars or cabs passed me on the way home. The residents of the New Town were safe behind their bolted doors, safe from their countrymen, safe from all the horrors that they love to read about in the Times or the Mail, about all the great unwashed, for whom the only emotion they held was a hateful fear. And they would vote for anyone who would suppress those they described as 'less fortunate' but whom they regarded as *untermenschen*. Yet they were no different; their money and private schooling could not hide the stench of their fear and vice. And perhaps some like Hastings revelled in it. Contrary to the lies they used to keep themselves warm at night, their proclivity to criminality was the same as the poor. The cab that had left with the boy was sure to take him back to Leith or Niddrie. My work was stained by evil and it had no barrier for wealth or status. Such evil was all pervasive and insensible to love and charity. This was my home, yet this was truly not me. I would rise above this place, and realise that for my whole life, I was always leaving.

The wet cotton of the combat jacket was buttoned tight around my throat. The knife hung on my belt. My first criminal offence. Harry would be proud of me. He would laugh and slap my shoulder, teasing me. If the police stopped me, I'd simply say I lost my dog and thanks to the old man, I had a complete description. My home was not far and they could check the address.

I stamped on through the rain. These hated streets are mine, and some days they shone like gold above the rats that infested them, but not tonight. Perhaps tomorrow the sun would shine.

Hastings would be in bed and perhaps asleep, if he could sleep. Did Campbell lay awake, thinking of the trust he had placed in me? He need not worry. He was a fool to think an old manual camera and film would be sufficient, but he was not a man of detail. He did not have my focus and diligence. Yet he knew enough to trust me in this crucial task. Although I'd take my own photographs, using suitable equipment. Under the broken streetlight near to Hastings' street would be a good place to park and observe in comfort. I have often thought of Campbell as a weak fool, although in this instance he had shown some mettle. Everyone else was part of the society, the establishment, the clubs, the old boy cliques, even the Masons. That was not my world. Other than teaching marksmanship at King George's, I had played no other role in the social life of pupils, and had no interest in doing so. The time spent in the company of their parents would be an absolute hell.

No, I was the only man who could see this job through to the end. Imprisoning these pederasts was secondary to stopping the abuse. Only when they were arrested would the abuse cease, at least at the school.

There was no room for failure. The thought of the boys and Hastings made my stomach twist and I let out a guttural noise and stumbled, holding on to a railing.

Everyone and everything would be against me. Everyone. A boy was already dead. Campbell had intimated suicide, but was that true?

My feet would not move. I sat on steps leading to a wide, porticoed door. I was up against the law. The establishment. Everything that had been my daily life for so long. And I had no doubt if I crossed their path, they would do anything to destroy me. A boy was dead. They might have killed already. They would break any law and justify it in their black souls. Carrying the knife was an accident, but had I also crossed the Rubicon?

It was of no consequence. There was no doubt that those above me, all the way to the Government in Westminster, would commit any sin and disregard any crime to stay in power and hide their evil. And now I was the childrens' law and their lawyer, and the government and the establishment were my enemy. Yet they would have no hold on me. The only time they would see the truth of what I had done would be as evidence presented in a court of law. Because, in truth, I would be protecting the law, and protecting the children.

Though the heavens fall, he had said. So be it. My God, they would kill me. I looked around. There was no one, although the urge to hide was strong. I held the railing tight and used to it to haul myself up. There was rainwater in my boots, but I kept going, then ducked into an unlit arched mews entrance between the terraced mansions. A broken, cast-iron drainpipe spewed out water down the edge of the wall and I scrubbed the camouflage cream from my hands. All around me was black, soaking stone and foul damp. I rubbed the back of my hands on my trousers, and saw where the mortar had decayed in the damp between the stones where it was shielded from the sun. Multi-million pound houses, slowly, ever so slowly, rotting in front of my eyes. In the rain and the darkness, you could almost hear it under the punishment of cleansing water. And if you looked up, or had crossed the roofs like I had, you would see the cracked, missing tiles, the gutters clogged with leaf mould and moss, rotting from within and barely clinging to the stone. The decay was all pervasive and the glossy black-painted railings rattled in your hands like old bones with no marrow. It was easier to paint over rather than confront the slow and inevitable death.

This was the old whore of Edinburgh, guarding her sleeping, filthy bairns and when she lifted her petticoats at night, she showed the rotting sickness within. Behind the shuttered windows, her bairns slept fitfully, terrified of any threat to their wealth, crouched over their money and their grasping children who they had made in their own image, waiting for them to die and find a lawyer to pick their bones. And for all the years this place had stood, it had always been the same, from when they cut the pasture and laid the first stone. But one day, the stones would tumble and the pasture would return. Only then would the rain wash clean into the Water of Leith and be welcome in the sea.

At the end of the street the view was clear to the north and across the Firth of Forth to the Kingdom of Fife, the gas flare at the refinery blazed into the sky, a burning beacon, brighter than a lighthouse, as if to ward off all the stench around me from reaching their shores. The road was quiet and wet, and there were no cars other than black cabs passing along Queen Street at the top of the hill. Then a car turned down the hill towards me, and pulled in to the side and killed the lights. No one got out.

My imagination was both a curse and a gift. And I imagined the knife in my hand.

I crossed the road and picked up the pace. All was dark, save the dismal streetlamps. I looked around at my neighbours' windows, those who love wealth and stature, but whose lives will fade and pass unrecorded, as had the previous occupants. They have nothing. Merely shallow existence. I am a messenger and will deliver justice. And I will deliver it from those who live in the belly of the beast who would kill me to protect the perpetuation of their privilege, their incestual circles and their justice for sale. None of them cared for the children, none of them cared for anyone but themselves and their vacuous lives, floating like scum on a fetid, stagnant pond.

It wasn't far now, and the car hadn't moved, although I could imagine a police car in front of my house, and knew it might come to that. They could try to track me, but it would be too late, I could be away and free over the roofs, my empire as a child, where Harry would lead me over each high mountain pass, over desert and endless plains, where no one would see me or find me.

So, what had to be done, had to be done with vigour, and before they heard the name of Hector Lawless. I doubled back, away from the car and running with pleasure and power, found a darker route home.

Chapter VIII

It was good to begin in the early morning when the flat was still cold. The hall light stung my eyes as if I had got up in the middle of the night. The winter dawn was yet a few hours away.

The box room door stood open, the table laid with the developing fluid, glistening in the trays. The photos of Hastings' front door hung to dry on a string above the trays: black, blurred and useless. The red light bulb hung down and the heavy blackout curtain was furled against the door.

The boxes taken from the box room were now stacked above cupboards and below spare beds. The thought had occurred to me, in the night, that there would be such interest in me after the trial, I could not assume all my personal documents would be safe. If the Press would hack a murdered girl's phone, they would have no hesitation in breaking into my flat. Most of the papers were functional and would be of no interest, but those that were, I picked up from the floor of the hall where they were stacked and carried them through to the sitting room, then placed them beside the fireplace full of cold ashes. Out of the glare of the hall, the darkness and shadows were comforting. The burning could wait. I needed tea.

In the kitchen I made a cup of tea, and focused on my pear bowl in the gloom while it brewed, then took the tea through to the dark of the sitting room and sat on a chair close to the window overlooking the street. The hot vapour from the tea condensed against the glass and I rubbed it with my cuff, and looked down as when I was a child, hot chocolate in hand on early morning weekends before my parents arose, wondering where all the people were going and what adventures lay ahead for them. I pictured them in the rain at Waverley, pretending not to take a train.

But there was no one, only a black cab idling at the corner. It pulled away and headed towards the town. Then I thought of the blood on the stone by the door. Perhaps a drunk had fallen in the street or a knife had been used. I turned away and focused on the darkness.

I was now in possession of useless photographs of the Secretary of State for Scotland. But I had witnessed a young boy entering his darkened house late at night. My knowledge and witness was now a threat to the Government.

If they came for me, it would be with reason and purpose, and if I were to deduce both of these things, then effective preparations could be made. My notebooks lay open in a line on the table. I longed to be writing in them, ordering my mind and decisions, and the joyful, gentle power that it gave, but there was some consideration of the topics required before that would be performed. That pleasure must wait. I sipped my tea.

The possibilities and permutations would then be determined through considered and ordered actions, though one series of connected events was quite evident. If the authorities discovered Campbell had any knowledge of the boys, Hastings or what I had found, then Campbell would betray and disown me without a thought. And then they would be through me, my life and this flat like a dose of salts. I would be hung out in a cage for all to see. And Campbell would watch me sway in the bitter wind and wring his hands and watch the Press pick the flesh from my bones.

For a moment the room was filled with the shadows of men opening drawers and pulling up carpets and leaning over and shouting in my face. I yelled out loud to make it go away and stood with the tea spilling onto my hands. My hands were burning but I could not put the cup down for fear of staining the carpet or the table, so I shuffled over to the fireplace and set it down on the hearthstone. Tears began to flow. My God, I thought, I am not a child, but the terror would not leave me.

I wiped away the tears with my wet hands and sat back and stared into the blackened fireplace. They would come, but that was irrelevant and that truth would strengthen me. Holding my fists to my fluttering chest, I took my mind to the form of a shadowing, empty room, with light edging through the windows, growing stronger, falling on ancient, dark-honeyed wood panels around the walls, and warm floorboards beneath my bare feet, surrounding me in gold as the light filled the room, then to the slight air from an open window, the sound of the sea, whispering as it broke on the sand.

My hands dropped and hung limp over my knees. Let them take it all, let them destroy it all, let them burn it all. I would not be here to see it. I closed my eyes.

In my mind, a door in the empty room opened, and I could see out to the far end of a corridor, where the sea swelled in the near distance, and I edged forward, through the open door, down past white plastered walls; warm iridescent wind rushed past me when I stepped out onto the sand and the sharp marram grass growing all around, dancing in the wind and leading down to the sea.

I opened my eyes. The salt was in my nose and throat as I crouched before the fire and the sour ashes. Everything around me would no longer be mine, anything they found would be immaterial, though they would interrogate my neighbours and colleagues. Let them talk, they would find little to slake their thirst. But they would lie and construct some scandal to feed their readers' emotional poverty and there was no escaping their bile. Even if I had left them an empty cardboard box, they would do it anyway. No, feed them enough to think they had it all, leave a semblance of everything then stand on the sand and laugh as the memory of them evaporates like a foul smell. They were worthless, and just so much noisy meat.

What was truly secret would never be revealed. Truly, they would have nothing.

Reaching over to the basket, I took two short logs and weighed them in my hand, finding their balance and shape, then began to build a fire. In my own bedroom, while Harry was away, and I was scared at night, I would spend hours building and rebuilding my fire before lighting it, so that the gaps between the stack of logs were just enough to allow the passage of oxygen, yet close enough so that the space allowed the air to superheat as it passed, and the logs fed off each other in a golden glow, burning so well it gave off no smoke. When the stack was perfect, I would light the fire then lay down on the hearth, a blanket around me, wishing that Harry was with me, pretending I was in front of a bonfire with him in the Highlands, both of us exhausted from the day's walking and climbing, with the warm fatigue in my bones and muscles as if I had crossed Rannoch Moor with a good pack and climbed Schiehallion. I would fall into a dreamless sleep, only woken by my mother knocking on my door in the morning.

I sat back. The fire was built well and would light easily. The logs were strong enough to take the weight of the paper. The box of pencil shavings for kindling was nearly empty and I stood, stronger now, and turned to a door at the side of the fireplace, the same as every other door in the flat. It was the perfect Edinburgh pretension, to build a useless cupboard into the wall, an Edinburgh Press, with the pretence it was a door to another room. I opened it to the shelves that were deep enough only for paperbacks, and took out a box of fire-lighters and matches. That's all they will find, I thought.

They would come and haul open the door to find a few copies of Ian Fleming and Lewis Grassic Gibbon. And if I couldn't get to the attic in time and haul up the ladder behind me, I could be behind this wall, in the box room, though a black curtain wouldn't save me. Picturing myself in the dark, hearing the shouting once more and waiting for them to open the door, I yelled out loud to make them go away. For a moment I was ashamed, but I was home. I could not be seen.

Once the fire had caught, I sat at my table and placed my hands on my notebooks that had lain there from the night before, all in order of subject. The fire burned well, and I looked again at the Edinburgh Press. If they hauled open the box room door and found the shallow shelves of a Press, there would be no surprise. Each room had one, another in the hall would not be out of place.

There was a hardware store in Craigleith, ten minutes away, where they cut wood to requirements. I had ample room in the garage to build the shelves, then hinge them inside the box room with a simple concealed latch. All I needed were the measurements.

The light from the fire grew and I reached over to a box of pencils, freshly sharpened the night before. The darkness outside was lifting. There was so much to be done. There was enough light to see the titles on my notebooks, and I opened one and began a new list, then placed the pencil in the box for resharpening. The fire shone over the stack of personal papers, and I walked over to the fireplace and lifted an inch-thick bundle, ignoring the contents, and placed it behind the logs where it blackened and smouldered before the edges sparked into orange and yellow flame. I returned to my list, the glow of the fire reflecting in the windows.

My laptop would contain nothing of interest, but they would think it contained my life and would take it for a trophy. A new laptop was required, and if I had to hide in the box room for more than a day, then I would need supplies. Bottled water and dried food. Perhaps the Army ration packs that Harry brought home from his exercises, which he would display as captured booty. A wave of warmth swept through me from my gut as I listed the items as fast as possible, then the pencil slipped from my fingers at the thought of us as young boys. There were reasons for what must be done, and I could not lose sight of that. They would never have the happy childhood I had in these rooms, my castle where I was safe from my fears and where I had built a lifetime of armour against the world outside, and the people, the noise and their filth. They did not have my powers. Their lives would be emptied by evil that no parents' love could fill.

I completed my list then got up and sat cross-legged before the fire, a child once more, my palms open towards the flames and the warmth. Plan the day. Build the armour. Strengthen defences and choose my weapons.

The box room could become my final redoubt. All I had to do was wait until they had feasted on what was outside the box room door and then slip away. The list of requirements was in the notebook. Working through it and building the shelves to hang in the box room doorway would take all day. Then I would rest, for the night would be long.

Hastings would be alone in Edinburgh. Would he take the boys from the school to his house? It seemed unlikely. I had a choice: recce Hastings' house once more, or Campbell had mentioned the school, the source of their victims. Either way, the correct equipment would be required. With superfast film it might be possible for night photography, if the subjects remained stationary. But it would be irrelevant. Campbell could have that film, whether or not it would be any use. The digital camera with specialist lenses would arrive today, and I could store the images on my new laptop.

My phone beeped. It was a message from a number that was not in my contacts.

The rear of the school is being used after lights out.

Campbell. He was using a burner phone. And desperate for revenge.

*

The light outside became grey and the morning was nearly upon me. I had to wash for the day ahead. I left the room and took my iPad to the bathroom and ran the bath, then stood until it had filled, checked the temperature, disrobed and lowered myself into the water. The Shipping Forecast played and I slipped lower, my hands folded across my chest, until the water lapped my chin.

My day was prepared. Of course, there would be situations where I would have to adapt. A shop assistant who wanted to make conversation. An inquisitive store clerk who would enquire around the uses of the wood required to be cut to certain lengths. Their questions would be answered politely and as succinctly as possible, until it was over, and I could return to the peace of my car and then home. Several journeys would be required and would take all day, when I would rest once more. My preparation was complete.

In the late afternoon, on my last journey from the car to the flat, fatigue set in. My hands were red and sore from opening the boxes, and hanging the new shelves in the doorway of the box room.

When I had completed my tasks, I pulled open the box room door to reveal another set of shallow shelves like any other Edinburgh Press. I knelt and placed a finger under the bottom shelf and pressed the release. It clicked and the door swung back to reveal the box room.

The old photographic equipment was now stacked in the hall and would be thrown out in the morning. The new laptop and digital camera sat on a desk. My shoulders ached and the darkness outside made everything brighter under the hall lights. The day was over, but my work was not yet done.

For what came next, I would wash to prepare and settle my mind. I ran the bath once more, to end the day and begin the evening. I stripped and folded my day clothes, for they would not be needed, then stepped into the bath. The Shipping Forecast washed over my mind, and at the mention of Forth, Tyne and Dogger, the thought of a beach in Fife came to me, where as a child I had walked out of the shaded forest onto a wide beach facing the North Sea. It was bright and sunny, but dark in the east, and I watched the rain come in fast from Denmark, then ran for the cover of the forest as it hammered onto the sand and the trees. Then the rain swept away, over my head and the forest, and the sun bathed the sand which turned from amber to gold with vapour rising in wisps. Around me, the drips from the leaves and branches was the prettiest sound I had ever heard.

The bath water was cooler now and I wondered if there was another beach like mine, far over the continent to the west and south where the water was warm and would lap over me, and I would close my eyes and listen as it washed me, and still feel the brightness on my face. One day, I would know.

Once dried, I stood naked in the hall. As with the kitchen, I had never stood naked in my hall before, but no one could see me, I thought. Before today such a thing would have been unthinkable. Things had changed. I would shed this flat like a skin.

Around me were boxes from my latest purchases. The box room door stood open, and the matt-white shelves still smelled of paint, but it was fainter and would soon be gone. I touched a finger to the edge of a shelf and the paint was almost dry, drawn into the fresh pine. I pushed my finger and the shelves stuck for a moment, then swung back to reveal the box room.

The ex-army cot lay against the wall with fleece blankets folded over the edge. The chair was under the small desk, the camera, laptop and printer on top. In one corner, a stack of shelves, with stationery, water and dried food. In the other corner, a camping chemical toilet, with more bottled water and dried food. The army ration packs would arrive tomorrow.

I turned off the light in the hall and let the darkness grow and it felt good. My eyes adjusted and as the shadowy presence of the stacked and cut boxes around me emerged, a flare of panic rose in my chest and I ducked into the bedroom.

Standing naked before my bed, my combat jacket and trousers lay folded, faded and soft from a hundred washes. I lay down on the bed and covered my face with the jacket. The smell of the old cotton and army stores filled my lungs, and I knew Harry was home. My eyes filled with tears and soaked into the soft cotton, and a strength grew in my belly and limbs, and my breathing quickened. Harry would know what to do. We would win. We always won. No enemy was left undefeated when we dreamed together.

The tears flowed and my sobs were soft and happy, and I held the jacket hard to my chest with one hand, and with the other stretched out to her pillow. The tears and touch brought warmth throughout me, and I lay there until I was perfectly still. I had all that was needed.

I stood and began to dress. The green thermal suit first, as it would be a cold night. Then the combat trousers, the thick green pullover and the jacket, zipped and buttoned to my chin.

I pulled the webbing belt around me with the pouches for the cameras and the combat knife, hanging heavy in its sheath, then pulled my trench coat on and walked out into the hall.

The sitting room was cold and felt good, as if I was no longer part of this place. On the table in the darkness, my notebooks lay closed. All my planned purchases had been accounted for, all my tasks completed. The night vision goggles and sensitive digital camera lenses that lay beside the notebooks had been unpacked and tested. Beside them were two burner phones. Hastings' wife would return soon to Edinburgh. Would she share the same tastes? It was not unknown.

I reeled at my own words. They are perversions, not tastes, call them what they are. It's an evil abuse that would ruin lives, or drive them to suicide, like young Alex Gillan who had confided in Campbell. The priority was the boys in the school. And the evidence.

When this was done, tonight would be another sleepless night. The thought of the abuse now figured in my dreams, with visions of disturbing retribution, but such a response was foolish beyond belief. The law is the law. I have read witness statements and psychological reports from every penal institution. Hastings would suffer in some of the most degrading conditions possible and would be under constant fear of violence, disfigurement and death, every moment of the day and night for his entire sentence. I would make sure it was for the rest of his life.

The boys would be in their beds at lights out and if their abuser arrived, I would be waiting. Perhaps boys would be told to sneak out, as many have done before, over the past hundred years, but this time perhaps a car would be waiting for them, not the privacy of the forest and illicit schoolboy activities. At night, if the weather was rough, they would hear the waves against the rocks on the shore, and see the lights of the bridges over the Forth.

I switched on a burner phone and brought up a map of Edinburgh, then moved the map north, to the shores of the Firth of Forth, and then west along the shoreline, towards the bridges to Fife. Switching to a satellite image, the roof of the school extended left and right in gracious wings, crowded by a dense tree canopy, all the way to the edge of the water. Five hundred acres that had held memories for the boys stretching back to the opening of the school. A vast mansion, taken in death duties from a Baronet ruined by syphilis and drink.

Now, children rattled around the grand halls and maze of corridors above vast storerooms, kitchen and servants quarters below ground level. Serving staff did not need daylight. And I did not need a map. My childhood adventures from the age of seven had explored every corner of the school and the surrounding woodlands. Any car approaching the rear of the school would use the service road through the woods from the back roads to Edinburgh or South Queensferry, under the giant, red iron web of the Forth Bridge, where every decade or so, a young boy would leave the school one night, slip through the dark forest to hear the waves crash against the shore, then climb up onto the railway embankment leading to the bridge, and out along the track to stand on the edge, to step off and be received by the sea.

Chapter IX

The wind pushed through the trees around me, and I could no longer duck under branches and limbs as a child. The forest around the school was left to grow wild and although a thick carpet of leaves cushioned my footsteps, the low branches and saplings made it slow going. My car was half a mile behind me in a clearing off the road, near the ruin of a fisherman's cottage and a crumbling wooden pier. Before me, the ground dipped, and I followed it down, the leaves becoming deeper and softer under my feet and I knelt to keep my balance.

The softness and warmth out of the wind gave me a rush of pleasure in the darkness. For a moment I was giddy with elation, but I had always distrusted such fragile emotions, though I would not forgo them, as long as there is a path back to reality. I understood their pleasure and function. Life is short and you must find your love where you may, yet I failed to see what function they had at that moment, and found it irritating. It passed, and I looked up to the blackness of the trees and the web of branches and brush around me.

This was madness. I could retrace my steps and find a better way, and the thought of it warmed me. The easier ground was closer to the road, although if a car came down the drive to the rear of the school there was a chance they could find me in their headlights. I buried my face in the buttoned-up collar of the combat jacket and the heat of my body rose, and the smell of the old cotton brought back the days of exercises in the Highlands, or by the forests near the coast of the North Sea, and the sound of Harry's voice and being brave. There is no power I can give you, he had told me, that you do not already possess.

I lifted my chin and it cooled in the air, but the warmth of Harry was still at my throat. I stood and the knife hung heavy at my side alongside the pouches.

As I climbed out of the hollow, the moon hid behind a cloud, and I could no longer see through the branches or find a path through the trees. It would be hard going, and still a half a mile to go.

No, it was no use. A schoolboy might weave through the branches like a fleet-footed imp, but I was now a lumbering ogre. I skirted the dip and turned back towards the shore. I could not see the way, yet I always could sense where north lies.

The sound of the waves came low around me, stronger when I stepped out onto the track that led to the clearing by the car, then down the path to the pebble beach which skirted the trees. The lights of the oil terminal danced across the black water and to the west, the red and white flashing lights of the tops of the bridges came over the brow of the headland that jutted out and blocked the view.

The path turned off and into the trees. The ground was flat and well-worn and my eyes soon adjusted to the dark, but branches brushed my face or tore at my combat suit. At the end of the path would be the high hedge that bordered the gravelled area at the rear of the school.

Only the sound of the wind was around and above me, and the cold, rushing air smelled of rain and salt from the sea and the damp of the forest. Keeping low, I picked up the pace but couldn't judge the distance. I stopped on the path and looked back; I could no longer see the water or hear the waves in the wind. Surely there would be no boys out tonight on an adventure? They would be punished, although that had never stopped the bravest of them. The night vision goggles were in a pouch on my belt. I lifted them out and switched them on, and the viewfinder came into monochrome focus. The path ahead was black and cold, and the fringes of the branches at the side showed as myriad ethereal fluttering fingers. A movement made me lift the goggles up, and a hundred eyes looked down at me. I dropped the goggles and there was nothing but blackness, then I lifted them again and up into the trees.

A murder of crows, roosting above me.

They didn't move, but kept their eyes on me.

Head down, I walked forward and kept going. I lifted the goggles again and all in front was dark. I turned and looked at the crows, and the crows looked at me.

A roar came over the wind and an orange glow spread over the sky, under the low clouds to the north. I trembled, as did the branches holding the crows. A tongue of flame in the distance thrust into the sky, the flare of the refinery on the far North coast, hissing as the wind changed towards me. I twisted around and headed down the path.

I came out towards the gravelled courtyard at the rear of the school, surrounded by an ancient high hedge that drooped back to form a green half-pipe hollow behind the branches. I ducked through the leaves to crouch below the curve of the hedge. The thick wooden limbs sprouted from the ground around me like a cage, just as it had when I was four feet tall. I pulled the hood of the combat jacket up, and settled on the flattened, damp earth. Around twenty yards in front, across the gravel courtyard, were the windows of the school kitchens.

The dark web that bent over and behind me had grown like a colossus since my youth, but beneath its canopy, each generation of boys had hidden here, all leaving their mark. Remnants of rolled cigarettes, matches, crushed cans and the rotting shreds of flesh-tinted magazines still hung in tatters from the hard, tight web of branches that encompassed me. And now at my feet, unfurled cardboard roaches and cough bottles.

I set up the tripod and fixed on the SLR camera, loaded with superfast film, set to take a photo every three seconds once activated. The flash functions were disabled. It was unlikely to be of any use, but the roll of film would go straight to Campbell. He'd soon see the folly of his ways. The digital camera viewfinder showed the double doors at the rear of the school, leading directly to the kitchens. One light, fixed to the wall above the doors, shone over the gravel. If they were coming, they would come here.

The front of the school was one hundred feet of high windows and Corinthian columns under a huge portico, accessed from a half-mile long drive, lined with a single row of trees either side, flanked by acres of lawn or sports fields. Even with the moon behind the clouds, there would be no cover for anyone approaching on foot or by car.

To my right was the lane which led out to the back road that circled around the woods and the school. On either side of the doors that led to the kitchen were a series of passageways and storerooms and then the original servants' quarters, flanked by two service stairways which led to a network of corridors originally used by the serving staff, but now the sole domain of the masters, and closed off to the boys.

Or so they thought. Each of the boys' dormitories was flanked by a master's bedroom, although many boys had sneaked past at night. As I was a day boy and had returned home each night with my father, I had only heard of these things, and of those that had been caught and paraded before the school.

I scanned each door and the high windows along the ground floor and saw a gap below one window. The windows should be locked shut. I stared at the gap, a few inches high, then sat back.

I checked that the tripod was stable on the flattened earth, but could not stop looking at the window. Sometimes my desire for order could be distracting. This really was not the time to be concerned about windows. Was that how the boys got out? And met someone in the woods? It seemed unlikely. Every other window was closed. It was twenty or so yards across the gravel. They were tall, heavy windows. If I closed it, then not only would all the windows be in order, but it might stop the boys. Both ideas twisted around my brain.

I could be there and back in under ten seconds. No, if that was the way the boys escaped, I had to record it for evidence. Then close the window and perhaps someone would come and try to open it again? I could record that too. Every door was closed and sure to be locked. And every window except one. But if a car turned off the road into the lane, the headlights would pick me out at the windows.

I fidgeted beneath the hedge, sharp twigs hooking under my hood. Why did they need to leave it open? If it was unlocked it could simply be pushed up. I could hear nothing. No lights, no traffic approaching. It was a back road in the countryside and headlights would give them away. I looked up at the window once more, then scrambled out from my hide and ran over the gravel, head down, stones crunching under my boots. I slid to a halt under the window, hard against the stone, then reached up and grabbed the edge and pulled the window frame. It wouldn't move. I tried again, putting my weight on it, but it was stuck fast. I put both hands in the gap and gave it a shake to free it from the frame. It would not move. Was it jammed open? I gave one last try and shoved hard with both hands and it whooshed down and clattered into place.

I turned, almost falling onto my face and scrambled under the hedge. My breath blew white through the webs of branches and I covered my face. I should have left it alone. I sat back, my head between my knees and let my breathing slow. I didn't even look up to enjoy the sight of all the windows closed in a line.

All I could hear was the wind and the creaking of branches around and above me. The images of the boys' faces filled my thoughts. But I couldn't picture where they were. Did they leave the school, or did the abuse take place right here? And someone must ensure that they were not missed during the night. Did a master count their empty beds?

When I raised my head the courtyard was in

darkness. Had the light above the double doors failed? I had never known it switched off before, and it had been some time since I had been here in the evening. No, it was switched off. I sat up and shuffled over to the camera. The viewfinder was black and empty, save a few shadows of the window frames.

Headlights filtered through the trees. The engine slowed and lights turned down the lane, illuminating the windows and double doors. A dark saloon drove past and swung around on the gravel, the driver's side nearest the doors. I looked through the viewfinder just as the brake lights came on and the red glare stung my eyes.

The rear doors opened and I saw the silhouette of two boys in jackets and kilts jump down and head for the door. As they entered the beam of the headlights, the double door opened a few inches, then the headlights died.

I could see nothing, my night vision ruined, when the car reversed towards me then spun around on the gravel and headed for the road, leaving the courtyard in darkness. A door closed and bolts were thrown home.

The light came on above the door.

I held my breath. My vision gradually returned and I lifted the night vision goggles and they shook in my hand but there was nothing.

I stuffed the cameras into the pouches, grabbed the tripod and scrambled towards the path and ran. The orange glow of the flare from the refinery and the noise of the waves grew and I ducked my head beneath the branches. The forest seemed to move and skreich around me as I held my hood down low to protect me from the crows, one hand over my face.

The clouds were low and my boots hit the pebble beach as the light from the roaring flare, high on the far coast, blasted high and shone under the orange clouds, bathing the surging water in hellfire. The pebbles gave way under my boot and I crashed onto the beach and lay there, the reek of the sea and seaweed and rotting wood under me, the thundering waves and the flare burning my eyes.

Chapter X

The lights of a black cab shone in my rear-view mirror. I pulled into the kerb outside my flat but it drove past without stopping. There was no one in the back. It turned at the end of the road, then accelerated towards the town. It's just a cab, I thought, then drove into the narrow arch leading to the mews behind my building.

The courtyard was in darkness, but the cobblestones showed edges of light from the windows of the apartments above, studded between the black drainage pipe work crisscrossing the undressed stone, unlike the polished sandstone of the facades on the street. On occasion, I had stood in the archway with my eyes closed and almost heard the hooves sparking on the cobbles and the acrid sweet smell of horses and leather.

I got out to open my garage doors, the same doors that a coachman had opened for horses a century before. Once the car was inside, I leaned against the door in the darkness.

On the buildings above and around me were the long, uniform ribbons of windows, some lit against the night. Most occupants had gone to bed. I knew all their names. The Scottish Land Register is very informative. On the east and west side, five storeys high and twenty windows long, and the north and south, forty windows long, forming a rectangular block. High walled gardens stretched out in a strip from the ground floor flats, and behind my own courtyard, separated by another high wall, a mews lane in the middle, running through archways to the street. On the west side, scaffolding climbed up to the roof. Repairs on the old buildings were constant and costly; the roofs had to withstand centuries of Scottish weather. Roofs that had been my secret delight.

In the darkness under the arch, I stood close to the wall before entering the street, holding my raincoat around the pouches on my belt. I had evidence. And a licence plate. Campbell's film would be useless, although my digital images could be enhanced. Holding my breath, I listened once more. The high headlights and the rattle of a black cab engine are unmistakable. But there was nothing.

My breath streamed out from the arch and the darkness. If they came for me and broke down the door then the evidence and my witness of abuse would be transmitted in a few keystrokes before they broke through to the shelves to the darkroom. But more was required. Cameras for each room connected to a secure wifi on my laptop. These would be next on the list in my notebooks. I had to see them coming.

Door keys in hand, I held the raincoat around me and ran out into the street, up the steps to my door then across the hall, my wellington boots squeaking on the marble and up the stairs to my flat. I bolted the door behind me and reached for the lights, then stopped. The raincoat slipped to the floor and I kept low and turned into the sitting room, stood to the side of the window and peered out. The street was empty.

Using the light of my phone, I opened the box room door. The empty shelves of the hidden door still smelled of paint but it would fade. I would add some paperbacks and dust to complete the illusion. My fingers slipped under a low shelf and found the latch and the door opened into darkness. I stepped inside and closed the shelves behind me, then switched on the light. My eyes burned as they adjusted.

I connected the digital camera to the new laptop and brought up the imaging software. Immediately it began to update and an anger rose in me. I should have checked the updates earlier. When a forty-minute estimate showed on the screen, my throat tightened and my head snapped back. I gripped my head tight, my hands over my skull and the soft cotton sleeves of the combat jacket pressed to my face, with the faint reek of the forest and the rotting smell of the pebbled shore where I had fallen.

It was no use, I thought. Frustration would be no help in this matter. The camera light blinked. The photos probably held no faces, but the software may reveal enhanced images. Was Hastings there? If so, he would be home by now. And was he alone? Would he repeat his perversions? Take the opportunity while his wife was away?

Outside his house there was a broken street light where I could watch from the comfort of my car.

I unplugged the digital camera and stuffed it back in the pouch. This time would be different. Hastings could switch off his light, but I would be waiting. However long it took.

Switching off the box room light, I pulled the shelves behind me, which went home with a satisfying click, and gave me more pleasure than I had expected. I grabbed the raincoat from where it had fallen. This night was not yet done.

I reversed between two parked cars, then shut off the engine and got into the rear and looked out, between the front seats. To my right was the junction with the road that dropped sharply towards Stockbridge, and facing me was Hastings' terrace; further down, the light shone above his door.

Under the broken streetlight, with a dark blanket draped over me, the rim of the night vision goggles peeked out towards Hastings' door. The vista seemed like a black and white movie, although the view was sharper than I had expected, and my breath quickened. It would be possible to see Hastings' face, but there no point confronting him at his door like some paparazzi, hoping for some bizarre *in flagrante delicto* as the young boy entered his house. If the door light went out, I had the night vision video camera by my side.

The black cab on the boy's last visit had come from the road to my right, the main route through Stockbridge. If it stopped at the same place, then when the boy left Hastings' house, he would walk towards me and I would see his face. First, I would record him going in and then leaving. There would be no doubt.

The car window was lowered an inch so I could listen for a cab and stop my breath from misting the windows. The engine had lost its heat, and damp air drifted across the tips of my fingers. The street was quiet, and the high hedges at the other side of the cobbled road were in darkness. I very much hoped the old man and his dog would appear, but only a few people passed, collars up against the weather, climbing the hill from Stockbridge towards the town.

The light above Hastings' door went out.

I almost dropped the night goggles and looked again. I grabbed the night video camera. There might be a glimpse of Hastings as he opened the door to the boy.

A smirr fell, threatening to obscure the windscreen.

The black cab came up the hill, its engine labouring in low gear then swung around and stopped at the corner, its engine rattling and the body rocking on tired springs. The interior light didn't go on. I lowered the video camera and peered forward. It was empty. I sat open mouthed for a moment before it came to me.

The boy was already here.

Through the lens, Hastings' door opened to darkness and a boy hurried down the street, the same white skinny jeans, the same sports top. He pulled open the cab door and jumped in.

I saw him.

The interior light came on and his baseball cap sat just above the edge of the seat and the back window. The light of the cab flicked off and it pulled away in a sharp circle and down the hill and out of sight.

I didn't need to check the video. I didn't need to see his face again.

Chapter XI

Three cars in front, heading north east. James Mauchline Torridon. The last time we'd spoken was on the Army firing range in the Pentland Hills. It was summer. His hair was longer. He was a good shot. Always relaxed and calm until the lesson ended, when he became sullen. Then he stopped coming. I never saw him again, or knew what became of him.

The automatic gearbox dropped a gear as I let the cab gain some distance from the lights, on the road to Leith and the sea. Amongst the new Michelin starred restaurants on the shore, the old Leithers lived where they always had, but now cheek by jowl with the new apartments belonging to incomers. When the eighteenth century bourgeoisie had moved out of their medieval Old Town flats, crammed along the Royal Mile, leaving the ascending poverty of fifteen storeys above them, they had crossed the Nor' Loch to the New Town, the paint not even dry on the grand front doors, and the division of Edinburgh was complete. The auld and the new. They left behind the low-ceilinged rooms, the sooty stone thick with grime, and moved across the loch to the high windows in the Georgian design, and golden sandstone fresh-cut from the earth. Centuries later, the bourgeoisie had now reached into the dark lands of Leith with new buildings of steel skeletons and vinyl cladding where the old buildings had fallen, or hollowed out warehouses rebuilt, for big flats with wee windows.

Money would win in the end, and the old Leith would shrink like a scab.

The lights in front turned red. I had to talk to him, I thought. The thought of it made me shudder and my hands gripped the wheel. But it must be done. Be who I have to be. Harry would have known what to do.

The lights changed. A horn blasted. I smiled, relaxed in the seat, let the traffic go, then took the gearbox out of automatic, dropped two gears and floored the throttle.

A car in front turned off. There was nothing between us now. Stone tenements and warehouses lined each side of the road, narrowing as they neared the harbour. It couldn't be far. Fifteen feet in front, James leaned forward to the driver. The black cab slowed then stopped, and I pulled in behind and got out, grabbed my raincoat from the seat and called out when the cab door closed.

"James Mauchline Torridon."

He slid to a halt, then turned, eyes wide.

Holding out my hands to show they were empty, I strolled towards him. The cab pulled away and he glanced after it for a moment, then turned to the open door of a tenement.

I stopped, feet wide apart and lifted my chin in the air. "You know me. You know who I am."

He looked at my combat suit and then down at his feet, then again towards the tenement door.

"I just want a word." I tried to smile, but my teeth caught on my dry gums. "Don't let the outfit fool you, son, I'm not on exercise." The knife was heavy on my belt.

His voice was weak, near a whisper. "What's with the blade?"

"That's my business. We need to talk."

His lips twisted into a smile and his eyes, sunken in their sockets, flittered and looked everywhere but at me. "There are boys at the end of the street, Mr Lawless, they'll give you what you want."

I shook my head.

His smile turned into a sneer, but it died as he spoke and looked down. "I never took you for a nonce, Mr Lawless."

The heat rose in my chest and neck. "Boys are not my scene, son."

"Aye, and dressing up as Action Man is?"

I laughed and my shoulders shook. "It's a long story. You don't want to know. But we do need to talk."

He seemed on the verge of tears. "No."

"I don't mean now. It's late and I'm tired. And so are you. Tomorrow, I'll buy you breakfast."

He looked behind me. "No, thanks."

"The café at the end of the road. Nine o'clock."

He sniggered. "I've got coin in my pocket. I'll be out of my face till lunchtime. Go home, Mr Lawless." He turned into the darkened doorway.

I strode forward. "James, I'm your way out of here."

He spun around. "Way out of here?" His face glared with spite. "Way out of what? You're talking shite."

"Aye, out of here. You could be in London tomorrow, where no one could..."

He came out at me. "I don't believe it. You're selling

me to some pimp in Soho? You and Hastings? Is that the deal?"

"No, son, it's not like that…"

"Did you follow me here?"

"Yes, I…"

He shook his head, staring down at the moss in the corners of the doorway. "I liked you. So did Alex. He thought you were a good…" He stepped closer, one hand slipping into his pocket.

I stood my ground and held up a hand. Saliva bubbled at the edge of his cracked lips. "I'm nothing to do with scum like Hastings."

He said nothing.

"I'm an investigator. A lawyer." I took a notepad and pencil from my pocket and wrote down the number of the burner phone. "Nobody else has this number." I held out the note. "James, son, we really need to talk."

He took the note.

"Breakfast, tea, it doesn't matter. Let me know when you're ready. This isn't going to get any better anytime soon. So I'll be here tomorrow. I'll wait."

He looked up. His eyes were red and wet.

I stepped towards the car. "It doesn't have to be like this." I held my raincoat in my hand and opened the car door. When I looked up he was gone. The wind blew hard and cold until my ears froze, but no lights came on in the windows above the tenement door.

The shaking started as soon as I closed the car door and gripped the steering wheel. Harry was back. I wanted to shout his name out loud and ask him so many things, but it was time to go. It took several attempts to turn the car around, yet when I needed him, he was there. My

Harry, it had been so long. I blinked away the tears and the oncoming headlights diffused in my vision.

A black cab passed and I grabbed the steering wheel and pulled myself up in the seat. There were lights behind me. A cab in front of me pulled out, a passenger in the rear. Other lights appeared and disappeared behind me. It was pointless. If they knew where I was going they didn't need to follow. At moments of stress, my imagination was a curse.

The road rose towards the New Town and I could see no pattern. No car or cab stayed behind me for any length of time.

The thought of James trying to sleep filled my mind. Did he take drugs? It would be likely. In the dim streetlight, his face was pale and drawn. He was just a boy.

I turned into my street, then the archway to the mews and parked the car in the garage. I listened for traffic, but there was nothing close. Were they watching? If my location was compromised, then so was the entry and exit from my car and the flat.

I locked the garage and stood looking up at the ribbons of lights and dark in the windows. If so, then hiding was pointless. The thought of the photos awaiting me made the bile rise in my throat. Whatever disturbed me was nothing compared to the pain suffered in the abuse of these boys. And James. He had been such a good lad, but now his spirit was gone. A spasm cracked through my chest and neck, lifted my chin and forced the air out of my lungs. I rested a hand against the moss-slick walls. There was work to be done. My legs shook, but with anger, and I strode to the front door, looking around as I held out my key. The street was empty.

What if they didn't have to follow me? What if they were waiting for me?

I opened the front door of the building, threw back the raincoat, grabbed the hilt of the knife and ran up the stairs.

Twisting the key in and out, the door flew open at the end of my boot. The hall was in darkness. They had the advantage of their vision being accustomed to the dark. I kicked the door closed behind me and smacked on the lights. Nothing moved.

I pulled out the knife and ducked into the sitting room, twisting around with the knife held close, then out, bouncing off the walls of the hall and into each room.

At last I stood in the hall. If they did come, the door was the only exit, save going over the roofs. But they wouldn't know that. I looked up at the attic hatch above me. It could be pulled behind me, although it would be unlocked and they might know, and they would find me.

The box room still smelled of paint, and I left the door open and sat on the stool to upload the images from the camera. In one image, the rear lights of the car had been blocked by the hedge, so the glare did not spoil the shot, but had reflected and backlit the rear window in red. In it was a man in the rear holding out a hand to a boy exiting the car. After a few attempts, I had the image enhanced and peered at the screen. A face was clear now, stark in profile.

Mungo Hastings.

I slumped in the chair. It was over.

Tomorrow I would stand witness to James Mauchline Torridon. He would tell me. And I would have it all.

The walls of the box room seemed to move closer

and I ran out into the hall, then dropped down to the floor and rested against the wall, facing the front door. If they knew, that's where they would come. More deadlocks would hold them, but not for long, I thought. Maybe enough for me to get to the box room. And then what? How many weeks could I survive before escaping, or discovery?

The only other way out was the attic, but they would follow. What if the hatch in the hall was locked from inside the flat? A simple padlock would suffice. If the attic hatch was locked from inside the flat, they'd assume I didn't leave through the attic.

Just fix the padlock to the attic then pull the shelves of the box room door closed behind me.

The box room door lay open. The roof above it would be traditional wooden lath slats and plaster. A small hatch into the attic would be of no consequence to construct. And with the box room door closed and bolted, there would be no obvious exit other than the front door.

Standing in the hall, dust fell into my eyes when I pulled down the folding ladder from the hatch above me, and I climbed up into the darkness. The air was cooler and chilly draughts from gaps in the roof slates fanned my face. The rafters below the slates sloped down on either side. The rectangular brick bulk of the chimney stack thrust upwards out of the rafters; below it was my sitting room on one side and the box room on the other. There was space to cut a hole and drop down between the rafters and into the box room. Several planks lay around to pull over the hole.

I pushed open the skylight and hauled myself up and over the edge and into the night sky. The noise of the traffic increased and the chill was harsh but welcome. I always loved the thrill it gave me, like stepping out into a strange Northern land. I lifted my legs out and stood on the lead gutter between the peaks of the roofs and the glass panes of the cupola, where the light shone from the communal stairwell like a pale beacon. It had been many years since I had stood here, and with Harry; the gutter channels our wild coursing rivers that led through the mountains to disappear off the edge of a cliff as waterfalls. I faced east, to the lights of the football stadium at Easter Road. I had been once with my father, decked out in green and white, but it was an experience so wonderful and disturbing that we decided to follow our team on television or radio. On match days, I would climb onto the roof and face Leith, holding a radio with an earpiece playing the commentary, and listen for the roar as it came over the rooftops then dance amongst the gutters.

But that world was gone, and in the north, the flare of the oil refinery spat yellow and red at the low clouds. Edinburgh Castle lit the south, the New Town lit the west, and only the east showed a line of clean black over the sea; behind it, another horizon where the sun warmed the earth. It brought comforting memories as a child when I had watched the haar roll in at night from the black sea and settle on the town to smother Edinburgh with a golden shroud from the streetlamps shining below.

But though a shroud, she would not die. Her lights burned until the haar lifted over the blackened, brittle, pockmarked skin of her houses that had yet to be cleaned. On the days when the clouds lift, and when the sun was low and blinding in the west, the fresh scrubbed Edinburgh sandstone burned with golden, healing light.

But we are too young to feel it, and the stone is too old to care.

I have walked the streets in the summer dawn, or come up here for sunset, and it filled my heart with a warmth that I held long and deep, eyes closed, soaking in the red, amber and gold of the gloaming. The memory has kept me warm during the short summer nights when it is never cold out of the wind, and the long winter nights when warmth is only a memory.

When this was over, I would go to the sea, and live with it every day outside my window. One night the haar might roll in, and envelop me in its salty, cotton-wool cold soul and I would truly sleep.

In my dreams, and sometimes during the day, in a certain light from the stones or in the glow of my pear bowl in the sun, I could almost touch this happiness. It is more tangible during the day. It is the sun and the sea, just out of sight, but as my happiness, it exists. It is the one thing that gives me hope and the will to go on. It has always been a constant, as far back as I can remember. I was always alone, and sometimes in the dark, but it was restful, and gave promise of a future when I would leave.

Looking over my shoulder, Edinburgh would be a golden city on a hill. Perhaps it was this understanding of the light that set you free, and then you may leave.

Before then, there was work to do, but that too was part of my leaving.

I picked my footsteps between the roofs and the gutters. Some of the grand houses had been built as separate plots, although all of them adjoined into a terrace with wide gutters marking the roofs to an unbroken line of glass cupolas, peaks and troughs of slated roofs, skylights and grey stone tiles.

The chimney stacks stood high as giants, and around me was the sharp tang of carbon monoxide from heating systems ventilating through old chimneys. Some had metal ladders fixed to the side, painted with red zinc, others had succumbed to the weather and rotted away.

I kept low, remembering the route where I would be unseen, and traversed the entire terrace then turned to the roofs of the east part of the block, to the house where scaffolding covered the rear of one set of flats, a permanent feature in central Edinburgh, given the age of the buildings and the harsh weather.

The wooden platform was level with the edge of the roof, and each level below had a cage of scaffolding and thick planks, with a gap to a ladder leading down, all the way to the garden below, where I had climbed every wall in the block as a child.

I ran back to the corner and looked out onto the square below. Two black cabs, their engines idling, waited next to a private residents' garden in the middle of a square, half hidden by the wide and high old trees that lined the railing. One had a clear view of my street. But then so did every other car on my street. Behind the gardens were two Community Cars that could be booked online and accessed via an app. If my own car was compromised, they would work. I could be down the scaffolding and into a community car, then out of Edinburgh. They might track me eventually, but I would be far enough away. But where?

In the west, the lights of the bridges over the River Forth blinked in the night. Heading south and west was the obvious decision, to major population areas, but Harry knew locations in the Highlands where we could remain hidden and live off the land, although the winter would be brutal and uncertain. No, if I made it over the bridge, I would head for the oil ports in the north east. There were several websites that arranged a cheap berth on cargo ships to ports all over the world.

But the photographic evidence must be secured. I pulled the combat jacket up over my face, and smelled the sweet smell of the old cotton. I would bear witness to young James, and if necessary, Harry would take me to the Highlands or the North East. The strength surged in my limbs. We would win. We must.

Chapter XII

Behind my eyes lay the leaden sleep that had escaped me throughout the night. Before me stood a smiling Syrian New Scot, his wife beside him, placing a coffee on the table. The cup and saucer were thick ceramic and sky blue, and the colour transfixed me. I blinked and he smiled, then ran a cloth over the gleaming pine table. Around me was sunlight from the window to the street, where the winter midday sun shone down on Leith and dried the stone. In my hands the coffee smelt dark and sweet, and the Syrian woman returned to the counter, her husband beside her and they faced out over the café, as if a New Leith Gothic of pride, joy and freedom.

My mother loved me and called me artistic, but I knew what she meant.

I had expected a greasy spoon, the walls sticky from years of fried food, but around me were pastel colours and the scent of sugar and cardamon that lifted me more than the coffee. The newcomers to Leith had travelled farther than I, and had brought with them their own sun and given it to the cobblestones outside and the broken door tenements across the street.

An old man in a torn overcoat pushed open the door a few inches, his eyes flickering back and forth, and he winced as the bell clanged above him. His grubby face and uneven stubble seemed to shrink together as the Syrian hurried forward, opening the door wide and ushering him to a seat. The old man lifted a wavering hand to point to where a paper coffee cup was suspended above the counter, but the Syrian's wife was already advancing towards him with a coffee and bannock. The Syrian buffed the table and waved a hand to the suspended coffee cup. No payment was required.

I set my coffee cup down and let the taste and scent flicker through my head as if a whisper of sweet, sooty smoke. Then I laid my hands flat on the table. Preparations were complete. I had the cash should I need to go north in a hurry and I had the app to use the community cars. Although it might be unnecessary. If I was trapped in the box room, a simple email to all news organisations with the evidence would save me. And if a gagging order stopped them, then social media would know. My burner phone data connection would suffice. Then a world of outrage would descend upon them and rip them open to their rotting core. The thought made me tremble, and I took deep long breaths to calm myself. Harry was not here. I would have to talk to James Torridon alone. My back and stomach tensed and my head flicked to the side.

No. It had to be done.

Conversation is not a gift that comes easily to me. I can mimic such things, and talk of the weather when required, remembering not to impart too much detailed information. It was several years before I discovered that people did not actually want to know the complete forecast details of that day, but saw it as a substitute for having to think of conversation, because we had nothing to say to each other.

The door opened and James entered, his pale skin blotched and red. I stood to offer him a coffee. He ignored me and held up two fingers to the Syrian, then pointed to the old man.

He sat down but did not look at me. The Syrian woman came over with his coffee, stroked his hand and whispered words in her own language. He bowed his head.

I leaned forward. "You alright, son?"

He stared into his coffee.

"Listen, James, I'm not who you think I am."

He looked up, and his eyes blinked then focused. "Always thought you were a bit weird, but not bad weird."

"I'm not a nonce."

James lifted his coffee, then placed it back on the table. "What would you know about that?"

"More than you think. I'm a lawyer. I've seen it all."

"Mr Lawless, just get to the point. If you were anyone else, there would be someone meeting you with a knife, so say what you have to say. One more lecture won't kill me. I know how that will happen. I know what I've done. So say what you like, but it won't change anything."

I pushed my coffee away. "This is not about the past, son. This is not about shame. You do what you have to do to survive. Whatever you have done, I'm not your judge. But I want it to stop."

"Ha, you..."

"I want the men who do this to stop. I want them arrested. Look, is there anyone I can call?" I remembered something about a mother being absent. "What about your father...?"

"He wasn't my father."

"Is there...?"

"There's no one! There's nowhere to go."

"Okay, let's just talk."

"No, you talk. If I talk, I'll be as good as dead."

"What do you mean?"

"This morning, I heard how Alex died." He leaned over, head down until his forehead almost touched the coffee.

"I understand it was an overdose."

"Oh, yeah." His voice was barely a whisper. He lifted his head, and I could smell drink on him. "Tell me, Mr Lawless, how does someone who's terrified of needles and catching HIV, inject himself?"

He kept his eyes on me.

I shook my head. "I don't know, son. I honestly don't know."

"Alex smoked heroin. Yet he's found with a needle in his arm? No, I stay quiet, I don't die. Simple as that. You can't stop them. They're probably watching me now. And you."

"Who?"

"Work it out." He leaned forward. "Alex was my friend. He was giving up drugs. He had it all worked out. He'd packed his bag. He was heading to East Anglia to work in the fields. He was going to go north but the Highlands are full of druggies. He was going to camp out at a farm, like we used to do as kids."

"We used to go with the school. You remember?"

"I remember. I hated it, but he loved it. He was packed and ready to go. He had money. Told me there was a man who was going to help him get out. He was going to see him then get the bus south."

"I know that man, we can trust him."

"He talked to that man and now he's dead."

"No, James, son, I know this man, he was helping Alex."

"Aye, then he dies from an overdose, from a needle. Mr Lawless, Alex would leave the room if someone brought out a needle. He was terrified of them."

I sat still, my skin cold.

James pushed back his chair and stood. "I have to go."

"James, wait."

"No." He turned away.

"One thing, why are boys arriving late back to the school in a private car?"

James looked down at the floor. "Chess club. Where it started."

"I didn't know you played chess."

"It wasn't about chess."

His eyes glazed over, and I thought he was going to cry. "James, Alex was your friend. We have to stop this. You have my number. Come and talk to me, give me the evidence to put these men away for life. If they killed…"

"Mr Lawless, I'm dead anyway. There's no happy ending for boys like me."

"I'll help you. I know how to disappear. I'll show you. They'll never find you."

He shook his head slowly. "They already have. I can feel them watching."

"James, wait. I have to know. Did Alex Gillan talk about me?"

His watery eyes found a focus. "Yeah. He said he was going to see you. That he trusted you. That's why

I'm here today. When you got here last night, I thought you were going to kill me."

"Jesus, son, I…"

"But you let me go, and I knew it wasn't you. Alex never made it, or he'd still be alive." He turned to the door and pulled it open. The bell clanged and he mumbled over his shoulder. "Thanks, Mr Lawless. Goodbye."

He didn't look back.

A black cab drove past.

Chapter XIII

The two black cabs were waiting at the end of the street. I turned the car into my street and the headlights flashed over my front door in the darkening afternoon.

Had other cabs followed me home? There were over a thousand in the city.

I couldn't remember running up the stairs but I slammed the door behind me and turned the mortice locks and the walls of the hall seemed closer together. Turning all the lights on against the growing darkness, I checked every room and the street below then returned to the hall.

James' words had come from his soul. He'd seen his own death next.

Dear God, I couldn't lead him into a trap. But he had nowhere to go.

The box room door and hinged shelves lay open. I worked fast, piling up all the ration packs and bottles of water, then my notebooks from the sitting room. The box room door had to be completed as my redoubt. Hands shaking, I took knives and utensils from the kitchen, then returned for my pear bowl and then her pillow from the bedroom. Nothing else from my life was required. I pulled back the shelves and they went home with a click.

Would it really fool them, or was it just a conceit of my intelligence?

If they came, they would pull out drawers and overturn beds. With the heel of my hand, I thumped the shelves. They did not move.

Then I hit it harder. And there was a slight, almost imperceptible movement. Kneeling, I held my head in my hands then stood up using the wall for support. Closing my eyes, I clapped my hands in time as I spoke. "Problem, solution, method."

Bolt the shelves to the wall. Padlock the attic. Entry and exit through the roof of the box room to the attic and down to the street on the scaffolding. Pretty shelves in a cupboard would not fool a professional.

First, I had to know how close they were, and whether my paranoia was as delusional as my ego.

The folding ladder slid down to my feet and I climbed into the attic, stepping over the rafters and then hauled myself out of the skylight and crouched in the gutter between the roofs. Keeping low and away from the glass of the cupolas, I scrambled between the roofs and chimneys, heading for the end of the terrace. Kneeling behind a wide chimney stack, I peeked out.

At the end of the road, two black cabs stood together under the bare-branched trees bordering the private garden, their engines idling. Were they the same ones as before? One driver had a newspaper spread out on the steering wheel and the other seemed to stare straight ahead, down my street. I memorised the licence plates. Next time, I would know. If they were still there in an hour or so, then I would know. But I felt it. I felt their presence, black and malevolent.

I sat down and leaned against the chimney stack, the cold of the stone seeping into me. Sometimes, to assuage any anxiety, I will give my imagination enough rope to hang, and therefore, taken to an illogical conclusion, my anxiety becomes unfounded. And then it can be dismissed, which gives me great comfort.

But this felt both right and terribly wrong at the same time. Two black cabs on a break, or two intelligence operatives hiding in plain sight? The taxi numbers would be genuine, or other drivers might be suspicious. And although they could see down the street to the front door, they were just out of sight from my flat. I'd have to lean out the window. In this neighbourhood, no one leaned out their windows.

To the east, the sky was already dark on the horizon. If they had killed Alex, they would kill me. After meeting James, perhaps it was now only a matter of time. That Rubicon was behind us both. I crawled back towards my skylight, then up into a crouch and headed for the gutter between the two peaked roofs, and shelter from the wind.

To the west the lights on the three bridges blinked in the slate grey sky. The roads west to Glasgow could be blocked, but once over the bridge, the roads spilled out into Fife and farm tracks across the Ochill Hills. I would take the community car and head north, then hide or dump the car in a loch until I could make my way to the coast and Dundee or Aberdeen. My burner phone held the website for securing accommodation on cargo vessels, but the names of the available ships was all I needed. Turning up at the dock with cash would work.

Cargo vessels won't know or care about fugitives, just the colour of my money.

But if they took me on the street, I would need a diversion to make them scatter, then take my chances through my childhood's hidden lanes and secret short-cuts of the New Town.

A gust of wind came over the roofs and chilled the back of my neck. Turning, the eastern horizon was darker still and I closed my eyes. A list of items was required, ordered by purpose and importance. I am a details man, I thought. I am a planner. The thought of writing in my notebooks warmed me.

The community car behind the gardens was out of sight of the black cabs. If I left the building on foot, I could cut through the mews lanes, hidden doorways and gardens and lose anyone trying to follow me. I know the paths the foxes take.

The lights on the bridge were now brighter. If they closed the bridge before me, I'd be trapped. They would hunt me down. And not stop looking until I was dead. But there had to be a way.

A train passed through the dark red lattices of the Forth Bridge, looking like a model railway under the massive diamonds of iron. Men died making the bridge, and over the hundred years it had stood, many died from walking along the rail tracks and stepping off the edge. The few that survived died from exposure and were washed out to the North Sea or found dead on the beach if the tide turned.

The wind made my eyes stream. The hardware stores on the edge of town and the diving shops near the shore would have what I needed. Cash was the way, there was no point in leaving a trail. And it opened up many possibilities. Ideas flashed around my head.

The water under the bridge shone black under the lights. They could not find me if I was dead. Just like the boys from the school who would rather fall into the sea than spend another day alive.

The road to the north or the sea to the east. The cold steel frame of the skylight bit into my hand, but the water would be colder.

Chapter XIV

Anyone watching the front door to the street would be disappointed. Below street level in these great buildings are a warren of store rooms, coal bunkers, cold rooms and wine cellars. In the last century, they were often used as bomb shelters. And in the mews lane behind, there remained access doors for deliveries and coalmen. Connected to this level was a narrow, enclosed staircase built behind the wall of the existing grand staircase that allowed servants and chambermaids to traverse the house from cellar to kitchen to ballroom without disturbing the nobility or the gentry. Over the years, the keys have been lost or the doors painted shut. But my father grew up in this building and passed me the key to the door outside my flat, next to the grand staircase.

This key had lain at the back of a kitchen drawer since my father died, but was now in my pocket as I exited through an old coal hatch into the dusk of the mews courtyard in front of my garage.

In a few moments I had scaled the wall using the hand and footholds of my childhood, and dropped into a cobbled lane that led from another row of mews houses out to an adjacent street.

Collar up and head down, I climbed the hill towards

the Old Town, then doubled back down the narrow lanes to emerge close to a community car, parked beside the private garden in the square at the end of my street. The grubby winter sun had died around 3 p.m. and the thin, grey dusk that remained soon disappeared under the weight of winter darkness.

The app on my phone unlocked the car. Through the trees and bushes to the far side of the garden came the rattle of the black cabs' engines.

I had to be sure.

My key to the private garden was stiff in the lock. The black railings around the garden rose six foot high, and the daylight barely penetrated the high trees and bushes.

I wanted to see their faces.

The tracks through the bushes of my childhood would make too much noise, so I kept to the shadows under the trees and bushes until the path turned and exhaust fumes filtered through the leaves. The leaves brushed damp against my face.

Both men were in their cabs, lights out and windows closed against the wind and cold. The first man had his head back and eyes closed. The other stared down my street towards the front door where the blood still stained the stone.

His stillness was that of a hunter.

My legs shook and I backed away, keeping low until the gate, then turned and got in the community car.

On my phone, the alphabetically ordered lists shone out, detailing the actions and equipment required. Plotted on the map were the route and the locations of the shops for chemicals or sports gear.

A visit to the woods around the school would be

the last destination before returning home. The thick undergrowth held many buried secrets for generations of boys, and would soon hold another for me.

I returned the community car to the same spot. The cabs' engines idled on the far side of the garden. From the boot I hauled out a wheeled kit bag packed with my purchases and headed up the hill through narrow alleys, the wheels rattling and bouncing on the cobbles, and then out onto the main road towards my flat before doubling back into the unlit mews lane behind my garage. I climbed up and looked over, but there was no one in the courtyard.

Lifting the bag across my shoulders I began to climb, the strap of the bag cutting into my neck and the stone tearing at my fingers. As I pushed up onto the top of the wall, the bag shifted on my shoulders and threatened to drag me down head first, then my boot found a foothold and took the weight, and I held still for a moment to find my balance. The thought of the bottles of chemicals being broken if they hit the cobbles sent a shiver through my chest. Driving my fingers into the ancient mortar between the stones, I slid around and dropped to the ground, then ran for the garage.

The door locked behind me and I let the bag slip to the floor. My trousers were cold and wet, and my hands were lined with deep scratches from the undergrowth and bushes in the woods around the school, bleeding where the stone had torn the skin. But it was nothing to what might lay ahead of me, and I leaned on the bench, letting my head drop until it touched the stained wood.

They could come at any moment. Why didn't they come now? I stood up and faced the door. Perhaps because they didn't know I had the evidence. The photos of the school and Hastings. But they would.

From the bag I lifted out the bottles and packets of chemicals and a small backpack. A simple binary device was all that was required. The correct mix of chemicals would have the desired effect. Selecting several of my father's tools pinned on the wall above the bench, I began the assembly.

Pushing open the door from the servants' staircase, I peeked through the gap, but there was no one at the door to my flat, or on the grand staircase. Once inside the flat, I bolted the door and checked every room. They would come, it was inevitable.

I placed my father's toolbox in the hall, then slipped off the backpack and moved it out of the way. My new laptop blinked in the darkness of the box room and the new wifi router flashed, looking for devices. From a box I took miniature wifi cameras with mics for all the rooms and attic, and a waterproof camera for the window to the street, with a monitor mounted in the box room. Perhaps I would see them coming. The shelves locked into place with a click and with a power drill from the toolbox, I screwed the frame of the shelves into the wall. I thumped it hard, but it did not move. Then I rapped my fingers on wood between the shelves. The blackout curtain behind deadened the sound. This time it would work. My cell was secure. I pulled down the ladder to the attic.

I was ready. After all, I thought, I am a details man. From my pocket I took a burner phone and switched it on. There were several in my backpack, to use once then discard. The burner phone bleeped in my hand

and I screamed, launching it into the air. It fell in the darkness, but I was able to find it before the screen cut out and I saw the text.

Mr Lawless, This has to end. I'll tell you everything I know. Then I'll go. I'm coming over. I know where you live.

I dropped to my knees and the breath stuck in my throat. It passed after a few moments. My hands opened where they had been clamped around the phone, and the blood returned to my fingers. Dear God, he was on the way here. My fingers jabbed the screen.

James, you were right. I'm being watched. Don't come to the front door, take the mews lane on the main road then walk down ten yards and stop. I'll be behind the wall on your right.

Chapter XV

The footsteps became louder behind the high stone wall, then I could heard him breathing hard.

"James?"

"Mr Lawless?"

"Can you climb over? There's a stone that juts out where you can get a foothold, then reach up for the top."

He grunted and his hand appeared, grabbing the top of the wall.

"That's it, son."

His legs appeared over the edge then he dropped onto the cobblestones. His face was pale in the thin light.

"Follow me. We won't be seen." I turned towards the coal hole door then stopped. "Do you have a bag?"

"No." His voice cracked. "I left everything. Not that I have much. Just wanted to be away before anyone knows."

"Good plan. This way." Crossing the courtyard, I pulled open the coal hole door and descended into darkness. James was close behind me and I locked the door, then shone my phone down a short corridor to the foot of the servant's staircase.

"Mr Lawless, what is this?"

"Old store rooms and a servants' staircase. Now

forgotten, like the servants. Be very quiet and use your phone as a torch. We're going to the top floor."

The wood creaked below our feet and cobwebs brushed my face as we climbed. He kept pace with my footsteps, turning at each floor until we reached the top and pushed open the door a fraction to listen. There was nothing, and I opened it for James and crossed over to my own flat door, then we were inside with the door bolted.

He was shaking and his pale skin was blotched from his tears.

"Stay away from the windows, son. Just in case. Don't worry, you'll soon be on your way. Let's get the kettle on."

He followed me into the kitchen and I began to make tea. "Have a seat. There's three grand in the envelope beside you. I've booked you a ticket on the overnight sleeper. You'll have a private cabin and bed. When you close the door they won't disturb you until London. The envelope also has a print-out of your ticket. When the train leaves, get rid of your sim card and lose the phone out the window. Buy a pay-as-you-go phone in London and text me the number." I placed a mug of tea beside him. "Careful, it's hot."

"Thanks, Mr Lawless."

I smiled. "Call me Harry."

He looked up but said nothing and sipped his tea.

"There are two black cabs to the west of this building beside a private residents' garden. But they're not really taxis unless they're the laziest bastards in Edinburgh. They're watching the door to the street. That's why we took the, er, tradesman's entrance."

He smiled and warmed his hands on the mug.

"I'll take you back down the servants' stairs, and you go as you came. If you leave in ten minutes you should make it just in time. No point hanging around a platform."

James picked up the envelope and stuffed it in his pocket.

"All we have to do first is make a statement. You write, I'll witness it. Be brief. Names and what they did. There will be time enough for the detail."

The mug nearly slipped from his hand and he managed to get it down before it spilled across the table.

"Sorry, son. That was stupid of me."

He wiped his wet hands on his jeans. "It's okay. What they did was no more than what some of the older boys did to me when I was a kid. When your dad is some posh Colonel no one gives a shit if you report them."

"I never knew. I've learned that some things pass me by, and I have no concept of them."

"We always thought you lived in another world. It looked like it was a nice place to be."

"Aye, sometimes. Look, is there nowhere you can go? Relatives?"

"No. Dad died in Afghanistan. He was actually my stepdad. We were close, but he was never there. I've no idea where my mother is, I think she went to the US. She said she would take me, but she didn't, it was just crap because I had wanted to stay with Dad. She drank a lot. She had me young with another soldier. Then she met Dad. And it was good for a while, then he got sent to Afghanistan. I was allowed in King George's because he was a Sergeant Major. I was going to go to my mum during the holidays, but she'd disappeared. I had no one. I just ran when I hit sixteen. They couldn't find me, because they didn't look. If no one is paying the fees, they don't care."

I couldn't think of a single word to say.

James pointed to a pad of paper on the worktop. "Is that for me?"

"Aye."

"Film me. If they somehow get rid of the statement, we'll have something else."

I lifted the phone and he picked up the paper and he talked as he wrote.

"My name is James Mauchline Torridon. When I attended King George's as a schoolboy I was sexually abused by older boys, who I can name, and by a man who ran the chess club. His name is Mungo Hastings. There was another man, a friend of his, but I don't know his name. It was always really dark in his room."

His voice squeezed to a barely audible whine, and he bowed his head and sobbed, pushing the chair back so his tears fell away from the paper and onto his jeans. He lifted his head and took long, shuddering breaths, and the spit bubbled from his mouth and the tears rolled down and over his lips. When the sobs subsided, he lifted the pen.

"When I ran from the school to the streets, Mungo Hastings found me, and the abuse continued so I could feed my habit." He looked up and seemed to switch off, then his whole body tightened and he stared out of the window, as if unable to speak or move.

"That's enough, son. That's enough." I didn't know what to do. I had never seen such pain. But it made me cold and still. He needed me. "Sign it, son. I stand as witness to your words."

He drew the pen slowly over the paper, carefully

signing his name like a child, then sat back. I took the pen, wet from sweat and tears, and added my own.

"It's over, son. Finish your tea and you can go when you're ready. I'll get you a warmer coat. Do you need me to make you a sandwich and a flask of tea?"

He stared at me then shook his head and stood up, holding on to the chair. After a few deeps breaths he straightened his shoulders and wiped his face on his sleeve. "A warm coat would be good. Just the coat. I should go."

I was about to turn into the hall, then stopped. "James, how did you know where I live?"

"Alex told me. He said he was coming to see you, 'cos he really liked you. There was no one else he could trust. They must have killed him before he got here."

I had no words. I had walked past his blood, the blood that had seeped into the stone around me.

The wind had sharpened, but the light from the floors below shone out of the cupola as I picked my way over the roof, to crouch behind the chimney stack at the far end. The phone buzzed in my hand.

Doors closed. Train leaving now.

I looked out from behind the chimney, to where the two black cabs stood together, lights out, engines idling. If there had been only one, then James may have been spotted. I turned away with my back to the cold stone and checked the train tracker on the burner phone. The train was still in the station. I pulled up the collar of my coat, and stared at the screen, willing the black dot to move down the line across the map.

It was over. I had the statement and the photos. And the video.

The phone in my pocket vibrated. I checked the train map once more, but the dot had not moved.

I pulled it out and opened the message.

Hector – This is Campbell. We must move fast. There are rumours of your investigations. Bring what evidence you have and meet me in the garage under the High Court. The garage door will be open. I have a senior police officer and a Channel 4 journalist waiting for us. You may be followed. Do not stop under any circumstances for anyone. I need you now.

One hand on the stone, I pulled myself up and the wind pushed me against the chimney stack. I pressed my head to the stone and checked the map.

The train had left the station.

Chapter XVI

I switched off all the lights and knelt in the hall, letting my eyes adjust until I was sure there was no light leaking from the edges of the shelves hiding the box room. It was time to go.

They were waiting for me to leave, sitting in their cabs in the dark, expecting their prey to run. They would be waiting for some time. And when they found out the deception, they would come through the front door. Then wait for my return.

But my return would not be through the front door. That was not the only route. Holding a torch between my teeth, I took a saw from the toolbox and a ladder and climbed into the attic. Between the rafters above the back wall of the box room, the saw tore through the old lath and plaster until the hole was big enough for me to squeeze through, then I lowered the ladder into the box room and placed heavy planks over the hole.

The skylight was unlocked so I turned back to descend the folding ladder into the hall. Once I'd pushed it back into place, I took folding steps from the pantry, reached up and fixed a padlock to the attic hatch. The trap was set, but it was not set for me.

In the kitchen, James' statement lay on the table, and I pushed it into the large envelope with the evidence then took another sealed envelope from a kitchen drawer. Should I not return, then my solicitor would follow my instructions. I had never written a will before.

To hell with them. I'd deliver the evidence and be home before they had any idea what had happened. But it might be my last night of peace before the hounds of the press would find me. One short statement on the front step would suffice, the rest they would hear in court. In the pantry, I took a bottle of Bordeaux from the wine chiller, cut away the dust cover then took out the corkscrew and pulled the cork. I sniffed the neck of the bottle then laid it in a dark corner of the pantry. By the time this was over, it would be ready to drink.

Campbell had said there were rumours. That would explain the black cabs. Perhaps if there were more than rumours, I'd be in an interrogation room. But as soon as my car left the alleyway to the street they'd be right behind me. Or so they thought. It was time to end this, and then the heavens would fall.

I pulled the door of my flat behind me, then unlocked the servants' staircase and moved quickly down to the coal hole, across the dimly lit courtyard into my garage then stood before the work bench and slipped on the bulging backpack. The thick envelope lay secure inside my jacket.

In the courtyard, with a glance towards the darkened arch to the street, I tightened the straps of the backpack and tucked the hanging cord into my jacket, then checked my footholds on the old stone. Falling from the wall and landing on the backpack was unthinkable.

The stone was damp but I clung on, then slid over the edge of the wall, and stone by stone, dropped down to the cobbled lane. Lifting the cord of the backpack to let it fall over my chest, I headed through the dark into the street and strode uphill towards the town, doubling back once more to the community car, pausing only to post the envelope to my solicitor.

The heat under my jacket had built up as I reached the community car and unlocked it with my phone, and sweat ran down the back of my neck despite the damp chill of the air. My breath was white, and I dropped the padded envelope of evidence in the footwell, then slipped off the backpack and placed it on the front passenger seat. I secured it with the seat belt, letting the cord hang down towards me.

Faint exhaust smoke drifted up from the far side of the gardens. Campbell said there was a journalist waiting for me behind the High Court. Perhaps when I return, I'll park the car and walk past the black cabs, just to see their faces.

No, such fantasies were for fools. Behind the cover of the gardens and the haar, I headed east out of the New Town then doubled back and up the slope of the Mound towards the Old Town, but no black cabs tracked me. The haar became heavier as I climbed the Mound and the top of the buildings were lost from view, and in front was the faint outline of the stone of the High Court, the stone where my hands had found cold comfort a few days ago, when I was innocent. Near the top of the Mound the buildings at street level were dark and cold, and in the thickening haar the streetlamps appeared as silver orbs of light. I stopped at the traffic lights and a black cab passed me from a road on the left but the driver didn't look at me and accelerated up into the Old Town.

To the left of the corner of the High Court lay the

garage door, but I could see no light or any figures through the haar. Although if they were waiting, they would be sure to remain hidden. Rumours, Campbell had said. There was no point driving into a trap. They would recognise me when I parked or drove by.

I screamed when the blast of a car horn surged through me and a black cab filled my rear-view mirror. I fumbled for reverse gear to ram him but the shouting in a broad Edinburgh accent and the green light stopped me and I spun the car left and down the hill towards Waverley Station, plunging into the haar until there was nothing but white in front of me. I pulled into the kerb. The taxi flashed past me towards the station. My whole body shook and I held onto the steering wheel, gasping for breath. Across the road lay an alleyway and steep steps that led up to the narrow cobbled road at the rear of the High Court. My heart slowed and I let go of the wheel. Two pinpricks of light shone from the alley as a couple of disorientated tourists appeared, clutching their phones and dragging wheeled suitcases – they kept tight to the stone of the building beside the alleyway then turned towards the station.

I pulled the backpack close to me, then reached down and grabbed the thick envelope. Campbell would be waiting. If I took the steps I could approach unseen, and it was only a short sprint to the garage on the other side of the road. I got out of the car, slipped on the backpack, draping the cord over my shoulder and down my chest, then crossed the road. I could barely see my feet in the haar, but I found the handrail in the middle of the steps that led all the way to the top and began to climb. The haar tumbled down over me and I was soon enveloped in a silver cloud, diffused by the streetlamps and darkening in the corners.

The effort of the steep climb stopped my legs from shaking, and through the silver mist around the lamps I could see the branches of trees looming above me, teardrops glistening on the tips, silhouetted by the darkness.

The steps turned right and the gradient increased, and my white breath blended with the silver mist. Then the handrail turned left when I reached the top, and I emerged unseen into the haar behind the High Court.

I kept low to the side, one hand on the cord to the backpack. Across the narrow cobbled road, the outline of the garage came into view, the rolling metal door lifted halfway, and a faint light came from within. A shadow appeared at the edge of the garage and a man stooped to peer under the door from within. It was Campbell.

Chapter XVII

Campbell ducked back inside. The cobbles were slick under my feet as I hurried over and was about to bend down to go under the half-open roller door when I remembered the bulging backpack. I rapped my knuckles on the steel and footsteps scuffed towards me. An electric motor groaned and the door clanked upwards.

"Lawless?"

The garage was empty except for a car with the boot open and I hurried in and turned to where Campbell's hand still rested on a green button beside the door. The door clanked to a stop.

"I wasn't followed. But I'm being watched."

The haar drifted into the garage and rolled over the floor. Campbell stood with his mouth open. His hand was still on the button.

"Should we close the door, Lord Campbell?"

He turned and stared into the silver and darkness. "No."

I pulled the envelope from my jacket. "Everything is here. Photos and a statement from James Torridon. He names his abusers, and I have signed it as a witness."

"Give it to me." He tore it from my hand and walked

126

over to the car, took a briefcase stuffed with papers and jammed it between them, then slammed the boot shut.

"He's safe. James Torridon is safe."

Campbell let out a low laugh. "I think not. That little shit is a threat to national security. You think the state will let him live?"

"But they don't…"

"Found dead in his cabin at Carstairs Station, the only stop before London, where they couple the Glasgow train."

"But he's… He won't arrive until…"

"Give it time. And you know who saw him last? You." Campbell pulled out his phone. "You had to kill him, didn't you, Hector? You gave him pure heroin for his journey south and he overdosed."

My throat tightened and the breaths came in wheezing gasps.

Campbell scrolled through his phone. "You're a bloody weirdo. Everybody knows that. Turns out you're a paedophile and a murderer too. That's certainly what the signed statement found on James Torridon's body says. And I witnessed that one." He tapped a number on his phone. "Monday morning, I'll be able to go to my chambers for the first time without you hanging around, you creepy bastard. What a joy." He turned away and lifted the phone to his ear. "Ah, Inspector. Your suspect is with me. Yes, me too. If he tries to run, I'll zap him." He cut the call.

My legs shook and my vision blurred. "Harry. Please, Harry…"

"Who the fuck is Harry? Anyway, the Inspector will be here in a moment. They were going to stop you when you tried to leave your house, but I was here just in case." He pulled a Taser gun from his pocket. "The Inspector left this behind in the event they lost you in the haar. He is aware of how dangerous you are. You know, being a murderer and all that. And a paedo."

I looked to the door.

"And I'll take great delight in shooting you in the fucking face with fifty thousand volts." He lifted the Taser. "We have it all. Photos of you trying to break into the school through a window. A signed statement. Posthumous, obviously, but then who's going to believe a fucking freak like you? You and your fucking pencils on your desk and sitting there humming a tune and pretending to be on a phone call. You should be in a padded cell. And then you gave us the cherry on the cake. James Torridon, rent boy and drug addict, arrives at your flat to be abused. It's all in his statement. We lost him in the fog, but then he turned up at the station with thousands in cash so we know you met up. What's the chances we'll find out who bought the ticket?" He glanced down at the knife on my belt. "Look at you. Like bloody Rambo. And you haven't got the balls to use it."

I stood still, and felt very cold. "It's you. You're the second man."

"Oh, well done, you win a fucking coconut."

I slowly wrapped my hand around the hilt of the knife and pulled it from the sheath and the odour of old gun oil drifted past me.

A car slid to a halt at the door and a man ran into the garage. "Put that down."

"Ah," said Campbell. "Detective Inspector Gilfeather, meet Hector Lawless. Murderer and paedophile."

Gilfeather kept to the side, glancing at the knife. "I

have cars blocking every road to the High Court. Drop it."

Campbell pointed the Taser, his hand tightening on the grip.

I blew out a long, slow breath and closed my eyes, then looked down at the knife, and replaced it in the sheath. The haar swirled around our feet. I smiled at Campbell. "I wouldn't fire that thing, if I were you."

Campbell smirked. "No?"

"No. You see, I've had a busy afternoon." I lifted the cord that led to the backpack and dangled it between my fingers. "You know, any garden centre or hardware store has a fascinating selection of chemicals."

Gilfeather's eyes flicked towards the bulging backpack.

My fingers twisted around the cord. "I think the Inspector knows what I mean. Hydrogen peroxide is so easy to buy. If there had been time, I could have ordered two litres from Amazon. Amazing stuff. And very unstable. Then the garden centre had shelves full of nitrate fertiliser."

Gilfeather cleared his throat and looked at the cord. "You're bluffing, it takes more…"

"More than a spicy cocktail of chemicals to kick off Guy Fawkes Night, no? You're right. So, what if I said the garden centre also stocked charcoal, potassium nitrate and sulphur? All standard items for gardeners. Just mix them in the correct proportions and we're ready to start the party. You with me?"

Gilfeather nodded. "I'm with you."

"What?" said Campbell.

"The three components of gunpowder," said Gilfeather. "As a detonator."

I wound the cord around my fingers. "And for ignition, a plastic bottle of gas and an electric candle lighter from eBay. Boom. Shake the room."

The Taser wavered in Campbell's hand. "You're a fucking psychopath."

"And you, Campbell, are a liar and a murderer. But, you fire that thing at me and all that will remain will be your expensive dental work." I turned to Gilfeather. "You won't be surprised to hear that I am entirely innocent of these crimes, Inspector. Unless you're part of his Establishment gang. You look like a decent copper, so probably not. But I've been set up by this sleekit wee shite. The evidence is locked in the boot of that car. Mind you," I cocked my head towards the backpack, "with this on my back, I'm not doing my case any favours, am I?"

"It's a lie," said Campbell. "There is no such evidence."

Gilfeather held up his hands. "Listen, Lawless. You're a lawyer. We can settle this in court. You know the system. Make it work for you."

"Fine words, Inspector. I haven't misjudged you. But either I walk out of here or no one does." I backed away towards the door.

"You won't get far," said Gilfeather.

"Might not need to." I slipped the backpack from my back and wrapped the cord around my hand. "I could end it all here."

"No…"

"Why not? I'm fucked anyway." I stretched out my hand and jabbed the red button to close the door and the door rattled downwards. Then I dropped the backpack to the ground and held it with my boot and lifted the cord until it was tight. "We'll burn together, right here and in hell!"

I tugged the cord hard and booted the backpack at Campbell then hit the floor and rolled backwards under the door and out onto the road. The door slammed into the concrete beside my face and I scrambled to my feet and headed through the haar for the steps. Behind the door Campbell screamed, but it soon turned to coughing as the smoke bomb took effect. One day I'd learn to make a proper bomb.

The railings beside the steps appeared through the haar and I fumbled for the handrail and hurried down blind, watching for the turn to the street and the alleyway. The knife was in my hand. Had they put a copper on the stairs? My feet slipped on the worn, wet stone, until I reached the cobbles of the alleyway. No, they had expected me to arrive in my car. They would have blocked the roads but not the steps.

In a moment I was in the community car and heading towards the rail station, then left towards the New Town. The haar would block the street cameras but it would take a while to find I had used a community car. My breath chilled and bounced off the windscreen.

I was prepared. Follow the plan. They would assume I had other transport when they found my own car. Gilfeather was no fool.

Head for the bridge over the Forth and north through the Kingdom of Fife and on to the Highlands or the North East then dump the car. Then while they were trawling the forests and hills, I'd be on a freighter to the Far East or a fishing boat to Spain. I switched on the fog lights and joined the traffic heading west.

*

131

Gilfeather rolled under the shutter and got to his knees, his chest heaving, leaning forward with his hands flat on the wet cobblestones, saliva dripping from his mouth as the smoke erupted from his lungs in racking breaths.

Campbell crawled past him, weeping and coughing until he collapsed in the road.

The shutters reached the top and clattered to a stop. Gilfeather knelt and watched the grey smoke tumble out the garage and curl over the top edge of the shutter and up the wall of the High Court. He grabbed his radio and spat out the saliva flooding his mouth, then thumbed the button. "He's gone. Done a runner. Smoke bomb. Block all the roads. No one gets through." A cough racked his body once more, and he waited until it had gone. "He's mentally unstable and may be armed. I repeat, may be armed."

He turned to where Campbell lay on the road beside a pool of his own vomit, and watched as Campbell tried to push himself up just as his hand slipped sideways on the vomit and he dropped face down, his nose cracking on the cobblestones.

"Campbell, what's his number?"

Campbell peered sideways, blood streaming from his nose and mixing with his vomit. Saliva sprayed from his mouth. "What?"

"His phone. Hector Lawless. His phone number. Do you have it?"

Campbell let out a racking cough, then dry heaved himself into silence and looked up. "Yes, but…"

"Give me your phone."

Campbell pushed himself up to his knees. "I'm afraid I cannot just…" He retched again, coughing at the same time until his body froze into a rictus of pain and he hit the road once more.

"Don't dick around, get me the bloody phone number. If he gets past the cordon or he's armed then…" Gilfeather pulled out his own mobile phone. "I've got a 24-hour sheriff to give me the permission to track him. If you'd given me his number before, I could be tracking him now."

A policeman came running through the haar. He stopped beside Campbell and gave him a sideways glance. Campbell raised a hand for a help up, but the policeman looked down at the vomit-stained hand and ignored him. The policeman handed Gilfeather a plastic bottle of water from his utility belt.

Gilfeather took a swig and spat it on the ground, then drained the bottle. "I'll get the Chief Constable to wake up the Sheriff and hope he's sober. We need a number tracked." He look around at the haar and the smoke, with the sound of sirens approaching. "Right now. In this shit a chopper won't get off the ground. Tracking's all we've got." He nodded towards Campbell. "When he recovers the power of speech, get the number and text it to me."

The policeman stood over Campbell and pulled out his notebook.

"And he's got evidence in the boot of his car," said Gilfeather. "When the smoke clears, bring it all to me. And get me a car back to HQ." He took a deep breath and stared into the haar. "Seriously, fuck this and fuck everything."

Chapter XVIII

A policeman pointed to the screen on his desk as Gilfeather pushed open the office door and ran towards him. He leaned over, the reek of the burned chemicals and smoke rising from his clothes.

"Sir, we've found his phone. Judging by the speed and location, he's in a car on the way to the bridge to Fife. He'll get there soon."

"Cameras?"

"Useless. It's the haar, sir, it's even thicker near the water." The policeman changed screens, to where the traffic cameras showed a pale grey, with the faint lights of cars passing slowly though the mist.

"So we've no idea which car is his?"

"No, sir."

"Shit. Right, block the bridge. Not our side, the Fife side. If he gets on the bridge he'll be trapped."

"Fife Police are nearly there, sir."

A police officer ran over and handed him a sheet of paper, thick with text. "MI5, sir."

"Fairbairn, just give me the headlines, I don't have time for the Gospel According to St Pompous of Twat."

"Sir, they've told our armed officers to stand down, and their officers will take care of any incident. They're treating this as terrorism. They want him kettled until their men arrive."

"Terrorism? Like, er, what our armed officers are trained for?"

"Yes, sir."

"Sir," said the officer at the desk, "Fife police have blocked the bridge at their end. Going by the tracking, the target will be on the bridge in five minutes. There will be cars behind him all the way. He'll have nowhere to go."

"Get me a car. And Fairbairn, tell the Fife coppers to shut off their blues and twos and nee-naws or he might see it as a trap."

"Aye, sir."

"Sir," said Fairbairn, "Why can't cops arrest him? If he is armed, they know they have permission to open fire if necessary."

"Good question. Probably because this isn't an arrest."

The city lights behind me faded into the haar. The line of cars in front made slow progress. If they blocked the bridge and I was too close, then I'd be trapped, but they'd more likely be scouring the haar-swept streets of the Old Town. The odds were in my favour.

The turning for South Queensferry, the harbour town below the Forth Rail bridge appeared and I swung left, the road rising to cross over the main carriageway. The haar dissipated for a moment.

The lights blinked on top of the red steel lattices of the Forth Bridge that carried the trains north, the pinnacles of the huge cantilevers jutting above the blanket of haar. To the west, the red lights at the top of the two road bridge towers flashed, and as I reached the top of the hill and slowed, pulsing through the haar were flashing blue lights at each end of the road bridges. Then they disappeared.

The faint sound of a police siren washed through the darkness behind me. No, this was impossible. How could they know?

My phone. The one used to text Campbell. I pulled it from my pocket. Gilfeather had the number tracked, and he would know I was heading for the bridge. Every road around me would be blocked.

I lowered the window and threw the phone into the darkness.

There was no choice, I thought. It ends here.

The glow of the street lights faded in the rear view mirror as I turned onto the narrow back road skirting the forest and down towards the sea. Atop the darkened hill to my left sat Dalmeny railway station, four hundred metres before the rail bridge left the shore and thrust out over the water. Once past the car park and steps up to the station, I took a right at the bottom of the hill along a narrow track next to the shoreline. The haar enveloped the car but the sea wall on my left and the forest close on my right where the branches brushed my window showed me the way.

Somewhere along the track was a long jetty and a house where the track was blocked by a gate. I slowed and spotted the gap in the trees where a stream ran down from the forest and under the road, then pulled the car into the side. The hidden forest path was not far from the stream. It was the path the boys from my school took when they walked into the night to climb the bridge and find peace in the darkness of the sea and end the agony of their childhood.

Now I knew why the boys had walked off the bridge. From the testimony of James Torridon, the abuse must have been passed down through the generations.

I climbed up the bank and pushed forward through the trees and found the track where the earth was hard, then hurried forward, searching for the two oaks that stood either side of an animal track.

After a few minutes the black mass of the first oak tree loomed above me and I turned along the track, stumbling over tree roots until the ground dipped, and I followed it down into a hollow filled with a soft mass of leaves. I had never been here at night before. As a boy, I could disappear at lunchtime and hide here, unseen from the track or the trees, burying myself in the autumn leaves. I began to dig into the leaf litter, down through the rotting layers until it was up to my waist, then found the kit bag and unzipped the cover. My purchases from earlier that day lay before me. My hands were freezing and the sweat chilled on my neck as I undressed, placing my clothes, boots and socks to one side, then pulled out the kit from the sports shop and the long-handled bolt cutters. Naked, I tugged on the neoprene wetsuit as best I could, falling backwards into the leaves several times. Once the legs were on, I stood exhausted, the vapour rising from my body and mixing with the cold haar that drifted between the trees, carrying the smell of the sea and the sound of police sirens.

I hauled on the rest of the suit and stood for a moment, catching my breath. All my strength would be required for what would come next. I pulled my clothes back on, with a bobble hat and a thick scarf to cover the hood of the neoprene suit, then took out a climbing harness covered by a high-visibility orange jacket. This time I wanted them to see me, but not what was underneath. On the cameras they would see me dressed for a cold winter night, not for what I had in mind. I tried to push away the thought of what awaited me. It was suicide. But that was the plan.

I kicked the leaves over the bags then turned back to the track. The distant sirens were clearer now, though the haar shrouded their location. Taking the car to the station car park had its risks, but there was no option. It was part of the plan. I hefted the bolt cutters over my shoulders and picked up the pace.

The outline of the car appeared at the foot of the bank and I climbed down. Inside was warm out of the chill of the sea. Lights off, I edged forward to a passing place cut into the bank and manoeuvred the car around. My eyes adjusted to the dark and I drove to the end of the track and turned left, onto the main road for a hundred yards, then parked near the steps that led to Dalmeny railway station, rising high above me. At the foot of the steps was one of the wide stone bridge pillars that stretched into the haar and I began to climb.

Halfway to the station, the path passed a courtyard at the foot of another stone pillar of the bridge, this time surrounded by a chain-link fence. Nearer the pillar I could see another fence enclosing the steel steps that led up the side of the stone to the narrow metal causeway that ran below the rail track and out over the water. I swung the bolt cutters around to bite into the fence and worked down the side of a metal stanchion where the links were fixed, then swung the bolt cutters up once more and cut along at head height until I could push through the links. Dragging the bolt cutters behind me, I approached the second fence. This was much more secure in construction, with thicker, closer strands of steel, but was no match for the bolt cutter. I began at the bottom and cut out a three foot square window then crawled through.

I dropped the bolt cutters and began to climb the steel staircase bolted to the side of the stone and into the haar.

The first camera was fixed at the top on the stairs as I stepped onto a narrow metal gangway with steel meshed sides that came up to my waist. Above me in the darkness were the thick steel girders that held the railway track. The haar swirled around me as I headed towards the shore and tried to picture the line of stone towers that led the bridge out to sea, before the first of the three mammoth diamonds of red latticed steel that stretched over to the Kingdom of Fife, each more than a hundred feet high. The water was shallow on the south side of the first massive concrete casements that supported the bottom of the nearest diamond, and depending on the tide, the water might only be a few feet deep. At low tide I had seen the sandbanks stretching out to the edge of the concrete but on the north side lay the first deep channel. The tide below could not be seen through the haar, but that was of no consequence. Anyone falling from the bridge before the deep channel would be killed by hitting the sand under the shallow water, fifty feet below.

I kept walking through the darkness and passed another camera. Whether or not they were monitoring me was irrelevant. A recording would be sufficient.

Then the haar grew bright and ethereal, and through a stone gateway the intricate red steel web forged out in all directions through a silver, sparkling mist. More than a century old, the bridge was lit as a tourist attraction, which I'd forgotten; I had imagined myself walking out into the wind and sea in darkness.

The light and haar were all around me, and shadows everywhere behind the red steel that seemed to burn in the night. They would light my way, but then a thought struck. I froze in fear. In the haar I would never see the north side of the concrete casement and the faster, deep channel. Too close to the casement and I'd smash into the concrete. Too far and I'd land in the deep channel and be swept away from the shallows. Survival in this water in winter would be measured in minutes. I hurried forward and the haar became thicker, reeking of the black sea far below. I stopped, with the light and haar all around me and brought out the fishing line attached to the climbing harness under my jacket. The drop to the water was a hundred metres. The fishing line was ninety five metres. My weight was 160 pounds, and the fishing line was rated for 100 pounds. It would be enough to slow me. The camera would not pick up the line before it snapped.

Standing with my mouth open, the stench of rust and rotting seaweed filled my head, a thought nearly stopped my heart. They would never know. The cameras would be blinded by the haar when I had planned for cameras being my witness. No one would see me fall.

I gazed around me at the intricate web of steel, to where the biggest girders and giant columns had ladders attached for maintenance workers, to paint the Victorian steel with the red oxide skin as a shield against the salt spray and northern winds. The ladders disappeared into the light below and my vision swam and I had to grab the steel mesh for support.

There was no need to jump. Climb down the ladders to the concrete casement and slip into the water. I'd have to swim like hell but that was always the plan. I'd be blind in the haar, but once in the water and keeping the light behind me I would find the beach. Unless a current took me out to the deep channels. I shook the thought from my mind.

Would they believe it? Well, they wouldn't see me coming back, and they'd find the jacket. Given the temperature of the water, survival would be unlikely.

I edged forward through the glistening haar to a gap in the rail beside me, steps leading down into the light. Wiping the damp and red oxide scabs from my hands, I held on and climbed down. Visibility was only a few feet and the descent seemed never ending, until the light became so bright I had to squint, and a low hum thrummed around me from the huge lamps, then a hissing as the haar kissed the hot glass of the lamps. The light was so strong I had to close my eyes and climb blind, feeling each rung, until the toe of my boot could not find a rung below. The ladder ended in mid-air and, and holding on tight, I lowered myself as far as I dared, until the tip of my boot brushed the stone.

Eyes closed and gripping the wet rungs, I placed one boot on the stone, then the other, let one hand go and covered my eyes, but the light dropped. I lifted the hands from my face and the light burst over my head, where I was shaded by the huge steel feet of the bridge.

As my eyes adjusted, the edge of the stone emerged through the haar a foot away from me, then the black of the water beyond.

I took off the high-visibility jacket and the harness and threw them off the edge, then took two steps back and ran into the haar.

Chapter XIX

The freezing black engulfed me and I thrashed and tumbled as if blind until the light flashed above me and I kicked hard. The breath shot from my lungs when my face broke the surface before being dragged under again, but I pulled and kicked at the water until I was into the air once more, then launched forward into a crawl. The cold was almost stupefying and my freezing arms moved as if in slow motion, with my chest working hard to drag in a breath. I caught the light to my left and turned away to keep it behind me.

Adrenalin pulsed with the rhythm of the stroke and I ploughed through the water, fighting the tide and current that pulled me north. Nothing mattered except keeping the light behind me and making stroke after stroke, on and on, the cold tightening around my legs and belly. The current's drag to the north weakened then returned fast, but I swam hard, keeping the light behind me, thrashing through the water until my right arm thumped into the sand of the shallows and my knees dug in below.

The water lapped around my waist as I stood in the dark and haar, hauling in freezing breaths, then turned to the glow of the lights of the bridge, pushing the water behind me and wading forward, the sand rising under my feet. The water dropped to my ankles and I ran, splashing like a child, before my legs sank knee deep in mud.

I tried to move but began to sink, so threw myself forward, my hand and arms extended, and fell face first into the stinking mud. I hauled my knees up and slithered frog-like over the mud. My muscles cramped in the cold until I fell into a channel of water. A few yards ahead a sandbank appeared and I stood and washed the mud from me, then crawled up the sand, the ground becoming firmer under my boots and onto the beach.

In front loomed the remains of a World War II bunker. I had played here as a schoolboy and in the darkness my hands followed the edge of the walls to where the beach rose through a cut in the dune that led to a track. I climbed, shielding my face from the gorse bushes, pushing through the grey and black shadows towards the path until my boots slapped onto the tarmac and I turned to face the bridge.

The bridge lights burned through the haar but the shore was in darkness. It was possible that the police would find the car and take the track along the shoreline. But they would use a torch and give themselves away, even with the haar. My night vision grew as the leaves of the bushes along the track appeared, and I hurried forward.

The haar dissipated in parts and the black trees loomed above me and I slowed, searching for a logging trail that would take me to the two oaks. A stack of cut logs appeared through the haar, and behind them, the track to the oaks. Jogging forward until the two oaks appeared, I ran into the dip until my shin found the kitbags and I fell sideways onto the soft leaves, and lay there for a moment on my back, staring into the darkness. I stood and cleared the leaves from the top bag and pulled out my combat suit and boots. There was no time, or strength left in me to take off the neoprene wetsuit. It was time to go.

I pulled out the folded electric scooter and slung it over my shoulder, then kicked the leaves over the bags.

To the south was a logging road that cut through the forest. It would take me to the school then out towards the suburbs and the back roads. I trudged forward through the leaves and the ground rose before me. The road would be at the top of the hill but the trees and bushes closed in around me. I stopped and pulled up the hood of the combat jacket, tied it under my nose then pushed forward once more, until the ground levelled onto hard tarmac. I unfolded the scooter and engaged the motor.

A faint rumble rolled in from the sea. A lifeboat or a tug. They'd be blind in the haar. Their radar wouldn't pick up bodies in the sea. A helicopter would be the biggest threat. Fifty feet high of cold haar may give me some protection but infrared cameras were very effective. I twisted the throttle and rode into the darkness.

Chapter XX

A stiff northerly wind had chased the haar into the countryside and the New Town slept, the night cold, but clear. I kept to the back streets and narrow Victorian alleys and stopped behind the private garden near to my flat. The black cabs had gone, and at the far end of the street, a police car sat outside my house.

The gate to the gardens was unlocked and I pushed through and folded the scooter. Kneeling on the soft earth, the stink of foxes drifted past as I stashed the scooter under the bushes, then crept forward to the railings and peered out towards the street.

The signal from my discarded phone would ensure that their attention was focused on the bridge. The dark mews lane behind my garage seemed deserted. I scrambled back through the bushes and out of the garden, crossed the road to the mews entrance then ducked inside, my back flat to the wall. The lines of windows above and around me were black, my own included. The mews courtyard and the coal hole access might be unguarded, but they could be waiting for me in the dark of my sitting room.

Over the wall behind me was another garden where the scaffolding clung to the back of the building and rose to the roof. Running my hands along the wall, I found the footholds and climbed up, then slid down onto the garden. A grey moonlight showed the edge of the scaffolding.

The entire metal cage had been sheeted in plastic against rain. The ladder to the first section had been removed for security, but the bolts and joints of the scaffolding pipes gave enough purchase for me to climb up behind the plastic screen to stand before a shuttered bedroom window. Speed was of the essence, but any light sleeper could call the police at the sound of a burglar, or alert the other occupants of the building.

At each level the wind blustering the plastic increased as I climbed, up and up, until the gutter and slates came into view, then clambered into a drainage gallery between two slated roof peaks.

I lay on my back and listened, but the wind picked up and obscured the faint sirens. A star appeared in the blue-black Northern sky.

Keeping low, I crawled forward to the corner of the block and a high chimney stack, and looked east. The haar had gone and the lights of the bridge shone in the night and the faint sounds of a helicopter drifted through the wind, the searchlight passing over the shore. I looked away and started shaking. Not far now. If they had worked it out, I would be trapped but there was no other choice. And although the attic was padlocked from within the flat, it might not fool them.

I scrambled over the rooftops, keeping to the drainage gullies and avoiding the cupolas above the grand staircases that shone into the night and then into the gully by the skylight. I pushed a hand towards the frame and my finger slipped inside. It was open.

Climbing in out of the wind, the warm blood seemed

to push up under my skin, swelling at each exposed area, but I locked the skylight with trembling fingers and, holding on to the rafters, slowly dropped to my knees.

I saw my future. And it terrified me. The blood in my head pumped so hard it shook my vision. All the plans I had implemented had brought me to this point, and whether I would live or die. My breath blew up dust, and in the moonlight from the skylight it sparkled, then settled around me, drifting into dark corners and sticking to my sweat-streaked face and hands.

I was home.

With my eyes closed, I tried to listen above the sound of my blood and ragged breath for sirens or the thud of boots, and thought back to that steel grey winter day, when the cold cracked the stone around me, and I had engineered my own death. If it worked, then this night might be my last. And the end of Hector Lawless.

The chimney stack rose up in front of me, two steps away across the rafters that shifted under my weight. I pressed my fingertips against the stone to steady myself. A handprint would be a giveaway. At my feet lay the planks of wood that led to the box room. This night I might pass into oblivion, unrecorded and unmourned. I would be a ghost, either forever tormented or tormenting.

Lifting the planks to the side, the soft red light from below warmed my eyes and I squeezed through the gap and stepped down onto the ladder until only my head was in darkness, then slid the plank over my head until it settled into place.

The four windowless walls seemed closer than ever, but now they were my comfort. I shuffled sideways past the old army cot and stood in the middle of the room and began to pull off my clothes. The wet suit unzipped easily, but taking it off was cumbersome and exhausting. Grabbing the knife, I slit down each leg and then up the chest, peeled it off and kicked it under the bed then stood naked, eyes closed, arms outstretched and my fingertips brushed the opposite walls of the room. The image of the room grew in my mind and those horizons were now my unseen shield, both my cell and my haven. Eyes open, the red light soothed me. My bed was made, as it should be. The small desk was clean apart from the laptop and my pear bowl. On the wall was mounted the monitor for the cameras. The shelves that took up half the wall space and stretched to the roof held water and rations packs, and in the corner, her pillow.

Through the wall to the street came the sound of diesel engines and van doors. But the engines did not roar, and the doors did not slam. I closed my eyes and let my head fall back. They would give anything to find me.

I rubbed my face on my cold hands then reached over and turned on the monitor. The picture was split into four images. The first camera showed the street outside. I had never seen so many people in the street before, although there were probably only ten in total. A small huddle of residents who had never heard of me before this day, who had never bid me good morning. Now, their faces were screwed tight with disgust. They began to back away when a TV van appeared, the satellite dish twisting, searching for a signal. After all, this was the New Town, it would not do to be seen on the street like commoners. Some retreated to doorways. Others peeked from behind lace curtains. I couldn't hear them, but knew they wanted to see me pulled down the steps to the street, so that for one fleeting moment they would feel the warm manifestation of their righteous anger, filling them with worth and purpose until it faded and they returned to feed on clickbait for another fix of outrage on whatever media gave them their cold, vicious comfort.

In another image, the attic was lit in pale grey by infra-red light. My footprints had vanished and the dust had settled. In the third image, one of my neighbours on the grand staircase opened the front door to the police. They moved quickly, but there was no rumble of hard boots on the stairs, just the low creak of wood under big men. They stood in front of my door but did not knock. One policeman hefted a heavy black cylinder and the door crashed open. On the fourth image, a man entered my sitting room.

Inspector Gilfeather. The copper in the garage.

The old floorboards sagged under his boots as he stepped forward and the movement on the other side of the wall sent a tremor through the soles of my feet. He looked around for a moment, and then walked towards me. He stopped, staring at the chimney breast, where an old painting of King George's school hung above the empty fireplace. He lifted a finger to the painting then turned to the side and opened the door of the Edinburgh press.

I stared at the wall above the monitor. He was two feet away.

Chapter XXI

The knife was tight in my hand. I switched off the red bulb, and now the only light in the room came from the camera monitor, and in my reflection, it glinted on the blade. Around me was the muffled noise of men opening doors, cupboards, drawers, and boots on the wooden floor.

Gilfeather's eyes flicked left and right, then he closed the press door and stood once again before the fireplace. Leaning closer, his mouth slightly open, he stared at the painting of the school and the woods, with the Forth Bridge under construction in the background. He mouthed the words, 'Eighteen Eighty-one', then stepped back and turned away. Head bowed, he crossed the sitting room and sat in my chair facing the empty fireplace, his hands together as in prayer, and through half-shut eyes, fixed his gaze on the painting.

My hand ached from clutching the knife, ready for the sound of hammers and fists that would breach my cell.

A policeman entered the sitting room with my laptop and the box of papers I had stashed at the back of a wardrobe. Gilfeather did not look away from the painting, but waved a hand to the side, and the policeman placed the box and laptop against the wall. Another entered with more boxes of papers and I recognized some that had been taken from my filing cabinet. Gilfeather called over the policeman and pointed to the painting. The policeman nodded, stood for a moment, then left the room.

In another corner of the monitor, the policeman strode out on to the street and into a waiting van. My boxes and papers remained stacked against the sitting room wall. Gilfeather tilted his head back against the chair, eyes closed. In the corner of the monitor a black cab pulled up and two men got out.

A few moments later, they entered the sitting room, and Gilfeather opened his eyes and pointed to the laptop and boxes. No words were exchanged as the two men picked them up and left the room. Gilfeather sat motionless, his eyes fixed on the painting.

The two men with the boxes left in the black cab and only one police car remained on the street, with the engine idling and white exhaust smoke blown about in the wind.

Gilfeather got up and walked to the fireplace once more. He stood before the painting, then closed his eyes and turned, leaving the room and switching off the light. He dragged the front door closed, where the broken wood dug into the carpet.

My hand began to shake and I squatted down until my fingers brushed the floor and let the knife slip from my grasp. On the monitor, the flat was in darkness. Gilfeather stepped into a police car and drove into the night.

I dropped to my knees and opened my new laptop, and the room flooded with light from the screen. The news sites would be slow to react, but social media showed pictures of police at a quay near to the bridge and along the sea wall. The haar had lifted and a video showed a tug slowly sweeping the water with a searchlight, then a police boat edging up to the harbour wall and a policeman handing over my high-visibility jacket.

Just a jumper, the social media messages said, while others fumed that the road bridges had been closed for a suicide on the rail bridge. I scrolled to the latest messages, but they had morphed into posts offering mental health treatments and inane comments.

The circus had moved on.

I stood up and began to breathe slowly, eyes closed, and mouthed the words, "I am dead." A warmth burst through me.

I was dead. But to their world, not to mine. My pulse quickened and the warmth pulsed once more. "Oh, Mother," I whispered, "I am free." My mouth dried on the words and my muscles hardened. What may come next horrified me, I thought. I know myself. I know what lies beneath the surface. The obsession and anxiety. The storm in my mind. The terror. My eyes flicked to the dark walls close around me. It must not happen.

Below the desk were several bottles of medication. Rest was required. Decisions could wait. I needed to weather the storm. Behind me was the army cot. There was no time to waste. The storm must surely come. And I must be ready.

I reached out for the medication and spilled out pills from several bottles and held them in my hand. They had been my shield against the storm.

Closing my eyes, I waited, but the storm did not come. I could not sense it. I had always been able to sense it. Hector could sense it. But Hector was dead. He died in the black water coursing under the bridge and out into the sea and the night. Perhaps all the wildness of Hector had died with him.

If so, who was I? Harry would die with Hector. I have no name. Why was I not scared?

Deal with the issue at hand, I thought. I reached for the water bottle and swallowed the pills. Wherever the terror had gone, it must never win. Not now. It must not find me wanting. Not tonight.

The social media page flickered and refreshed. Some speculation continued, but the consensus was that survival was impossible. The tide was going out, and the currents that sweep out to the North Sea would mean the body might never be found.

Hector Lawless is dead, I thought. I now inhabit his body. I breathed in deep and it was as if tight ropes that bound me fell from my chest. Maybe this was part of the leaving.

No, not yet. Not yet. Hector has gone with the darkness and the sea, but the boys remain. Campbell and Hastings remain, the murders and the abuse remain. And in front of me was the laptop, with the photos of Hastings' house and the school, and the video of James Mauchline Torridon dictating his testimony, with a photo of the statement of abuse.

But if I sent it, then they would realise I was alive. That must never happen. For once in my life I was free. This birth from the sea onto the sand near the woods could not be undone. The warmth and calm prickled my skin and flowed through me, naked and free. I smiled, which was unexpected. Suspecting it was a result of the medication, I closed the laptop, switched off the monitor then pulled on the combat jacket and lay down, holding the knife soft to my chest.

The cotton of the jacket was cold against my skin, but it would dry and warm with me. Hector had died, and an outlaw had taken his place. Outwith the law, like those men and women of old who had hidden in the gorse of Holyrood Park and Arthur's Seat, outwith the town walls and no longer bound by their laws.

And now there was no law to which I was beholden. That had died with Hector.

And Campbell and Hastings should be next. The thought sent a bolt of energy through me. I could find weapons and kill. Of course I could. And in detail. With imagination. There is no law, so why not?

No, too much attention. They would know I was alive. But the thought of killing was of no consequence, and held no consequence. Guilt did not exist, anymore. There was no law.

If there was no law, then there was no guilt. And no limitations to action.

But there were other ways to achieve what had to be done. I am a man of detail and planning. And they wouldn't be looking for me, whoever I am.

My breathing deepened and my fingers relaxed around the knife. I would remember. Hector and Harry. And we shared one thing. Our first occasion of freedom and joy, a subdural memory that now passed through them to me. It was a sensation that has never left me and the warmth and happiness were locked in a room that I could visit in my mind, heightened by the soothing substances that now slipped through my veins. The blade slid through my fingers and lay cold on my chest, near as cold as that day.

That bright early winter morning where, as a young boy, I had woken to gleaming, low-lying mist shimmering in the sun and hiding the snow-covered roads and fields. Slipping out from our holiday cottage in the farmlands of Fife while my parents slept, I walked into the shining white mist that came up to my chin, as if my head bobbed on a silver sea, the tops of the fence posts my only guide.

The road dipped and I was lost in the whiteness burning my cheeks until the outline of a gate appeared. The metal was frosted and stuck to my hand. I pulled it away before the skin tore from my fingers. At my feet was a track and my shoes crunched on the hoar frost and I followed it down until the white ice of a lochan spread out before me. The mist was thinner over the lochan, and the sunlight sparkled on the frosted branches of the trees that ringed the ice.

For a few moments it was all I had ever wanted to see, but my eyes flicked to a movement on my right. A few yards away, on a branch over the ice, a robin redbreast sat, fluttering his wings. He looked at me, chest out, and then fluttered harder.

I stood transfixed by the fresh blood red of his chest and his stare, then I understood. The frost had gathered around his claws and held them tight to the branch. He fluttered harder again and I held up my hands to calm him, but it was no use. He was waiting for the morning sun, though in mid-winter it might never warm the land for days. The higher branches might see more sun but he was too low, and in the mist. He would die here.

Edging forward on the ice, I slid towards him, and he struggled hard, then stopped and stared at me, his mouth open, wisps of anger drifting from his beak.

I whispered to him, then reached out behind and above him, and let my hand drop to cup his whole body, leaving his head free.

He was cold in my hand.

I leaned forward and blew through my fingers, the white breath surrounding us, until at last, one claw lifted from the branch, then the other.

I wanted to kiss him, his bloody chest, but slipped him and my hand into my jacket, under my arm, and slid backwards to the frozen grass.

Standing, hunched over, breathing long and hard, holding him tight but allowing warmth to drift over and through my fingers, my hand became our world.

There was no movement, then the fine push of a wing to test his bonds. I turned from the low mist and gleaming white ice of the lochan and up the slope to the gate, onto the road, and soon my head lifted above the mist, and the sun dazzled me and I stopped, and pushed my head into my jacket, breathing warmth around my hand.

Most robins fly south in the winter. Some stay. The brave, or the old.

The sensation of feathers pressing against my palm grew, and I pulled out my hand and opened it.

The robin looked up and threw out his wings, turning them to the sun. I lifted my hand and he leapt off across the whispers of white, then dropped just below the mist before he flashed up into the sky, higher and higher, then turned and dipped towards me, his chest blood red, wheeling across the mist then up again to the sun.

The tears froze on my cheeks.

In a room in my mind, is kept that day of silver, white and red and cold, and the brilliant sun and white mist where I can hide from the terror and the storm. But it was no longer needed.

I had flown like the robin. Now the sun was on me, and the knife slipped from my hand.

Chapter XXII

The rosy light of the power socket shone across the floor and showed pink on the blade of the knife where it lay on the floor. The rest of the room was in darkness. The blanket was up to my chin, and warm. I was hungry.

Sitting up, I wrapped the blanket around my legs, hearing the faint skeletal creak of the building as heating systems engaged and pipes and wood began to warm and shift. It was 5 a.m.

I sat for a moment, tightly wrapped, listening for the storm in my soul. But it was nowhere. There had never been a time like this. There was always the storm, and though far, you could see and hear it if you looked. It was not a good idea to look. It would come soon enough, and I would hide. All I wanted was time to hide.

The bottles of medication were dimly lit by the red power light. They had saved me and sheltered me. Would it come again? Bravado and false assumptions would not make me fail. I had weathered the storm too much. There was no fear lurking within me. No terror. My habits had gone, and now touching the thistle seemed of no consequence.

Perhaps one day it would be amusing.

I picked up the knife and dropped it on the bed

then stood and let the blanket slip away and I seemed heavier on my feet. Stronger in the belly. I expected the medication to dull my senses, but my tongue tasted the warming air of my breath and my fingers and palm pushed the air aside as I brought them up to my face. The morning was here. I was alive, and Hector was dead. Perhaps the storm left with him.

I tapped the keyboard and the screen and camera monitor came to life, dazzling my eyes. My pencils were beside my notebooks, misaligned and disordered. I instinctively reached out, but let my hand drop and ignored them. I held my eyes shut for a few moments and let the light filter though my eyelids, then opened them to the monitor. The cameras showed the flat in darkness, save for light of the cooker clock in the kitchen. The heating and power were still on and would remain so for some time until my solicitor processed my requests, written in the event of my death. In a few hours, he would be at his desk, not far from Campbell's chamber on the Royal Mile. And in a few hours too, I would have touched the stone of the High Court. My desk would be empty, and voices muted, though not in respect. In shock and disgust.

The thought of never again having to walk down that piss-reeking close that led to Campbell's door made me smile. My day now began in darkness, but of my own choosing.

Pulling the kettle from a shelf, I filled it with bottled water and set it to boil. Social media had moved on, and only a brief mention on the BBC said that the bridges had been briefly closed for an alert. There was no mention of a young boy's body being found on a sleeper train to London. The news of a rent boy dying of an overdose would go unnoticed and disappear like a snowflake engulfed in a wave far out to sea.

My hand trembled when I poured the water into the teapot. For once it was not fear. It was anger, which would not help me, unless as a power to be unleashed. Anger must wait, alongside revenge. Prosecution and confession could not.

The faint scent of the tea cheered me. I looked around for a timer, but stopped. The tea would be fine.

I bunched my pencils together and dropped them on the notebooks. After breakfast, the planning would begin. After all, I remained a details man. Only the prosecution of the plan had relevance. The law did not. These things had been left behind.

The tea was cool enough to sip, and it soothed and strengthened me. Looking around, I choose an army breakfast ration pack and poured hot water into the self-heating pouch to activate the chemicals, then sealed it and set it aside.

On the screen, the page for the shipping forecast had an audio link, though I did not need to hear it. Winter storms may affect my departure over the North Sea, but today was of no importance. The day after may be different. I would check then.

The camera outside was still dark and would be for some time on such a winter's morning, so I pulled on my combat trousers, took my tea and turned to climb the ladder into the attic, pushing aside the plank with one hand and up onto the rafters.

Then with tea in hand, I slid out of the skylight into the freezing morning air and crouched in the gulley between the slated roofs, my bare feet wet on the grey lead and tiles, yet I did not care. The lights of the bridges sparkled in the distance. The boys that had walked off the edge were forgotten, like Hector, except in the torn hearts of those who loved them but did not protect them.

Further to the west, down the river, lay the port of Grangemouth and the container ships that took trade routes over the North Sea to Denmark, the Netherlands and further to Germany and the Baltic Sea. The weather was clear and cold. The change from the haar of yesterday was not lost on me. I had also changed. Birthed from the waters of the Forth and onto the sand, unseen in the night. And now the waters were calm. It was a strange sensation, yet not unpleasant. As if in suspicion, I looked over my shoulder to the east and the sea from where the haar had come, but the horizon was clear.

On the roof opposite lay the scaffolding that clung like steel ivy. The builders would be here soon to work through the short span of daylight. When they left at the end of their day, no one would notice another builder in a hard hat and hi-vis jacket making his way down from the roof, a scarf over his face against the cold.

Prosecution and confession. Then the boys would be safe. The confession would come from the grave, but it would not be Hector's grave. There was a path to prosecution that would keep me safe, where I could leave unnoticed and forgotten. Yet there would be no prosecution in a court of stone and wood, cloaks and wigs, or revenge and damnation. No, the law had betrayed me. I had already left all those things behind, as if they had been washed off, like filth from my boots and skin.

*

My tea was cold by the time I set it down on my box room desk and ate my breakfast, then boiled the water once more, and laid out my notebooks and sharpened the pencils. There were many factors to consider. Shop opening times, locations and building plans. The internet would provide the bulk of the information to form a plan to execute the prosecution. Houses sold online had images of their rooms and floor plans hidden in some internet cache, or a database of council planning applications. I began listing everything that came into my head. Objectives, assumptions, methods, risk and execution, then brought up information on the screen as required.

By the time the notes and planning were complete, I sat back, hungry once more. And it was a good hunger, born of work. My notes filled many pages. I set the ration pouches to heat and sat back. On the monitor, the ivory sun had passed over and was now dropping towards the horizon. But a plan had emerged. It would work, if executed with purpose and vigour. And then the prosecution would begin. If you could prosecute a corpse.

There was time. I got dressed, in boots, combat trousers and the hi-vis jacket. With my hood up against the cold under a builder's hard hat and with a mask covering my face, I lay back on the bed, waiting for the dark, my armour complete.

Beside the bed was a flask of hot tea. All I needed was a sex shop.

Chapter XXIII

The commuters on Princes Street had thinned as I hurried from the sex shop. Head down against the bitter wind, no one looked my way. Even the shop assistant had not made eye contact as her efforts to close the shop were interrupted.

I turned south and headed down the hill to my flat.

The darkness was growing now, but the lights of the windows shone bright around me and glistened on the wet stone under my boots. Climbing the scaffolding would be too dangerous, with people home after work and children in their rooms.

The dimly lit lanes took me to the private garden. There were no sounds of taxi engines, and I took off the hi-vis jacket and stuffed it inside my combat jacket, then unlocked the gate and headed to the far corner, where a gardener's hut sat in the corner under the trees. I had acquired the key from a gardener now long dead, and the cold black iron turned in my hand. Pulling the door behind me, I held my phone low to light the way. In the corner was a long potting table. As a boy, I had found a dry corner hidden behind a hessian cloth that hung down from the table. Although as a man, this space was too small, so I lay down on the floor and stretched out.

The scent of earth and wood, both sharp and sweet surrounded me.

By tomorrow night, I thought, winter storms allowing, I would be on the North Sea and the leaving would be complete when my boots stepped from a container ship onto the harbour at Hamburg or Rotterdam. A ship to the Middle or Far East would leave me at sea too long. In the event of discovery, they would track me, but the extensive travel network of Europe and the connections to the east would be my salvation. I would not see a border post until Romania, which I would avoid. Then over the Carpathian Mountains, and the land route to India.

Everything was ready. Campbell had to be alone in his house. If not, then I would wait until the next night. I placed the flask of tea beside me, then closed my eyes and dreamt of the sea.

The door of the hut clicked behind me. The sky was dark and clear and I pulled on the hi-vis jacket once past the garden gate and headed deeper into the New Town, the temperature dropping fast, with the streetlamps and the bright lights from window showing me the way.

My mind was set. When the penitent had served his penance, I would return to the hut and wait until the early hours to creep up the scaffolding once more.

My boots thumped on the pavement and I wanted to hear it rain. I wanted it to cleanse me, to wash Edinburgh and the betrayal from me but also to wash the buildings, so that by these actions, the golden stone may shine a little brighter when the sun arose in the morning. Yet these emotions and old memories at once became faint and ethereal, and had vanished when I turned into the darkness of a narrow mews lane.

Behind me, the streets of the New Town were mostly empty, save a few late commuters, delivery bikes and local shoppers. Collar up and cloth mask on, I turned towards Stockbridge. The buildings once so familiar to Hector now seemed to be that of a foreign city. Buildings no longer towered over me and the stone was just stone. Different colours, clean or dirty, wet or dry. I no longer cared. And I did not belong here anymore. Everything that I had used as a shield had been my prison. Structure, society, law and their justified morality.

I should have seen it coming. I should have known, although I hid it from myself. Why? Cowardice. I refused to recognise my enemy and so lived in fearful comfort. But no more.

The water ran high and fast from the rain on the hills around Edinburgh as I crossed the Stockbridge and the Water of Leith swamping the banks and the footpaths and turned left up the hill bordering the river. Lights spilled out from tall windows and sparkled on the ice forming on the cobbled street. Near the top lay a row of grand houses, and halfway along, a mews lane bisected the terrace to lead to the low-roofed mews houses behind. The ice also sparkled on the walls of the houses where it lay tight against the crumbling stone and in the cracks, as if studded with diamonds. In that moment, I loved Edinburgh and all her faults, and forgave her as I forgave myself. But she was no longer mine.

Campbell's house lay on the corner of the terrace and the lane. Forgiveness would not visit here. The grand, ground floor room of the townhouse was the only room lit, a chandelier spewing light out onto the street.

The plans were listed on the council's website where Campbell had applied for upgrades to the plumbing and kitchen. The front door opened onto a hall and wide staircase to the next floor, and a landing bordered by heavy wooden balustrades, looking down onto the entrance hall.

I turned into the mews lane, walking past his house, and then stood before the head-high wall of his garden, and pulled myself up to look over. A weak light shone onto the grass. A kitchen window stood to the side. I slipped off the hi-vis jacket and hauled myself up and over and moved to the back of the garden, then edged into the cover of an overhanging hedge.

I could see straight through to the room to the front, but there was no movement. A toilet flushed near the back of the house and water coursed out of the pipes below the kitchen and into the ground. The kitchen light came on, and Campbell appeared and took a bottle of wine from a cupboard, then moved through to the main room and sat at the far side, near the main street. There was no other light into the house. He had once been married though it had ended when he was young. He was alone.

The back door looked secure, but it was only required for exit.

In the garden was a rusted Victorian clothes pole leaning at an angle out of the grass and a dirty clothes line hanging down. I took out my knife and cut it down, winding it around my hand and arm to use as a rope. It would be a welcome detail to the story I was about to weave.

Looping the clothes line around my shoulder, I climbed over the wall and walked to the corner with the street, then checked the battery on my burner phone. The front door stood to the side of the bay window. I rounded the corner and climbed the steps to the front door, turned my back to the window and pulled up my collar, then pushed the intercom. After a few moments, a distorted voice came back.

"*Hello?*"

I covered my mouth with the hand. "Delivery." His voice sounded tired or drunk.

"*I'm not expecting a delivery.*"

"I have a package for Campbell. I was given this address. Signature required. Is this for you?"

"*One moment.*"

I pulled out the knife.

Chapter XXIV

The door unlocked and opened a few inches then burst back on the end of my boot. I shoved the heel of my hand hard up under Campbell's chin and his head flew back. I flung the door closed with my knife hand then stepped forward and placed one foot behind him and shoved him again, and he fell to the floor.

He looked up, eyes wide, his open mouth and lips stained purple with wine. He mouthed my name but could not get the words out.

"Good evening," I said, and placed a boot on his neck. "I'm sure this must be somewhat of a surprise. When you have gathered yourself, stand up, go into the sitting room and draw the curtains." I pressed down on his throat then stepped back and held the knife out towards the open door to the sitting room. "Your cooperation would be appreciated. There are other options." I tapped the knife against the door frame. "Which I will not hesitate to employ."

He clambered to his feet using the door frame for support. "I... Hector, look, if there's..."

"Move." I lifted the knife to his chin.

Grasping at furniture, he stumbled into the sitting room and drew the curtains. He turned to face me, swallowing hard and trying to lift his unimpressive frame to its full height. "I assume..." He choked and cleared his throat. "I assume you have come to arrest me."

The room was decorated in purple and gold, its heavy, dark, gleaming furniture displaying generous scrollwork, with a wide marble fireplace where logs burned in lazy yellow flames. It was hideous. And he had no idea how to build a fire.

I turned the knife in my hand. "Arrest you?" I shrugged. "Of course. Why not?"

"I mean you're not a man who..."

I strode forward and held the knife to his groin. "Whatever assumptions you are making at this very moment, I can assure you that they are rather wide of the mark."

He trembled, his hands flapping, afraid to move.

"Sit." I pointed to a chair beside a round polished table. "We have work to do."

He shuffled forward and dropped into the chair.

In front of the fire lay a winged armchair, a freshly opened bottle of wine and a stained glass. Pulling a handkerchief from my pocket, I lifted the bottle then the glass and placed them in front of him on the table. "Drink. You'll need it."

The neck of the bottle rattled on the glass as he poured, then he downed half a glass, cleared his throat, and tried to relax in the chair. "You know, it'll come as no surprise... Well, I mean, a man of your talents, it was to be expected that..."

"Shut up. Time to confess your sins."

"Look, let's talk about what we can..."

As I stood over him, he seemed to shrink in the chair. I spat the words at him. "Bless me, Father, for I have sinned. It has been many years since my last confession. These are my sins."

"What?"

"Not a Catholic, then."

"Eh? No, Church of Scotland, but Hector, you know a confession under duress will never stand up in court."

"We'll see."

He took another drink, then refilled the glass. His shoulders relaxed. His lips pursed and barely twisted into a smile. "Indeed we will. Then let's do it. I will confess and take my chances in court. You understand your position? How difficult this will be to prosecute?"

I leaned over him. "I understand very well, and in some detail, the methods of prosecution I intend to employ."

"You've never tried a case in court, Hector. You flew a desk, remember?"

"There will be no trial."

He smirked and sipped his wine. "No?"

"Only an inquest."

"What? A Law Society inquest? In your shoes I'd take my chances with a jury."

"Who cares about the Law Society?"

A gilded escritoire sat against the wall of the room. I opened the drawer and took out a sheet of writing paper. It was embossed with Campbell's title and address, and I placed it on the table in front of him.

"I was betrayed by the law and now you threaten me with the law?" The tip of the knife touched his nose. "Give me an excuse and I'll open your face to the skull."

The wine glass trembled in mid-air.

"You killed Alex Gillan when he threatened to expose you and Hastings. Then you killed James Torridon, or

171

had him killed, because he was the only one who could expose you. Then you set me up to take the fall. Very clever, I must say. You played me exceptionally well. You took into account my fears, weaknesses and my strengths. But you did not consider my imagination. You forgot my attention to detail." I let the knife drop to my side. "My plans do not include using this knife. That can change."

The glass in his hand clattered to the table, wine spilling over the rim.

He stared at the table for a few monents, then looked up. "You have stated your case very well, Hector. I look forward to the Law Society expressing their deep admiration for your, er, imagination. Oh, and the impressive detail, of course."

I placed the paper and pen in front of him. "Write."

He picked up the pen. "You know…"

The back of the blade rapped against his fingers and knocked the pen from his grasp. "If you're looking for inspiration, let me say I can change my mind and that you don't need all ten fingers to write."

He picked up the pen once more.

When he was ready, I began. "To my colleagues at the Campbell Chambers, and fellow members of the Law Society of Scotland, I wish to confess my crimes."

He wrote slowly, with a wavering hand, no doubt in the hope that to a jury this would be evidence of duress rather than emotion.

"I was expelled from school for the beating and rape of a young boy."

"That's bloody nonsense, it was just…"

I laid the back of the blade on his fingers. He squealed and the pen flew from his fingers.

"Next time I'll use the blade."

He grabbed the pen and resumed writing.

"I continued the abuse at King George's School. In later life, I used my power and influence to form a chess club, where I took boys out of school and abused them. Murdo Hastings, the current Secretary of State for Scotland, was a schoolfriend, and joined me in this abuse. We also abused homeless and drug-addicted young boys in Edinburgh. I abused Alex Gillan and Hastings abused James Torridon. When Alex Gillan threatened to expose me, we had him killed using officers of the state. When James Torridon threatened to expose Hastings, we had him killed by officers of the state. James Torridon confided in Hector Lawless, who I manipulated so it appeared that they were the perpetrators of these crimes with a false witness statement from James Torridon. Hector Lawless is not guilty of any crimes, his only intention was to catch the abusers."

He looked up. "Please, Hector, we can work together to find a solution. It's not too late. As a lawyer, this is morally wrong. You must…"

I leaned over him. "You have spent a lifetime abusing children and you talk to me of morality?"

"Hector, I have no idea how you faked your death to fool those stupid policeman, but you have no idea what you're up against. It's not just me or Hastings, it's…"

I placed my hand on his head and pushed his face down on the table and held the knife to his eye. "My patience is not limitless." I let him go. "I know exactly who I am up against and have planned accordingly. Now, write." He picked up the pen. "I confess these crimes of my own free will and accept my penance." He finished writing. "Sign and date it." He attempted a ridiculous flourish of his name. I picked up the paper. "*Alea iacta est*. The die is cast."

"I know what it means, I'm a fucking lawyer."

I pulled from my pockets a pair of pink, fluffy handcuffs.

He laughed. "My God, are you going to fuck me to death?"

"Put them on your ankles." I stood close behind him.

He looked over his shoulder and grinned. "Did you choose them especially for me?"

"Yes. They don't chafe the skin."

"I am genuinely touched at your concern."

"You shouldn't be. I have no concern for you at all, except as that of a penitent. I will prosecute your penance." I opened my jacket and took out the rope from the garden. It was mossy and damp, but that would make the knots easier, and I began to make a loop.

He didn't look around. "You could just guard me until the police arrive, this charade isn't helping your case. I mean, pink fluffy handcuffs?"

"Hands behind your back." I took out another pair of fluffy handcuffs and fixed his hands tight.

He sighed and sat up in the chair. "Well, let's get this over with. You had better call the…"

The words were squeezed from his throat when I looped the noose over his head and pulled hard, hauling him backwards off the chair. He hit the ground. His eyes bulged and his mouth gaped open, while his handcuffed arms and legs thrashed around. I flipped him over onto his front and sat on his back, tugging the rope tight until he began to weaken and the strength drained from his body. I let go and pushed the noose loose with my fingers. He lay gasping and coughing into the carpet.

I patted his pockets then took out his phone, and unlocked it using his thumb, then walked out to the hallway. To the left, a corridor led to the kitchen at the back of the house and to the right, a wide staircase ran up to the first floor and a balcony of thick wooden balustrades. They had not been changed from the online photos for the most recent planning permission and would be adequate for the task.

Campbell rolled onto his back, saliva sputtering from his lips. "What the hell are you doing? You could have killed me! Are you trying to concoct some sex game injury? I was right all along. You're a fucking weirdo. You belong in an asylum, you mad bastard!"

I took a copy of James Torridon's confession from my jacket and laid it on the table then used his phone to take a photo of both the statement and Campbell's written confession. Using my own burner phone, I brought up the video of James making his statement and sent it to Campbell's phone then knelt down beside him, wrapping the rope around my arm. "Your chambers has a WhatsApp group. All the lawyers were included, except one. Me. You thought I didn't know."

The noose was still tight around his neck and he stared at the rope looped around my arm and his phone in my hand.

"I didn't mind."

I brought up a new message for the WhatsApp group on his phone and attached the two photos and the video and typed a message. *I'm sorry. God forgive me.*

I pressed send.

"What have you done?" he whispered.

"What was necessary, penitent." I looped the rope over my shoulder and stood, using my weight to pull hard, lifting him up by the neck and dragging him along the floor to the hallway, then I returned for the chair and placed it below the balustrades on the first floor.

He frantically jerked his neck against the carpet, trying to loosen the rope. His mouth opened but no words came forth. I tightened the noose until his body went limp then lifted him into the chair. Holding the other end of the rope, I climbed the stairs to the first floor and tied a bowline knot around a balustrade then took up the slack. Below, the breath wheezed out of him and he clambered onto the chair. I pulled hard until his feet stood firm on the seat, then fixed the rope.

When I ran down, he had kicked over the chair and was choking, his face bright red and turning blue around the neck. I picked up the chair and placed it beneath him, then lifted his feet to take his weight off the rope and held him steady until he had stopped shaking. His trousers were soaked with urine. His breath was ragged and his eyes bulged.

I stood before him. "Tell me, Lord Campbell, what will the police say when they find you in this position? I mean, if you fall from the chair, it's all over. An ignominious death, and your name wiped from history, save as a pervert and paedophile."

His eyes were vague, then he found mine and focused, and the pleading began, but his swollen throat could not form the words.

I unlocked the handcuffs on his ankles, then walked behind his back and undid those around his wrists. His hands flew up and grabbed at the rope, trying to loosen the noose.

"Do you repent your sins?"

His hands clawed at the slippery rope, his fingers tearing into his skin and rope. "Yes," he croaked.

"Do you accept your penance?" He didn't reply. Urine ran down over the chair. "Whatever." I booted the chair down the hall.

He dropped and his hands tore at the noose, but his strength was gone. His face turned blue and his tongue protruded, first cherry red then the colour of dried blood.

"I'm a details man. I have read many post-mortems. Fluffy handcuffs will not show chafing or signs of a struggle. Your clawing at the noose will show your hands were free at the time of death."

I looked past him to where the kitchen door led to the garden. "I'll let myself out."

The cold wind chilled my scalp as it flashed over the tops of the slate-lined gully on the roof, and I bowed my head and sipped my tea. To the west, blue lights pulsed over the rooftops of the hill above Stockbridge. Somewhere in those grand terraces, the police would be deciding whether to cut him down. It was a dilemma for first responders, I had read in many documents that had crossed my desk, whether to protect the crime scene or to cut the body down. Those that cut the body down plead they are preserving the dignity of the dead. But having examined photographs of these scenes and the effect of gravity and strangulation, the swelling, purple-blue skin, the eruptions from burst blood vessels, the grotesque, black protruding of a tongue three times its size, the blood-red eyes bulging almost out of their sockets, and, given sufficient time before discovery, the evacuation of bowels, there is little dignity to be preserved. The more experienced coppers would let the body hang until SOCO arrive. It's less paperwork.

I had no doubt Inspector Gilfeather would be summoned, and attempts would be made to contain the scene, but everyone in Campbell's chambers had a copy of the evidence, and his suicide note, so containment was a lost cause. And my name, or that of the late Hector Lawless, would be cleared.

A storm was building which would blow over the house of cards, that tower of privilege, abuse and power. And I would watch it from afar. It would begin with resignations, with some plausible excuse, but no matter how deep they buried it, the stench would follow them and the truth would emerge. The news would be global.

A spatter of rain hit my face and I turned to the east, where the sea was being enveloped by black clouds sweeping in from Norway and Denmark, stretching across the horizon. It would be a wild night, and in some grand houses in Edinburgh and London, it would bring darkness and terror.

To the west, the red lights on the top of the bridges shone as if in remembrance of the dead. Further up the river lay the container port of Grangemouth. The ships for Hamburg and Rotterdam would be leaving soon, sailing head first into the storm. Tomorrow, with minutes to go, I would register my ticket. The website was Romanian and would not coordinate with UK systems. They may find out later, but too late.

My rucksack was packed with only my bowl and her pillow to be added. I'd walk to the suburbs then take a taxi to Grangemouth. Just a few steps to freedom, and the leaving. But not tonight. Tomorrow they would be distracted and trying to recover the situation, which would be the perfect time to walk away.

My tea was cold and I poured it into the gutter where it rolled away through the leaves and down a drain to the street. I was a murderer. Although it was much less dramatic than I had imagined. On the walk home I had had to stop a few times to catch my breath. The power was intoxicating, the core gratification in my mind and body of revenge and fulfilment almost overwhelming. I had been to the edge of my mind many times, in fear and terror, but never like this. It was glorious.

Tonight I would dream of killing Hastings, even though it was impossible. Perhaps in the future a penance would visit his door. It was a thought to be nurtured and treasured. And perhaps I would not have to hide the fact that it would be an execution.

My body trembled at such a thought, and I closed my eyes for a moment and took long, deep breaths. I would save it for my dreams. Soon I would be on the shoreline in those dreams, of the sunlit rooms and the sand, and the water whispering as it broke on the beach. Perhaps then I would need different dreams. I stood and faced the west. This was my leaving, of which I had also always dreamed. And below the stars being engulfed by the dark clouds from the east, the lights of Edinburgh sparkled a little brighter, all the way down to the ice diamonds and grains of glistening quartz embedded in her stone.

This is how I would remember her.

Chapter XXV

I couldn't remember the last time I had slept without an alarm. And such a dreamless, healing sleep. A camera on the monitor showed daylight on the street and by the lack of shadows, the sun was high in the midday sky. I sat on the edge of the bed and rubbed my eyes, then set the water to boil for tea and to cook my bag of army breakfast rations. In the corner, my rucksack bulged with rations and tea. The rations could be eaten cold, if required, but I had a camping stove for my journey, should it be necessary to go off the grid. A late lunch would suffice to tide me over until darkness. The train network from Hamburg or Rotterdam could take me anywhere in Europe, though the east would be safer.

I resisted the temptation to check the news and sat still, my eyes closed until the food was ready. I ate slowly and sipped my tea. Like the sleep, I could not remember a day when there was nothing to do but wait. My cell was warm with the sweet smell of sleep, and I would wash later when it was time to leave. My hands reached for the keyboard, then I pulled them back. There was no news for me. I did not exist. And Hector was dead, so the news meant nothing to him. I missed Harry. Maybe he had made it over the bridge and was now safe in the Highlands, deep in a wooded glen, eating his wild salmon from the black pools below the falls.

I lay back and closed my eyes. The leaving was here. I had often wondered what it would be like, to take the first steps on the journey over the cold, dark waves and across the mountains to my far shore, and now it was here. And I would leave a better man. I had found an unknown strength and peace. For some men, the guilt of Campbell's murder would be a torturous sentence for the rest of their lives, but for me, it was an act filled with light and purpose. The childhood of those boys who would have descended into abuse would be saved. It was an extraordinary achievement and it made me happy. But happiness is ephemeral and fleeting, I thought, and too fickle a mistress to waste time chasing it to fill any emptiness in your life. True joy is finding a purpose that you can call your own and which drives you through life. If there is happiness, true happiness, then it lies there.

I awoke and threw myself up, twisted my head to the monitor. Was I dreaming? A thump shook the walls and I jumped to my feet. I listened, but there was nothing. Then another hard thud shook the floorboards. On the camera in the hall, the front door swung open and a man filled the doorway. He was wearing a boiler suit and carrying a hammer.

I stood up, stared at the monitor, then saw the tool bag on his waist. He took several nails from a pouch and hammered them into the door jamb where it had been ripped from the wall by the police. Then he closed the door behind him. After more thumps and bangs, it opened again.

Dropping onto the bed, I rubbed my face. Just a man fixing the door. My solicitor had received the keys in the padded envelope through the mail. It must have arrived on his desk this morning. He did have a reputation for efficiency. I waited until the shaking had stopped, then laughed.

I set the kettle to boil and poured my tea as he worked. The sun was now casting shadows on the street camera. Yes, he was a very efficient solicitor, a fine man. I would miss him. At least the flat would be safe. If Gilfeather came back, he would need keys. He couldn't kick the door down twice. I laughed again and sipped my tea, both hands around the mug.

You didn't think you'd be here to see it, I thought. You hadn't planned for this. My gut tightened, but I stood up and lifted my head to stretch my neck, then placed the mug down on the table. I'm not here, Hector is dead. They can't harm him now. I let out a quick breath then sat at the table and brought up the news.

They had moved fast. The stories talked of a tragic death but it was not being treated as suspicious and did not name the deceased. That would change soon enough. Everyone would want to know who and why. Campbell's neighbours would be tight-lipped. If he ever talked to his neighbours, or if they ever talked to each other. And if they did, it would not be something so middle-class as gossip.

Social media had more clues, though nothing definite. The WhatsApp message from Campbell may have been shared amongst legal friends, but none had stuck their head over the parapet to share it on social media. They all liked to know something that others didn't, or at least pretend. Their public school cliques were tight knit, and they'd pretend that discretion was more valuable than knowledge. And so they would talk.

Although Hastings would know and the rumours would soon run amongst the cliques, that Campbell's past had come back to haunt him, and so cast a shadow over the office of Secretary of State for Scotland.

The Press would not be so discreet. Lawyers and civil servants all over Edinburgh and perhaps London would soon be turning off their phones. There was blood in the water, and the feeding frenzy would begin. Allegiances would be tested and relationships strained. Favours would be called in. The rumours of Hastings and the schoolboy scandal with Campbell would be proffered to get the press off someone's back, and then the predators would identify their prey. A live victim was more satisfying than gnawing at a corpse and sold more copies.

The politicians in London and the Tory establishment in Edinburgh would protect him until they watched the blood-soaked water reach their feet, then they would throw him to the sharks.

But Hector was dead. He would not see it, and knowing how it would play out, I did not care to witness it, the long, drawn out result and slow, excruciating evisceration of Hastings until he appeared in the dock at the High Court in Edinburgh for all the world to see. Alone and abandoned. Then they would talk of Hector Lawless and how he died because of this man and Campbell. And no matter what the public thought, the establishment would ensure Hastings never again be a free man.

It all died with Hector. My journey, this leaving, would not be stained by it.

The sun was stronger in the camera to the street, and I could imagine the warmth on my face as a boy when I sat on the roof with my hot chocolate, out of the sharp wind. At my feet, the rucksack was packed, and only to be shoved through the gap to the roof as soon as it was dark. The next container ship was 7 p.m. to Rotterdam, and I would book my ticket at the last moment with a false passport number, swapping two digits. If it was checked, which was unlikely on a Romanian booking system, it would be seen as a simple error. If not, cash would ease the way. Few people knew of how to traverse the world on cargo ships, and in the morning, on a railway platform in Rotterdam, the route to freedom would lie before me: three lines to France, Germany or south to Austria. Vienna would be my next stop, and the gateway to the East and the Carpathian Mountains.

My head flicked towards movement in the cameras. The front door opened. I got to my feet. A man in a suit entered, inspected the door frame then switched on the light. I trembled as the face was lit. AJ Shiresman. My solicitor.

He closed the door behind him and walked down the hall, opened the door to a cupboard, then closed it and turned to open the box room door. He stepped back when he saw the shelves and stood, holding onto the handle, then slowly closed the door. He turned on his heels and crossed the hall to the kitchen and opened the pantry door then set down his briefcase on the table and examined the electricity meter.

The padded envelope had contained instructions and my will, and he was simply acting upon my wishes – this action was preliminary to selling my flat. This is what I wanted. He knew where to send the money, or at least what enquiries should be made to make it happen. It may take some time due to the lack of a body, but he was well-versed in these issues. And hopefully the flat would be sold to a new family, who would treasure it as a home, and be happy here as I had been.

After taking readings from the meters, he sat at the kitchen table then answered his phone, which contained no names, only initials. The only name was stencilled on his battered briefcase, faded and almost illegible. AJ Shiresman.

He sat very still, eyes closed, then looked around him, then down at the floor. The thought of his being sad at my death hurt very much. He is a man I greatly admire.

A solicitor devoted to his clients; the keeper of many secrets and few friends. Known as the most discreet lawyer in Edinburgh who shunned the wine bars, clubs and cliques, he was the only man I had ever talked to of topics other than law. A sadness bit into me. I would never talk to him again, and was surprised by the depth of sadness at such a thought. Perhaps one day, long in the future, we would talk once more. For it was sure he would never tell. I pictured his tiny office and his secure filing cabinet where, like his phone, clients only had initials. Only he knew the names. I remembered climbing the winding medieval stairs to his office overlooking the Royal Mile, where he had begun his trade as a young English lawyer arriving in the capital. Having discovered he had not gone to the right schools, he shunned the snobbery of the other lawyers, until his secrecy gained a reputation. And then the clients came to him.

And now he had come to serve me for the last time.

I held my face in my hands, knowing I had lost the only man in Edinburgh I admired. On the monitor he was talking into his phone. Pulling headphones from the desk, I plugged them into the laptop and switched on the mics on the cameras just as he cut his phone call. He got to his feet and walked out into the hall.

The intercom buzzer at the front door stabbed through my head and I almost fell from the chair. When I looked up, Shiresman had answered the entryphone and pushed the button to open the door to the street. Turning down the mics, I leaned forward to the monitor. Who on earth could it be? I sat back. Of course, Inspector Gilfeather. He had come to snoop around. But it would do him no good. No, by dark I would be away from here, and Edinburgh would be a memory, one that I would cherish, for all her sins, blood, beauty and glory. Gilfeather would be forgotten.

A young woman appeared in the doorway. Her hair was short and jet black, set against her pale skin, her ears and nose pierced and what seemed to be a tattoo on the hand that she held out to Shiresman.

A buyer? The flat could not be on the market already, I thought. And she's not police. Shiresman's voice was muffled as they approached the camera at the end of the hall. I clamped the earphones to my head and strained to hear them talking. She turned and pointed back up the hall.

... to the door?

Ah, I shall explain that in a moment. A very unfortunate event.

The place looks great, I bet it cost a bloody bomb!

It is most certainly not without value. You have the

sitting room here, and all the other rooms open onto the hall.

What's this? Ah, just a cupboard. Bit of a fancy door for a cupboard, yeah?

Cupboards are often disguised as such. It gives the impression of more rooms. Edinburgh, my dear, is full of surprises.

Mate, today has been bloody surprising, I can tell you that for sure.

That you were in London was also quite unexpected.

I'll bet it was!

I understand this may have come as a great shock to you. And am I to also understand this is a complete surprise for you? He didn't inform you of his intentions?

Hector Lawless? I didn't know his name until you called me.

Really?

No, I never knew my father.

Chapter XXVI

I grabbed the edge of the table with both hands but the shaking would not stop and the headphones slipped from my head.

No, it's too soon. Please, just go. Please. Go.

It was never meant to be like this. I grabbed the headphones and had to use my palms to push them in place, and the blood thumping in my ears drowned out their voices. Her lips moved and she laughed. Please, it was so long ago. She looked towards the camera and her eyes were her mother's, and my eyes flooded with tears.

I clamped a hand over my mouth to stifle the wheezing from my chest and my head flicked back in the air. No, not now. Hector is gone and you are not here. I clamped my jaw shut and drew in long breaths through my nose to stop the terror from growing as her voice came through the headphones.

"I've always rented. This is totally weird."

Shiresman smiled, "I'm sure it will take some time to take everything in. Tell me, how do you pronounce your name? Is it Aylee or Eelee? I always think it so rude to get a pronunciation wrong."

Eilidh gently punched his arm which made his eyes open wide. "It's Ay-lee, but no worries, mate. Ellie is fine. No one in Oz knew how to pronounce it. Just me and my mum."

"May I say, it is a beautiful name."

"And got me called Smelly Ellie my entire childhood, so it's good to be back where my name is known."

"Thank you, Eilidh. Now, I am always here if you need advice on such matters. And I am proud to say I was a friend of Hector's, perhaps his only friend, although we saw each other infrequently. He left funds for you to use my services as required in this matter."

"Yeah, thanks. I've no idea what that might be, but, yeah. I'm still kinda stunned."

"As am I, Eilidh. I had expected finding you to take months, yet here we are."

"I live not far from Kings Cross Station. I share a flat with some other Aussies."

"Are you working there?"

"Freelance, yeah. I'm a stringer for a few Australian newspapers, just took a sabbatical to come over and see the old country and write articles on politics and culture. Look, I worked out that my dad was Scottish, but my mother never mentioned him, except to say I was a love child and my real father would never know. She said it was best to keep it that way. You don't always find what you are looking for, yeah? I told her I wouldn't look, and I kept my word. I kinda meant to come to Edinburgh for a weekend, to see where my mother was born, but I'm a reporter. I knew if I did then I would start digging. And she didn't want that. So I stayed in London. Of course, she's passed away now. You never really get over it. And then I got the Facebook message this morning and jumped on the first train. I mean, you made it sound like this is a big deal financially so I moved my arse. Of course, I don't mean…"

"Oh, Eilidh, I understand. Indeed, it is a big deal, but not without an emotional cost."

"Well, he's dead or I wouldn't be here, so yeah, that's emotional. Sorry, I'm not dealing with this very well, I don't know what to think or feel." She looked around, the soft afternoon light gleaming off the copper cooking pots that hung on the wall. "What was he like?"

"Hector? A complex and gifted man. I admired him immensely, and shall miss him a great deal."

She laughed. "That says everything and nothing."

He bowed his head and smiled. "You have your father's gift for lucidity."

"So? Hector? Who was he?"

"Simply, he was a lawyer. A very gifted lawyer. But not one you see arguing cases in court. Hector, shall we say, shunned the limelight."

She sat up in the chair. "Hector. I never knew his name. That's a funny name, no?"

Shiresman smiled and shrugged.

"The only time my mother spoke about him was when she told me my step-dad was not my real dad. It was a really hot day in November. But, hey, I can count, I already knew, and could see she didn't want to talk about it. So I never asked her. I reckoned if she wanted to talk about it she would. Then on that day, the only time she mentioned him, she said he was a really lovely bloke, but very shy. Most of my life I've never really thought about him. Just sometimes when I saw my mother looking at me. Weird, eh? Did he ever talk about me?"

Shiresman bowed his head for a moment. "Only briefly."

"Yeah?" She sat back.

"Yes. I think it caused him great sorrow that he could not be part of your life. I can say, with some certainty, that he loved you and your mother with enormous and undying passion. And he was extraordinarily proud of you. Not being part of your life was too difficult for him to express or, quite clearly to me, even to consider. He was a very sensitive man."

Eilidh turned and looked out towards the sunshine. "I never really thought about him."

"Other than the social media profiles where he thought I might find you, he did not have a phone number or address, as he did not want to interfere in your life, but he did confide to me once that he wished things were different."

"Yeah. Me too." She turned back to Shiresman. "So, why are we here?"

"Well, let me first say that this inheritance, for which he gave me very clear instructions, was to be given to you on his death. However, he updated these instructions in the past few days, and as to why, I can only surmise, but I'm afraid we will never know."

Eilidh leaned forward on the table. "Just give it to me straight, Mr Shiresman. I'm a reporter. I've seen some shit."

"Indeed. The reason we are here is not a pleasant one. I'm afraid your father took his own life."

She sat, her mouth open, then looked out the window, her eyes blinking in the light. "Oh, Hector. I didn't even know him. For fuck's sake... Sorry, I mean..."

Shiresman waved a hand and turned away. "May

I say, I am also deeply affected, though like Hector, I have a tendency not to show such emotions."

Eilidh wiped her eyes. "Okay." She blew out a breath. "What happened?"

Shiresman lifted his head and pushed back his shoulders. "You're a journalist, and as you've said, you've seen some things, so I won't insult you by sugar-coating this. I will only say that some of what I tell you, I believe, in my hearts of hearts, to be a monstrous lie." His lips tightened, and then he spoke slowly. "A monstrous, heinous lie."

"Look, I've spent four hours on the train searching social media and following threads. I reckon I know where this is going. Go for it."

Shiresman took a deep breath. "Your father is said to have killed himself because he was to be arrested for child abuse."

Eilidh stared at Shiresman.

"There will be an inquest, but it will be without a body."

"What?"

"He was last spotted on a camera..."

"Wait, why...? Look, how did he...?"

Shiresman closed his eyes. "I am about to tell you strictly confidential information which has been relayed to me by certain... people in the know."

"Cops. They always talk."

"Perhaps. Your father was to be arrested not far from here, but he escaped the police. Once they had found the phone he was using, they tracked the signal to near the road bridge crossing over the River Forth to the Kingdom of Fife. It is believed he was trying to escape north to the Highlands."

"The bridge?"

"Yes, there are two road bridges and the old Forth Bridge for trains."

"Did they catch him? Did the coppers…?"

"No. They blocked the road bridges before he could cross."

"Fucking hell."

"Indeed. Hector knew the country and… I think if he had made it, he would be alive today."

Eilidh pushed back her chair and stood. "What happened?"

"I believe he saw the road was blocked. He parked his car out of sight of the police, away from the road bridges, then climbed up onto the old rail bridge. It was very foggy, but he was last seen on a camera heading out over the sea. The cameras recorded nothing more. He never came back."

She turned to the window. "Could he have…?"

"No. Even if he survived the fall, the Firth of Forth is an estuary of the North Sea. Water temperatures are such that survival would be measured in minutes. When last seen, he was heading to the deeper channels and strong currents which would take him out to sea."

"You said there is no body?"

"No. It's possible his body may yet be found, but it is unlikely."

Eilidh sat down on the chair and leaned forward on her arms. "Why didn't he contact me before?"

Shiresman sat back. "He was a good man, Hector. A great man, but he found relationships with people very difficult. He was also very kind and thoughtful, yet painfully shy. His anxiety… Well, he had his own demons. Though they were his own and kept to himself.

He lived his life here, in this flat. I am going to miss him very much. I am very sad that you did not know him. He was, as my East End mother would say, a good soul."

"He never married?"

"I am sure that your mother was the only woman he ever loved."

Eilidh lifted her head, her eyes red. "Jesus."

"However, it is my duty…"

"Have they stopped looking?"

"Possibly. I'm not sure, but the North Sea is very unforgiving."

"And they're saying he's a paedophile?"

"In so many words, yes."

"And that's how his story ends?"

Shiresman leaned over the table and took her hand. "I only saw Hector perhaps once or twice a year. But he was my friend. Whatever confidences he shared, and there were very few, he shared with me. Whatever you hear about him, and whatever he was supposed to have done, do not believe it."

She smiled. "I know you're being kind. But sometimes life is shit."

Shiresman sat back and opened his briefcase. "I have a copy of his will here. It is brief. I'll leave it with you."

"Will there be a funeral?"

"No. Unless a body is found. The process for declaring someone dead without a body is somewhat lengthy and convoluted. The state may try to claim his wealth. But your father was a clever man. He is not leaving his house to you in a will."

"What? I thought…"

"No, his estate is selling you this apartment for one

194

Scottish pound. He knew how long the legal process can take. We can sign the papers…"

"Did he know what he was going to do? What was going to happen?"

"I cannot say, though as a lawyer, Hector was always one step ahead. He was a man of process and planning. We can sign papers later, but once you have given me a pound, the house is yours. And then I can sell it for you and send you the funds." He reached into his pocket and pulled out a Scottish pound note, then laid it on the table.

Eilidh stood and walked around the kitchen, her hand brushing the worktops. "You know, I have a cold reporter's heart. And I see something that has been planned out. He changed his will, or these instructions, in the past few days?"

"Yesterday."

"Shit. He bloody knew. But they caught him at the bridge?"

"Yes." Shireman stood. "I'm afraid I must go. I have High Court meetings I must attend. You have my number, please do not hesitate to contact me. And you have the keys, you can come back here any time. Hector left funds to pay for the heating and…"

"I'm staying." She picked up the pound note from the table and handed it to him.

Shiresman took the pound, then nodded and picked up his briefcase. "As you wish."

"I need to know who he is. Was."

"I understand. But any investigation may already be terminated. The police may have moved on. Whatever information they may have is unlikely to be made public."

"So the case dies with him?"

"Perhaps." Shiresman turned to the door. "I have some rather discreet contacts and confidantes who value my discretion. Let me see what I can find."

Eilidh watched him go, then turned to the window and looked out into the sunlight.

I couldn't see the monitor from below the desk, my arms wrapped around my face, and my body sore and racked with the sobs bursting through my chest. When they began to subside, I clamped my mouth shut and lifted my head. On the monitor, she knelt before the ashes in the fire and picked up a blackened scrap of paper, then dropped it.

In the hall, she found the wifi router and the plastic tag that slid out, holding the password, then pulled a laptop from her bag in the hall and took it into the sitting room and opened it on the table.

The door buzzer sounded and she looked up, then walked to the hall and listened for a moment.

"Yeah, come up, top floor."

She opened the front door then returned to the sitting room and opened her laptop. She looked around, then stared out the window.

In the doorway of the sitting room stood Inspector Gilfeather.

Chapter XXVII

Eilidh turned as if a spell was broken and smiled. "To what to do I owe the pleasure, handsome stranger?"

He held up his warrant card. "As I said on the intercom, Davey Gilfeather. Police Scotland."

"Well, then not really a pleasure, Inspector."

"No, I'm afraid not."

She stuck out a hand. "Eilidh Strathmartin. But you can call me Ellie. It's close enough. Not many in Oz knows how to pronounce my name. Come in."

"Yeah, I know what you mean. My first name is Ruaridh."

"Roo-ree?" She closed the door.

"Yeah, made me sound like a posh public schoolboy so I ditched it."

"So, Davey from the block?"

"Something like that." He looked down at her rucksack. "I hope you don't mind me asking, are you family?"

"You're a sharp copper, Davey. Come into the kitchen, I'll make you a coffee."

"Thanks. I didn't know there was any family."

Eilidh filled the kettle and turned towards, him, leaning back on the worktop. "That makes two of us."

"Eh?"

"You might also call me Eilidh Lawless. Hector was my dad."

"You're his daughter?"

"Yeah. You look as surprised as I was." She began opening cupboards and searching through jars of herbs and condiments. "C'mon, Hector, where's the java?" She opened the last cupboard and stepped back. "Wow. That is the most impressive and slightly threatening collection of tea that I've ever seen."

Gilfeather relaxed in his chair. "Tea's fine."

"Maybe for you, but I could kill for a flat white."

"Will I have to report a murder?"

Eilidh laughed and took two bags from a wooden tea chest. "You're making my day better, Inspector Davey, you can come again. Milk?"

"Just a spot."

She made the tea and placed a mug in front of him with a spoon to remove the bag, setting a saucer beside him. "So, red-haired king from the streets, tell me something."

Gilfeather smiled and lifted his cup, blowing on his tea. "You know your Gaelic names. Yes, I do have a wee touch of red in me, if that was your question."

"I think with our blood, we all do, but tell me, what is a man who was going to kill himself doing with two pints of fresh milk and a fridge full of food?"

He sipped his tea. "That is a very good question. And here's another one. Why were you surprised to learn you were family?"

Eilidh leaned forward on the table. "Ladies first, eh?"

He shrugged. "You know what coppers are like. Nosey as hell."

She tasted her tea and sat back, looking down at her

cup. "I don't want there ever to be a day when I get used to this. It's just warm brown water."

Gilfeather sipped his tea but did not reply.

"Okay, I'll come out with it. I'm Hector Lawless' long lost love child."

His eyebrows lifted and he held the cup in mid-air.

"I was conceived just before my mother, still a teenager, left with her family to move to Oz. I never knew who my father was, and my mother wanted it that way. My Oz father, Jonny Strathmartin, made me who I am, and I wear him every day like armour. He was a great bloke and he loved me and mum with all his heart until the day he died. But I didn't know the name of Hector Lawless until ten o'clock this morning, sitting in my rented room in London with a decent cup of coffee and checking my Facebook messages. A message pops up telling me I have an inheritance. I was one click away from deleting it as a scam. Then I saw Edinburgh in the message and a bell rang in my head. I answered the message, then jumped on the first train and got here about half an hour ago."

Gilfeather placed the cup on the table. "Wow."

"So, I'm sitting on the train and this solicitor dude is on the blower and tells me I've inherited the estate of my long-lost father, Hector Lawless. He thought it was gonna take months to find me. But I had a father, Jonny Strathmartin, and we were closer than two coats of paint and I knew him more than I know myself. Hector Lawless, I don't know. Though from what I see around me, he wasn't a man who was going to kill himself."

Gilfeather sipped his tea.

"The heating is still on, which is one thing I've learned to detect very quickly in this rain-swept madhouse of an island floating off the coast of Belgium. Also, he has enough tea to, as my father would say 'keep a battalion of the Black Watch going for a month', and he's taken a bottle of fine Bordeaux wine out his wine cooler, and opened it so it can oxidise and come up to room temperature. Last night, I assume. He planned to come home and drink it."

Gilfeather looked over to the bottle sitting on the worktop.

"I'm an Aussie. We know wine. And whatever Hector was planning to do, it wasn't to kill himself."

Gilfeather nodded. "You'd make a good cop."

"I'm a reporter. We think the same."

"Yeah, I suppose we do. Sometimes."

Eilidh leaned back in the chair, drank some tea then placed her cup on the table. "So, before I die of brown water poisoning, what brings you here, Inspector Davey?"

The wine cooler hummed into life behind them. Gilfeather rested his elbows on the table. "Curiosity."

"Really? No investigation? Like, you know, a detective?"

He shook his head. "No. Listen, Eilidh, what I'm about to tell you is rather unpleasant…"

"I'm way ahead of you. I had four hours on the train to work on this. Social media, rumours and legwork. The solicitor dude hinted at something nasty. Hector was going to be arrested for child abuse, right?"

He closed his eyes for a moment. "Right. And I think I was the last man to talk to him."

Eilidh didn't reply, then stood up and walked to the window, looking out at the sunshine. "What did he say?"

"He said he was innocent."

"Was he?"

Gilfeather leaned back in his seat. "The case against him was very strong."

"Strong?"

He looked down at his tea. "Watertight."

"What else did he say?"

"That he was set up."

"Maybe he was…"

"Eilidh, he was armed with an IED."

"What?"

"An improvised explosive device, it…"

"I know what it means. What the hell was he doing with that?"

"He told us he was going to blow us all to bits rather than be taken. Turned out it was a smoke bomb and he used it to make his escape."

"Fucking hell. And then he ran for the bridge?"

"Yeah."

"But why go so far to kill yourself? He could have jumped out of this bloody window, we're four storeys up."

"We think he was trying to cross the river into Fife then escape to the Highlands. But he was trapped on both sides."

"Maybe. So, if it's all cut and dried, why are you here?"

Gilfeather didn't reply for a moment, then nodded his head back towards the hall. "A painting."

"What?"

"I was here last night. Your father has a painting next door. It show the bridges over the river. Or one, I mean."

"Show me."

She followed him down the hall and he turned into

the sitting room, then crossed to the fireplace and stood before the painting.

"This one."

She stood close by his side.

"There's only one bridge here," he said, "the rail bridge, but it's an old painting. Now there are three. Two road, one rail. One bridge for each century. Nineteenth, twentieth and twenty-first."

"The big red rail bridge? It's that old?"

"Yeah, massively over-engineered. They had to instil confidence it wouldn't fall down like the one over the Tay, north of here. Lots of people died. So they went absolutely tonto with the steel. One of the wonders of the world in its day. And down there, that fancy house in the woods, is where your dad went to school. He also taught the boys that… Well…"

"I get it." Eilidh spoke in a low voice. "Was it you that kicked the door down?"

"Yeah. Sorry about that."

"And did you find what you were looking for?"

"The place was empty."

"Yeah, but the fridge is full. So where's Hector's computer? Laptop? Papers? This place is cleaner than a nun's browser history."

"Ah, taken away for any inquests or investigation."

"Right. Am I getting them back?"

He didn't take his gaze from the painting. "I'm afraid I don't know, it's out of my hands."

"So, you just came back to look at the painting."

He looked towards the window. "Aye."

Eilidh leaned closer. He didn't move. She smiled. "I don't believe you."

He turned and faced her for a moment, then lowered

his head and stepped back. "Look, there was concrete evidence against him."

"He was a lawyer. Why didn't he fight it?"

Gilfeather shook his head. "I don't know. But I'll tell you what I do know. He was a man who lived alone all his life, had no friends, had a history of mental illness and was facing signed witness statements from two former pupils naming him as an abuser. They have photographic evidence of him trying to break into the school at night. If you ask one of his colleagues they'll say he was a really sweet man. Ask another and they'll say he was a weirdo. And he came at us with what could have been an IED. He told me how he could make a real one. And he could. That's some serious shit. It takes research and preparation. He was ready for us. And when we trapped him, he chose to walk out over the bridge instead of facing the music. Looking at it as a copper, he was an emotionally disturbed man on strong medication who took his own life. I'm sorry, but that's the way it is."

She looked up at the painting. "That's okay. I understand."

He moved a little closer. "I wish it was otherwise. The few words I had with him made me think he was a good man. Though everyone has demons."

"Yeah. Maybe. But he did have a friend. And he did have a family. He just chose to keep it quiet."

Gilfeather took out his card. "In case you need to call me."

She took the card and handed him one from her pocket. "In case you need to call me, Roo-Ree."

He nodded and headed for the door, then stopped in the hall.

She walked over. "Still here, Davey?"

He was looking at the attic hatch in the roof. "Didn't notice that last night. But then we weren't really looking for him."

She laughed. "You want to search the attic?"

"Do you mind?"

She threw out her arms. "Knock yourself out. If you find a pot of gold, let me know."

"Got a key? For the padlock, I mean."

She sighed, then turned back to the kitchen and grabbed a ring full of keys from a hook in the pantry. In the corner were a set of folding steps, and she carried them into the hall. "Here you go."

He stood on the steps and found the key, then unlocked the padlock and pulled down the hatch. A folding ladder unloaded to the floor. He looked at Eilidh but she shrugged, and he climbed the ladder.

She watched him disappear. "So?"

He looked down. "Nothing."

"Dead end, mate."

He climbed down and pushed the ladder home and the hatch swung shut. He looked at the padlock lying on the steps, then Eilidh picked up both and took them through to the kitchen.

"What's next, Davey? Under the beds?"

"Sorry, just had to be sure." He smiled and headed for the door.

Eilidh watch him go and when the door closed, she pulled out her phone and tapped the keypad. "You awake? Yeah, thought you might be. I'll be quick, 'cos a mobile call to Oz is going to bankrupt me. Listen, boss, there's some weird shit going down here. I'll send you an email. In a nutshell, my real dad is dead, I've just inherited a super-expensive apartment and... yeah, real dad. He topped himself and I'm sitting here wondering what the fuck just happened. They say the case is closed, but there's a cute copper sniffing around and all sorts of shady shit. This might be a real cut and shut case, but my spidey-sense is tingling. Yeah, I'm gonna kick over a few stones, see who Hector really is. I mean, even if he wasn't a kiddy-diddler, then... yeah, Hector, tell you about that later. Tomorrow I'm gonna do some digging, start with the neighbours, then track down who he was. Anyway, look, what I wanted was two weeks leave, to kinda see who the hell he was, and who the hell I am? Yeah, thought I'd mention all that first, get your newspaper man glands swelling before I popped the question. Yeah? Thanks, boss, you're a good bloke, I'll email you later. Eh? No, the bloody sun is already going down and it's only 3 p.m. Being this far north sucks. I'm gonna jump in a cab and get out there before it's dark, see the bridge where he jumped. Yeah, yeah, the House of Lords article, I know, I'm on it. Got most of it done on the train. It's unbelievable, but it's real. I'll make the deadline. Ha, ha, yeah, see ya, boss."

The knife was loose in one hand and the other covered my mouth, both wet with tears. On the camera, she grabbed her coat and headed for the door. I stood looking up at the roof. I was trapped. If I went out onto the roof, the men working on the scaffolding where I had climbed down would see me. Then what? The attic was unlocked, but there was no way out other than the servant's stairs. The main door was too risky.

In the camera to the street, she stood outside talking

into her phone, then raised an arm towards the corner and the street up the hill to the Old Town.

I knelt down on the floor and wrapped my arms around my head. She was nothing to them. Hector was dead. But the news would soon be out and she would know who Hector was, and so would the world, and she would be safe.

I looked over at the camera and she stepped between the cars as a black cab pulled up. She opened the door.

Chapter XXVIII

The oak-panelled room was empty and portraits of grey-haired men stared down at him. Outside, from the Royal Mile, the muted sound of bagpipes and tourists drifted into the room.

A key rattled in a lock and a door opened in the corner of the room. A shiny-faced man in a grey suit looked through. In his hand was a long iron key, brown with age, but shining with oil. "Inspector Gilfeather?"

"Yes."

"This way, please. And may I see your warrant card?" Gilfeather held it out and the man examined the details. "Excellent, come this way. Apologies for the décor, though if you like a touch of vintage chic, you'll be in heaven."

Gilfeather followed him through and the man locked the door behind them. Directly in front, spiral metal steps of steel mesh twisted down into darkness.

"I know, Inspector, it looked like a cupboard, but it holds the path to the underworld. Edinburgh, eh? You never know what goes on behind closed doors." He flicked a switch on the wall and bare, dim lightbulbs lit the steps. "I hope you don't suffer from vertigo, Inspector. I shall lead the way, although the only way is down." He laughed at his own joke and began to descend.

Gilfeather looked down at the steps. A line of bulbs lit a shaft descending into the depths until it was obscured by the winding steel mesh. He followed the man, treading carefully, his hand grasping the cold metal handrail by the wall and turning constantly down the steep steps.

He stopped and glanced up, but the entrance was in darkness. Then the man stopped in front of him and pointed a to lightbulb.

"That's been there for eighty years. Never failed. Fascinating, eh? They don't make them like they used to."

Gilfeather nodded and kept his eyes on his feet, each step echoing in the shaft.

"A hangover from the last war. They went down deep. Still, we have all mod cons." They emerged into a corridor, one wall of dull, stained plaster, and the other rough-hewn foundation blocks. "You'd be amazed what they found. An absolute warren of early medieval rooms from when Edinburgh was but a boy."

Edinburgh's more Lady Macbeth, thought Gilfeather, not a boy. She holds evil and love in equal measure. And dispenses them as she sees fit.

Above them ran cast-iron pipes alongside fibre-optic data cabling. "This way. The Secretary of State and your Chief Constable are waiting." The man stopped before a door. "I'm Mr Sussex. We shall be working together." He pointed down the corridor. "There are other entrances, but they're on a need-to-know basis." He opened the door.

The room was low, narrow and vaulted with rough,

hand-hewn bricks. Three desks took up one side where technicians sat before screens. Three rusted metal hooks hung down from the wall. Sussex murmured to Gilfeather as he closed the door. "Yes, that's what I thought, turns out it's a medieval butcher's shop. Next door was a pub."

At the end was another door. The technicians ignored them as they walked to the far side of the room. Sussex gestured to Gilfeather, who opened the door. Inside was a larger room, and a huge fireplace along one wall. Above it was a wide screen TV, showing a network of phone masts and streets, with mobile phone numbers flashing up when they connected to the network.

At the end of the room, sat behind a cheap plastic desk, the Secretary of State for Scotland, Mungo Hastings, leaned forward as Gilfeather approached. To his side stood the Chief Constable of Police Scotland. Gilfeather nodded to him, "Chief," then turned to face Hastings. There was nowhere for him to sit.

Hastings had the only chair in the room. He played with a pen on a blotter and stared at Gilfeather.

Gilfeather turned to the Chief Constable. "Sir, am I here for a theft of furniture?"

The Chief glared at him.

Hastings stood up. "You have been allowed access to these rooms due to your involvement in this case of national security. In future, you will never speak of this location. Further access depends on your performance. If I have to impress upon you the seriousness of this operation, and its value to the State, then you will be dismissed."

"Well, impress away. I'm all ears."

"Your street copper attitude has no place here," spat Hastings. "You will address me as Sir."

Gilfeather glanced to his Chief, who nodded, his lips so tight they blanched against his florid skin. "Alright, Sir Secretary of State, what's up?"

"Gilfeather," growled the Chief. "Just fucking behave. You're playing in a different league."

"Indeed, Chief Constable," said Hastings, "where failure is not an option."

"Yeah, I get that." Gilfeather shrugged. "Okay, thanks for the pep talk, what's this all about?"

Hastings' chin trembled and his jaw clenched tight for a moment. "It is about Hector Lawless and Lord Campbell."

Gilfeather said nothing but relaxed his shoulders and widened his stance.

Hastings lifted his chin. "Lord Campbell could not have killed himself. Hector Lawless did it."

Gilfeather didn't move. "Really?"

"Yes. Really." He enunciated his words slowly and the veins in his foreheads bulged purple. "I knew Campbell since he was a boy. We were at school together."

"Yeah," said Gilfeather, "I heard you were close when you were young. And Campbell got kicked out of school for a serious offence, but you stayed."

"Don't you dare insult me with rumour! It was a schoolboy prank that went wrong, and Campbell took the blame."

"I heard a young boy was beaten and raped. But that's all in the past for the late Lord Campbell. So, what's this about our jumper, Hector Lawless? Lord Campbell was alive and presumably well when Hector Lawless took a leap of faith off the Forth Bridge, so how could he have killed him?"

"That, Inspector, is what you have to find out."

Gilfeather blew out a low breath that ended in a faint whistle. "I'll be honest, sir, you don't need a detective, you need a fucking clairvoyant." Spittle flecked the edges of Hastings lips. He took a deep breath, but Gilfeather continued. "Hector Lawless walked out on the bridge. He was caught on camera. He didn't come back. Is there a possibility he jumped and survived? Yes, although it's more likely that Shergar ridden by Lord Lucan comes through the door behind us than Hector Lawless surviving that jump."

Hastings spat out the words. "Did you find a body?"

"No. If he went off before the first casement he'd hit the shallow waters and break his neck. If he went off after the first casement he'd be swept away in the current and out to sea. Even if he survived, he'd have minutes before the cold killed him."

"That's conjecture. I repeat, you haven't found a body."

"Perhaps, but saying that he killed Campbell is also weapons grade conjecture. However, if you like, let's entertain the idea. Just for fun. What makes you think it was Lawless?"

Hastings jabbed a finger at Gilfeather. "You were there. In the garage under the High Court. Campbell told me. He wanted revenge."

"Ah, he never said that. However, if Hector Lawless was still alive, then yes, Lord Campbell would not be on his Christmas card list. But are you saying that after he survived his attempt at suicide, he comes back into town and fakes the suicide of Lord Campbell?"

"I don't care which scenario you choose, I can tell you that Lord Campbell was murdered. He would never have taken his own life."

Gilfeather shrugged, "Okay, we'll go with that. Did he leave a suicide note? Campbell, I mean, not Hector Lawless. He was probably in too much of a hurry."

"Don't concern yourself with faked notes, concentrate on Lawless. No one else would want to murder Campbell."

"Faked? So there is a note. When can I see it?"

"It's irrelevant! Find Lawless."

"You're asking me to find Hector Lawless with one hand tied behind my back? At least throw me a bone. Mind you, the late Lord Campbell's post mortem will be out later today, that should help as to whether he was murdered."

"Inspector, the post mortem will tell us what Lawless wants us to hear. Campbell told me about him. He was a lawyer of many years' experience and had seen every type of death and how it was caused. He was a man obsessed with planning and detail. I'll make this easy for you to understand because you have mistaken this for a discussion. It is not. It is an instruction. You have the local knowledge required, and if it was not required, the Security Services would have performed this task. Find Hector Lawless. This is a matter of National Security."

"National security? In what respect?"

Hastings face turned puce.

The Chief Constable stepped forward. "Look, just do it. Turn over every stone. I don't care who you upset, I'll cover it. Find him."

"Okay. Can I have bugging and tracking?"

The Chief pointed to the door. "Already authorised. They're outside."

"Well, it's a start. I'll get all the phones that were in the vicinity of Campbell at his time of death. Once the post mortem tells me he's dead."

Hastings squeezed his eyes shut. "Gilfeather, if it helps, I can assure you that success in this matter will result in significant career opportunities. Now, get out and do your job."

Gilfeather spun on his heels and marched to the door, then turned. "He has a daughter, you know."

"What?" Hastings' mouth dropped open.

"Hector Lawless. She's cute. Aussie girl. I've got her number. Standard police work. Just doing my job. I'll give it to the techs outside."

He left the door open, then strode over to the table. "Track this number for me, lads, and I'll have another request later."

He turned back and poked his head into the door, "Sussex, old bean, could you show me the way out? I don't want to wander down the corridors and discover Bomber Harris with his hand up a Wren's jersey."

Sussex smiled and left the room, closing the door behind him, then handed him a card with a phone number. "This is the number to call for access to these rooms. It changes every day."

"Of course it does."

Chapter XXIX

The bottle of pills were in my hand when a black cab pulled into the kerb. I held my breath until the door to the flat opened.

Eilidh strode in carrying a pizza box, threw her coat and bag on an armchair then dropped the box on the dining room table. She opened her laptop, took a tin of Irn Bru from her bag, then opened the box and grabbed a slice, eating it with one hand while she opened the tin with the other.

My eyes flicked from one camera to the other, checking the street then watching her eating and wiping her hands on a tissue from her pocket. The street was quiet.

My chest ached and I could not look at her any more. In my mind she was a thousand miles away, yet if I spoke now, she would hear me. She is of another world, I thought, not mine, and a world I left behind that has now come back to tear me apart, dangled in front of me by the terror that never left, but slept, waiting to punish me.

The dreams I had were now crushed by reality. Had she come before, I would have submitted and found the strength. I would have answered her questions, learned how to laugh when she joked or teased me, for she would always tease me, and I would thaw before her love. We would walk the streets in the sunshine and the sparkling golden terraces, the filigree of the statues and tenement tops in rose-coloured stone and climb the hills of the town and Arthur's Seat to look out over the Pentlands and Fife, Portobello and the beach, and the blue sea where it melted into the sky.

She tipped the tin back to drain it then belched and stood, dropped it into the pizza box and walked out into the hall.

In an hour, a boat was waiting to take me away. But no more.

It was not time to leave, I thought. It was not over. And I must say her name. I held my hands to my face and closed my eyes. "Eilidh." Then I looked up as if a spell had been broken.

She stood in the doorway to the bathroom, then stepped in and ran a bath. In her hands she held the thermometer then laid it behind by the taps, took a towel down then turned back to the hall towards the bedroom, pulling off her clothes.

I switched off the bedroom camera, and in a few moments she emerged wrapped in a towel and headed for the bathroom, leaving the door open. I turned off the hall camera and sat back.

The table was littered with a pizza box, empty tin and discarded tissue. Her phone lay beside her laptop. Gilfeather had the number, I did not. The phone screen lit up for a moment, then died. The processor light on her laptop flashed twice and a green light pulsed at the top of the lid next to the camera. I peered at the monitor, it flashed again, once, and then stayed on with rapid bursts of light. It didn't make sense. I turned on the hall camera. She was lying in the bath, head back and eyes closed, the water deep in soap bubbles, but the wifi router light was blinking off and on, and then stayed on for several seconds.

Gilfeather. He had her number and this address. She was being hacked.

Holding the towel tight, Eilidh pushed the pizza box aside and pulled the laptop towards her. A moment later the face of a man appeared on the screen. She waved, the other hand holding a cold crust of pizza. "Hey, boss. What's happening?"

"Same old shit. You going into the shower?"

"Nah, just had a bath! I haven't had a bath in a year, the bloody digs in London only have a shower. God, I missed it so much."

"I'm gonna get a screen shot and show the boys in the office."

"You dare! Anyway, I'm heading out soon, wanted to catch you before you leave the office."

"Like that would make a difference."

"So, I just got back from the rail bridge. It's quite a sight. It's about twice as long as the Sydney Harbour bridge, and over one hundred and forty years old. It's massive."

"Yeah? Maybe get a look someday if I want to go back and drink warm beer, eat soggy chips and freeze to death in the rain."

"Oh, you would. I whacked the heating up, and there's also a real fire, so I'm gonna burn the shit out a whole tree to get warm. Or do they use coal? I have no idea, I'm in a Victorian winter wonderland, and I'm freezing my tits off."

"Then put some clothes on. What you got for me?"

"This rail bridge is something else. I talked to the locals and it used to be the place where people took their final walk, but now they do that on the two road bridges. The rail track is now monitored twenty fours a day so they send the cops as soon as you step onto the track. And they told me that there is a maintenance gangway hanging below the track, and you can see it from the road. The lifeboat station is right under the bridge, and the dude there said that's the route Hector must have taken, because they didn't stop the trains. Plus, the whole thing was covered in thick fog on the night, so no one really knows. They call it haar, it's like massive sea fog, can be a hundred feet high and thick as hell. Kinda like a really spooky horror film fog that just rolls in and smothers everything. So Hector, he just went out into the fog and didn't come back. The coastguard guy said if he went off over the shallows near the shoreline, they'd have probably found him drowned with a broken back, but the deep channel would take him out to sea. But the thing is, because of the fog, nobody saw him drop and there's no sign of a body."

"That's only half a mystery. He's probably gone under."

"Maybe. Anyway, I'm in his flat now and there's nothing here."

"Eh?"

"No papers, no old bills, no receipts, no photos, not even a takeaway menu for the local curry house. The cops kicked his door in, looking for him, but why take it all?"

"Coppers can be weird."

"Yeah, though they left his medication, and I

recognise some of it from a story I did last year. I'm gonna help myself to get a good night's kip, 'cos my head is buzzin' with this shit."

"You sure this is worth your time?"

"I don't know. I might just sell up, take the money and run, but something's bugging me. This is his home. So where is his life? And after all, he is my real dad. I want to know. And something is not right. I can feel it."

"It's your holiday, Eilidh."

"Yeah. Anyway, I'm going to put on all the clothes I have and head out. I promised my old mum that if I ever made it to Edinburgh, I'd light a candle for her in the Cathedral. She'd have liked that."

"Maybe light one for him too. Reckon he needs it."

"Yeah, reckon he does."

She was going out on the streets. At night. But now they could track her phone and know where she was going. Would they take her? She knew nothing, only what she told her editor. And Hastings would be suspicious. And terrified. It was me he wanted. Although the post mortem may say otherwise, Hastings would realise that an immoral coward like Campbell would not take his own life. He enjoyed the evil too much. Either Hastings was looking for the evidence sent from Campbell's phone, or looking for me. The evidence should appear soon. The lawyers would be discreet, though the evidence would leak. But to whom?

The street was dark outside. She moved through to the bedroom to get dressed. She was the bait. It was me they wanted. My head flicked back and an anger rose and the heat of my blood spread across my face and neck. This was no time to cower. I stood and felt the strength descend as if from above. If the terror was back and holding onto Hector, then Harry would know what to do. He would always help me.

If they came to take her, I would be waiting. The only camera they had was on her laptop. They would never know. But there was one thing I had to know. Would they take her?

The combat jacket felt snug and warm, and I pulled on a woollen hat down over my eyebrows and ears, then fixed a dark cotton mask over my face and throat until only my eyes were visible, lifted the knife and climbed the ladder to the attic.

The cold wind made my eyes water as it gusted between the gutters in the roof. This wasn't the plan, but there was no other way. And I would know for sure. I kept low, skirting the cupolas and skylights, until I reached the end of the block and the high chimney stack, then peered out.

Below, beside the private garden, a black cab stood, its engine idling. The driver sat in darkness.

I kept low and scuttled over the roof and back to my skylight and had just got in when I heard the front door close. She was gone. I was too late, and I gripped the steel edge of the window for a moment, unable to move. But I had to know. Pulling myself out, I crawled back to the corner of the block.

The taxi hadn't moved. Then a faint light came on in the cab and the driver lifted a phone from his lap, looked at it for a moment, then killed the light and the engine.

I ducked back behind the stone. They could track her by her phone. They don't need the taxi. A door closed and I looked down. The driver was out of the cab, a toolbox in his hand and heading towards the front door to the street.

Scuttling over the roof, my skin tore on the stone as I pulled myself head first into the skylight, then dropped down into the room, slipping on the ladder and landing hard on the box room floor.

The hacking was not enough. They wanted more. They wanted to set a trap.

I grabbed the rucksack and opened a side pocket, pulling out a burner phone. I set it to airplane mode and switched on Bluetooth then shoved it in my pocket. If she had to be warned, there was no other way. On the monitor, her laptop lay closed. They had lost vision. I scrambled up the ladder into the attic then pulled the leaver to release the ladder to the hall, and it extended and thumped onto the floor below. I dropped into the hall, then ducked into the sitting room and took the burner phone from my pocket, pulled open a drawer in the escritoire and pushed the phone to the back.

A card with a phone number sat on the leaf of the escritoire. Inspector Gilfeather. I slipped it into my pocket as a faint creak of wood came from the main stairwell. I turned and ran.

My chin cracked on the rungs of the ladder as I dived for the higher rungs and pulled myself up, then turned and hauled the ladder back. It hit the rafters with a thud and as the hatch closed, scratching sounds came from the front door.

The blood dripped from my chin as I stepped down into my cell and pulled the wood over the gap to the attic. A man on the monitor pushed open the front door and returned his picks to his toolbox.

He closed the door, then placed his toolbox on the

hall table and examined the wifi router, then took out a small black box with a thin cable attached. Taking out the data cable from the router, he inserted it into the box, then attached the cable from the box to the data socket on the router, peeled back a plastic tag from the box then pressed a button on the side and stuck it below the table.

They had her laptop bugged, why go to the trouble of bugging the router? Then the man took a small bag from his toolbox, and it made sense. From the bag, he pulled a device similar to the self-adhesive cameras I had installed, and placed the first above the front door, pointing down the hall, and then did the same with the sitting room, moving down the hall to the bedrooms, bathroom and kitchen. These cameras did not need to transmit far or have a powerful battery. The black box under the table was the receiver and all data would be transmitted through the internet.

There was nothing I could do. His cameras were already active. Even if the power was cut to the flat, his system would function. And I was trapped. I couldn't go down the attic ladder or the servant's staircase. No doubt they would bug the garage and the courtyard. The only way was down the scaffolding and that would require all the inhabitants of the block to be asleep. One wrong footstep outside a bedroom window and the police would be called. They'd work it out.

The man closed his tool box and stood in front of the front door. I saw the screen light on the phone in his hand. He raised a hand to the camera, then left through the front door.

I sat back on the bed, holding a hand to my chin to stop the blood. They had set the trap. For her, and for me.

I made to grab my notebooks to list my options, then remembered the blood and took out my first aid kit from my rucksack and dressed my cuts. I washed my hands with wipes and picked up my pencils. Only severing the data cable would stop them. It ran outside the kitchen window to the ground, but there was no way to access it. Even if I did, they would immediately be suspicious. It would only attract attention.

But once the evidence came out, she would be irrelevant. They would be fighting fires all over the media and Eilidh would be safe. It was only a matter of time. They would leave her alone and this would be over. Then my leaving could begin again. Another ship would be waiting.

Yet the Guardian had nothing. The BBC had not even reported Campbell's death. I pushed the pencils and notebooks away and sat on the bed. Perhaps they knew and injunctions were already underway. But they were pointless. Social media and scandal were always lurking, and with a word in the right ear, Twitter would erupt.

It was only a matter of time. It had to be. They weren't the only ones waiting. I dimmed the monitor then lay back on the bed and closed my eyes. I would hear the front door when she returned. I would hear my daughter come home. Then the tears flowed free and I turned to bury my face into the bed.

The morning sun shone through the kitchen window and into the hall. The bathroom door was open and I looked away. In the sitting room two pizza boxes and empty tins littered the table. Over the sofa lay my tweed overcoat, which she had worn the night before against

222

the cold. It was too long for her, and it had made me cry when she came in with the collar wrapped under her chin.

She had dressed in the bedroom, then brought her coffee through to the sitting room and sat before the laptop to read the screen. A ping sounded from the laptop and she sat back. In a moment, her boss' face appeared on the screen.

"Hey, Ellie, you finished the House of Lords piece yet? And yeah, good morning, afternoon, or whatever Pommie time it is."

"Yeah, morning, Boss, did it last night, gonna send it right now. It's incredible. They made the son of a KGB agent an actual lord 'cos he's mates with some Tory wanker. Now this dodgy geezer can vote and affect the laws of the country. That's not the worst. You can just buy your way into the Lords with cash. Totally unelected. It's a fucking banana republic in the 21st century. But, oh, tradition, right? The Poms are crazy. They just lie back, sing God Save the Queen and take it up the chocolate spider."

"How dare you criticise the Mother of Parliaments, you young colonial pup!"

"It's not even the Mother of Parliaments, that's Iceland. But the Poms keep voting for the same old shit rubbed in their face."

"Welcome to the Empire. Anyway, I've got another one for you when you're finished your holiday. I need two thousand words on the rise of the right wing in the over-fifties and permanently-offended on social media. See how many times they mention the Blitz."

"Can I just cut and paste the words 'fucking gammon' one thousand times and send it in?"

"Ha, very good. No."

"Okay, deadline?

"Two weeks. If you finish it before that you get extra brownie points."

"Jeez. Okay, leave it with me. First I'm gonna go and see the place where my dad worked. Some legal chambers. Find a few names and faces, see who wants to talk and who doesn't. Lawyers are all treacherous bastards so someone is bound to throw me a bone. Gonna kick over a few stones and use some Aussie cheek to charm my way in."

"Good, that'll drive them mad."

"Oh, yeah. Right, the sun is shining, so I want to get out of here before I forget what it looks like."

My tea spilled across the desk. No, don't go. Don't ask questions. They're listening, they'll…

She had the tweed overcoat on and was heading for the door. She grabbed the keys from the hall table before I could move.

I brought up social media, but there was nothing. It had to be soon. Please, it had to be soon. The swine in the chambers would say nothing to her, the bloody swine, but Hastings would hear every word she said and see every step she took.

I knelt down on the floor and held my head in my hands.

Chapter XXX

Above the narrow entrance to the close was a Latin inscription, and she thought for a moment then typed it into her phone.

Fiat justitia ruat caelum 1605

She pressed enter.

Let justice be done though the heavens fall 1605

Yeah, she thought. Lawyers. Start like you mean to go on, with over four hundred years of total bullshit. Her nose wrinkled at the sharp smell of urine, and the damp walls made her hold her breath until she had climbed the worn steps and was past the studded wooden door.

On the wall was a brass plaque that had been polished until the words were almost indecipherable. "Campbell Legal Chambers." A few steps down the corridor she saw a woman behind a desk, just inside a room, focusing on a screen, but she had a view of the door. A button below the plaque instructed callers to ring for attention with a command to wait.

Well, thought Eilidh, who doesn't like a bit of attention? But I'm not waiting for it or getting fobbed of by some bloody secretary and a few snooty lawyers. They could talk to me for hours and I'd learn nothing.

She pushed open the door and took quick steps past the secretary and turned into a low room. Several people sat behind desks looked up, and others turned towards her.

"Hi. I'm Eilidh Strathmartin. But you can call me Ellie Lawless." Several mouths opened and others fixed her with a stare. "Yeah, I'm getting used to that reaction. Okay, brace yourselves. Big news, I'm Hector's daughter, so pleased to meet you all, but if you like we can do all the handshakes and hugs later."

A secretary hurried in behind her. "I'm so sorry, she didn't…"

"Never mind, love, it's like I'm part of the family. Ellie Lawless." She held out a hand.

The secretary ignored it. "You have to leave. Right now."

"Hold your horses, love, we're just getting acquainted." She turned back to the room. "Okay, I know Hector was a bit Marmite, and I'm hearing lots of different things about him, but I'd kinda like to build up a more complete picture by talking to the people who knew him best. The ones he saw every day. You guys. Who wants to go first?"

No one said a word. Some looked towards the doorway.

Eilidh pointed at one man staring at her, his face reddening by the second. "Yeah, you look like a good sport. What was old Hector like, eh?"

The secretary rounded her and stood directly in front. "You will leave now or I will call the police."

"Relax, sweetheart, I just want to hear about my old dad."

The red-faced man stepped forward. "Hector Lawless was a very disturbed man. He was tolerated here only out of the charity of Lord Campbell. From what I hear of his activities, his death is not unwelcome."

Eilidh held out her hands. "Aw, mate, you had to go and spoil it, didn't you? There must have been something nice you could say about him? You fucking prick."

The red-faced man stepped forward a half pace, then stopped. "You will leave now, or I'll take you outside by the scruff of your neck and throw you down the steps."

Eilidh laughed. "No, you won't, mate. You try that shit and I'll put you in a fucking wheelchair then take the sentence in court and send flowers to your ICU bed, so you wind your fucking neck in."

"Please," said the secretary. "There's nothing here for you."

Eilidh didn't move. She smiled at the secretary and took several business cards from her pocket. She dropped them on the nearest desk, then clicked her fingers and pointed to the group. "Call me. Anytime," as she pointed her finger at the red-faced man. "Not you, arsehole."

She turned into the corridor with the secretary close behind her, then stepped into the close. "Look, babes, I'm sorry to wind them up, but I'm not taking any shit from an old scrote in a shiny suit."

The secretary half-closed the door, then stopped. "Hector was a lovely man. A kind, gentle, caring man. But you won't hear that from them."

"Lawyers, eh?"

"I'll miss him, and I don't for one moment believe the rumours."

"To be honest, I don't know what to think. I thought I might get something from them. Maybe someone will loosen their knickers and call me. I'd appreciate it. Can you let them know? Poor old orphan trying to find out about her long lost dad?"

The secretary's lips tightened and she looked behind her. "They can't."

Eilidh shook her head. "Can't or won't?"

The secretary turned away. "Can't." She made to close the door.

Eilidh placed a hand out and held the edge of the door. "Listen, I never knew my dad. I don't know what to think. If you ever want to chat, have a cup of tea, I just want to know a bit more about him. Anything, really. Call me anytime."

The secretary glanced down the dark close then towards the High Street, her face flushed. "I can't."

"Okay, but you know, if you…"

"They took our phones." She closed the door.

Eilidh stared at the blackened metal studs hammered into the door before the smell of stale urine drove her towards the narrow entrance to the High Street.

An old man stood just inside the entrance, a little unsteady on his feet and his cane out to the side, half-blocking her way.

What the hell did she mean about the phones? She stopped behind the old man. "Excuse me."

"What?" His head was bent down and he turned, shuffling to one side, then the other as Eilidh tried to squeeze past. His cane slipped and she caught his arm. "Oh, thanks, m'dear! I thought I was a goner then."

She grinned and stepped into the street. "Watch out for yourself, mate."

He smiled and turned down the dark close.

The wind was biting on her neck and she pulled the tweed collar up under her chin and shoved her hands into the deep pockets. Her left hand brushed against a piece of paper. Weird, she'd thought the pockets were empty. She pulled out a small, folded piece of heavy, watermarked paper.

Don't turn around. Keep walking. Head to the Castle. Search for Sgt. Lawless. Royal Scots. Died Italy, 1944.

What the actual...? She stopped herself just at the moment she was going to turn and look for the old man, then pocketed the paper and headed up the Royal Mile. She weaved around the crowds of tourists, until the cobbled street became narrow, hemmed in by high gothic buildings, then emerged into a wide parade ground that faced the castle.

To the north side of the parade were Celtic crosses, engraved with ornate carvings and symbols, and the names and dates of fallen soldiers and long forgotten battles. Two Highlanders with rifles guarded the entrance below the stone ramparts, and she followed a line of tourists over the drawbridge and through the gatehouse into the castle, climbing up the steep cobbled street.

At the ticket office, she took the ticket as it was passed to her under the glass. "Where would I find a Sergeant Lawless? Died Italy, 1944."

"Scottish? Or served in a Scottish Regiment?"

"I think so."

"Then you want the Scottish National War Memorial. Up the hill, follow the signs."

"Thanks."

The hill was steep as she trudged behind tourists, through another gate with a spiked portcullis suspended over their heads and into an esplanade lined with cannons facing out over Edinburgh. Signs pointed the way, and she followed the paths into a courtyard of ancient, high stone houses. In front, lay a sombre, fortified building, like the gatehouse of a Highland castle. She followed an old man through the door. It seemed like a church, but with the names of regiments and battles carved in the rosy, gilded stone surrounding her.

She stopped when she saw high above, picked out in gold, wide over the stone, the word ANZAC.

Another candle would have to be lit.

On a long plinth that stretched around the length of the walls, lay books bound in red leather, some open. She approached and saw the pages filled with names, dates and places. There were so many books, and so many pages. Above the books were the names of the regiments and she walked along until she found ROYAL SCOTS carved deep into the stone.

An old man stood before the book, pages in his hand, then turned and smiled at her, closed the book and stepped down.

Eilidh stood before the book and lifted back the heavy, embossed cover. On each page, two lines of surnames were listed in alphabetical order, and she turned the pages until she found the page listed for L, and hesitating to touch the paper, found the name.

LAWLESS, T. W. Sgt., Monte Casino, Italy, 18th June, 1944.

The page was bowed, as if something was behind it. She turned the page to find an envelope with the initials EL written on the front. She glanced back, but the old man had gone.

She drew back the page to cover the envelope. Why here? Her fingers found it under the page.

No cameras. Not in a war memorial. And she was

just looking up a relative who had died in the war. Like any tourist in Edinburgh. She leaned forward and slipped the envelope into Hector's old jacket. Was this desecration?

The envelope was snug behind the tweed. The men and women in this book had died so that others may live. Maybe what was in the envelope meant the same. She closed the book and bowed her head, then followed a shaft of sunlight to the door.

The wind caught her hair and chilled her face, and she pulled the collar up once more then stopped in the middle of the courtyard. Highlanders in combat jackets and kilts marched towards her, then out of the courtyard. This was an Army HQ.

Shiresman, you beauty. You deliver the goods with no witnesses right in the heart of the State, because the army is separate from the State. No wonder Hector trusted you.

The toilets were clean and bright. Army efficiency, thought Eilidh. She took a cubicle and sat down, taking the envelope from her coat. Three folded pages emerged with a note.

These are copies of photos that were taken of a phone screen and a WhatsApp message. They show the suicide note of Lord Campbell, in which he admits his guilt as a paedophile and murderer, and exonerates Hector Lawless, who he manipulated to take the blame for child abuse. They also show a witness statement signed by a murder victim, witnessed by Hector Lawless, that confirms the guilt of Lord Campbell and Mungo Hastings, Secretary of State for Scotland for child abuse and murder. A video of a verbal reading of the statement also exists. The evidence is being supressed under a gagging order or a D-Notice. Publication will mean conviction and imprisonment. Assume your phone is compromised.

Her fingers held the paper so hard that they left dents when she released her grip. She read the suicide note and stared as the cubicle door. He mouth was dry and the breath rasped in her throat. She looked down once more. "Oh, Hector," she whispered, "what have they done?"

Her legs shook as she stood and folded the papers and slipped the envelope back in her overcoat. She pulled out her mobile phone from the pocket of the coat. The battery had already dropped ten percent. If they were using Pegasus variants of hacking, the camera and the microphone were live. They'd expect her to be looking at her phone. But it wasn't perfect. When she had talked to the secretary, the phone was deep in the pocket surrounded by thick tweed. She was safe. And he was one clever man, Mr AJ Shiresman. No witnesses, a plausible destination right down to the name of her relative, and nothing with a digital footprint.

The north wind was cold, but this time it cooled the blood in her neck and face, and excused the tears that welled up in her eyes. Her hand rested on the wide black barrel of a cannon by the ramparts overlooking Edinburgh. To the west, obscured by a hill, lay the bridges over the Forth, and on the other side of the river, the Kingdom of Fife and the road north, through the rolling hills to the Highlands. He tried to make it over the bridge, Gilfeather had said.

She turned away.

Chapter XXXI

She was not the same. Her walk, her look, was both hunter and prey.

On the hall camera, I watched as she shrugged the coat from her shoulders and threw it on an armchair in the sitting room and dropped a fresh pizza box on the table with another can of Irn Bru. She turned away then stopped, walked back to the coat and took the phone out of the pocket, checked the screen then stuffed it deep into the coat and headed for the kitchen.

She hauled open the pantry door and stepped inside, and stood, looking down at the floor.

They could not see her. Their camera was in the corner above the pantry door. But I could see her as she pulled folded paper from inside the waistband of her jeans. She opened the paper and held it in front of her. There was a picture of a phone that filled the first page and then the next. The camera focused in, but I didn't need to see the words on the page. I had written the words. Campbell's confession. She had the evidence.

My skin chilled. It was happening. If she had photos then someone was leaking. Someone would talk. Then she would be safe. Although she went to the chambers. Did someone from the chambers give her those papers?

It was possible. A printed photo would not leave digital evidence of the phone.

She folded the papers and stuffed them in an empty pizza box and then placed the box in a bin bag, and set it by the bins and walked out of the kitchen. She knew she was being monitored. That's why she left her phone in the overcoat. She went to the pantry because it's where the bins are kept. She did not know about the cameras.

In the sitting room, she opened the laptop on her desk.

My heart seemed to judder and my mouth dried. She did not know they were listening. If they knew she had the evidence, they would come for her. If she told her boss, they would shut her down in an instant.

The contact page for Campbell's chambers came up on her screen, then she started a virus sweep. As it ran, she took her phone from her pocket and began to dial the numbers listed on the page for Campbell's chambers.

The first call rang out. No voicemail, no response. She stared at the screen for a few moments, then tried the second. Same result.

The landline phone was in the hall, on a table beside the wifi router. She left the antivirus running, then took the phone from the hall table and dialled the numbers, each one in turn. But there was no answer.

The antivirus completed with no result.

She brought up Zoom and her boss appeared on the screen.

"I was just going to bed," he growled.

"You don't sleep."

"Well, ain't that the truth. What's up? You found something?"

She stared at the screen. "No."

He didn't reply for a moment, then nodded. "Okay."

"Just some weird shit."

"Yeah?"

"I went up to the place where Hector, my dad, worked, the legal chambers?"

"I remember."

"Well, I was as welcome as a fart in a spacesuit. But here's the thing. All their phones... I mean, I've got the web page up for the chambers, and I'm trying all their office mobile phones, and there's no reply. Then I call them back, and the phone's disconnected."

"Try another."

"I've tried them all."

"All of them?"

"Yeah. All disconnected." She cleared her throat. "Okay, but I've got nothing. The phones are dead and they didn't tell me shit."

"Well, maybe there's nothing to find."

"I can tell you something that's not news, except to the wider public."

"Yeah?"

"Yeah, this Lord Campbell dude, the guy that Hector worked for, he topped himself. Took a long holiday on a short rope."

"Why he'd do that? Is it connected?"

"It is if you're an incel on Twitter, though it's probably bullshit. But Campbell had a past. Hector was up on charges of child abuse, right? I talked to a man, who... Well, I went for a walk around Campbell's parish, stopped a couple of unfriendly locals and one gave me a name. I checked it out, and the word is, Campbell got kicked out of school for sexually assaulting another boy.

235

He got canned from the school, but his mate got away with it."

"His mate?"

"Yeah, Mungo Hastings. Which already sounds like a paedo's name. He was a lawyer too, then climbed the greasy pole in Government."

"Ellie, Mungo Hastings is the Secretary for State for Scotland. He's in the cabinet at No.10 Downing Street. You're winding up the wrong people. And then the phones are disconnected. Ellie, you know what a D-Notice is?"

She paused for a moment, then shrugged. "I get the feeling it's not good news?"

"Remember, I spent four years in my misspent youth in London drinking shit lager and watching cricket in the rain. A D-Notice is Kryptonite for pommie journalists. The Government can shut you down. You find out something they don't want to know, they shout that it's a National Security issue, judge issues an order and that's it. You can't print it, talk about it or share it with anyone. And I mean anyone. Otherwise, it's straight to the Tower."

"But I'm an Aussie."

"They won't give a shit. Christ, the arrogant arseholes still think we like them."

"Jeez. Is there anything on the wire? PA? Reuters? They won't care."

"No, there's nothing. If there was it would be flagged up, as with a caution. What I'm saying is, if you find something, be careful who you tell. 'Cos you can't tell anyone from prison."

"You serious? Like a High Court Injunction?"

"Yeah. Don't blow the biggest scoop of your life by

being a blabbermouth. If you need to leave, then leave. Fuck London, just get off the island. I'll cover it."

She didn't reply for a moment, then cleared her throat. "Yeah, no worries, it's all internet gossip, total bullshit as usual. Just 'cos you know someone doesn't make you a paedo, right?"

"Exactly, so don't go around upsetting people. As usual."

She gave out a high-pitched laugh. "Not me, Boss. I'm done with all this conspiracy bullshit. I've got nothing. Okay, you go to bed, I'm gonna go for a walk. I need to find the local pubs, chat to the neighbours. Hector is still a mystery man."

"Take care."

The daylight reflected off the table and diffused the camera picture on the monitor. She stood in the glow from the screen, then closed the laptop and shut off her phone. She knew they were listening, and I stood, shaking but happy. She had let them listen, to show she had nothing and I was proud. If she had researched conspiracy sites then she'd know about Hastings when he gave an alibi in court for a man accused of sexually assaulting a boy, and Hastings had proudly testified that he was a hundred miles away with the man when the alleged assault took place. And the man who walked free was now the Prime Minister.

On the monitor, she pocketed her phone and lifted the overcoat. Would they believe her story? It didn't matter, she had to leave the country. Get out right now.

I grabbed a burner phone and switched on the Bluetooth. I could message the phone hidden in the drawer of the escritoire. Tell her to forget everything, pretend to go for a walk and run for the airport. They might work it out, but too late. I looked up and she was pulling on the overcoat as the front door closed behind her.

Chapter XXXII

Hastings' voice could be heard behind the door when Gilfeather stepped into the tech room. He turned to Sussex. "Who's pissed on his chips?"

Sussex sighed. "It seems surveillance has picked up his name in relation to Miss Strathmartin, or Miss Lawless, if you prefer."

Gilfeather pressed his lips together to stop himself from grinning as Sussex opened the door.

The Chief Constable was just behind the door and stepped back as they entered. "Where've you been?"

Hastings stood up from behind his desk, his face blotched pink and white and his neck a bright red, bulging over his shirt collar. He jabbed a finger at Gilfeather. "Hector Lawless is alive!"

Gilfeather stood in the middle of the room and looked around. "Still going with the minimalist furniture, eh? Or did you expect me to kneel?"

The Chief Constable stood right behind him. "Fucking behave yourself!"

Hastings held up several sheets of paper. "This is a surveillance log of her calls. She has my name. She's been talking about me to her editor in Australia."

"So, this is about you?"

The Chief Constable bawled in his ear. "This is about Hector Lawless. Where the fuck is he?"

Gilfeather looked straight ahead. "I have found no indication that…"

"She must have got my name from Lawless. He's feeding her information."

"Ah, no," said Gilfeather, "you don't have to look far to find a link between the unfortunate demise of Campbell and your past, which is being handled with remarkable restraint by the press, I must say, so I assume someone has had a word. However, your name…"

"It's him, he's…"

Gilfeather held up a hand. "Gotta stop you right there, Sir Secretary of State, a Google search using the right words will link both of you very quickly, especially amongst the kind of chat rooms that think the Royal Family are space lizards."

Hastings stared open-mouthed at him.

"They go into it in some detail, which is not…"

"What? What words?"

"I'm sure you can work them out. You and Campbell, I mean. Not space lizards."

The Chief Constable's chin jutted against Gilfeather's shoulder. "What did you tell her?"

Gilfeather turned his head until his nose almost touched the Chief Constable's cheek. "Nothing."

"I'll make it clear," said the Chief Constable, "her conversation with her editor went from Campbell to Mr Hastings very quickly. She's being fed information. She's a journalist and…"

"Yeah, I know. Can I see the call log? The transcript?"

Hastings laid the papers face down on the table. "No."

"Why not?"

"Need to know," said the Chief Constable, "and you don't need to know. Find Lawless."

"Gentleman, I don't know how to say this.. Well, I do, but…"

The Chief Constable edged closer. "Gilfeather. She is also aware that aspects of this investigation are under a D-Notice and an injunction. She didn't get that from the internet. She's a journalist. Hector Lawless is no fool by all accounts, and he's using her."

"Sir, with all due respect, would you mind backing off a few paces? I can tell what you had for lunch." Gilfeather stepped forward to stand before Hastings. "The story of you and Campbell at school is well known."

"Damned public school and dinner table gossip!"

"Whatever. Anyway, tell me about this D-Notice. What don't I know? It's hard enough to find a dead man without doing it blindfold."

Hastings placed his hand on the papers. "None of your damn business."

"For fuck's sake, how am I…?"

Sussex sidled up beside Gilfeather. "Gentlemen, this is becoming unnecessarily heated. Inspector Gilfeather, any information you might seek to judge its relevance is contained within information that is very sensitive and has the highest classification. It is impossible to split the two. That is why it cannot be revealed. I'm sure you understand that any information that can be revealed most certainly will be. We have the same aim."

"We do?"

"We do. In the meantime, it is essential to this investigation that you find Hector Lawless."

Gilfeather smiled. "Mr Sussex, that must have been a very expensive education to allow you to talk such beautiful pish."

Sussex gave a brief nod. "It was. Now, it would be of benefit to us all if you could…"

"Find him!" Hastings slammed his hand on the table. "Before she knows too much. Or just damn well deport her."

"Yeah, that'll work." Gilfeather turned to the door, brushing past the Chief Constable. "She'll be utterly convinced there's nothing in the story when that happens, eh? Got any other brilliant ideas?"

Sussex held up both hands towards Hastings. "Inspector, I understand the passion for your job, but this is a career-defining moment for you. Success will propel you forward, and one day this will be water under the bridge and we'll share war stories over a drink."

"No, we won't. Now I'm going to…"

Hastings' lips whitened and his eyes bulged in their sockets. He pointed to the Chief Constable. "I want someone who can follow orders."

The Chief Constable turned, then jumped aside as Gilfeather advanced towards Hastings and stopped when his thighs hit the edge of the desk. Hastings took a step back.

"I'll do my job. Whatever opinion you have of it, I couldn't give a fuck. There will be another faceless suit in your position next government but I'll still be on the streets doing my job. You want to get someone else, you go right ahead. And they'll be asking the same questions as me. 'Cos that's what we do. We're coppers. And then there will be two detectives who think this stinks like a pot of burning shite."

"How dare you..."

"I'm a Detective Inspector of Police Scotland, you're a lawyer in a shiny suit. You better talk to me with a civil tongue in your head or you might find yourself face down in jakey's piss in the back of a meatwagon." He cleared his throat. "Now, I'm going to go and see Miss Strathmartin, and using all my policeman skills, persuade her that there is nothing to this story. I've talked to her. You could say we have a basis of trust in each other. And if there is any indication that her father is alive, I'll follow it up. And if I find anything, you'll be the first to know."

Sussex followed him as he headed for the door. "I think, Inspector..."

"Fuck off."

Chapter XXXIII

She kicked the door closed behind her then jumped as the entry buzzer sounded. "Jesus, that's loud."

She grabbed the handset. "Yeah? Oh, Inspector Davey. What a surprise. Of course, are you alone? Okay, come up."

She replaced the handset and looked quickly from side to side, then tore off her jacket and ran to the kitchen and hauled open the pantry door. Opening the bin bag and pizza box, she pulled out the papers then folded them again and stuffed them down the front of her jeans, walked to the hall and fixed her hair in the mirror, then opened the door. "Inspector, nice to see you again. Here for another art tour?"

Gilfeather shrugged. "I was passing, and thought that, er, maybe..."

"Of course you were, come in. Can I offer you some hot brown water?"

"No, coffee is fine, thanks."

He followed her to the kitchen and she nodded to the table, nudging closed the pantry door as she passed to fill the kettle. "So, why are you really here?"

He looked down at his hands, then lifted his head. "I was actually just passing, and thought I'd ring your bell."

"Yeah, progress on the case?"

He shook his head. "No. That's why I'm here. There is no progress. There's no case. That closed when your father…"

"Yeah. Oh, one moment, just got to find my phone. Do the coffee, will ya?"

She marched down the hall and grabbed her phone from the overcoat and then ran back, slowing as she entered the kitchen.

Gilfeather brought two cups of coffee over to the table.

Eilidh sat down and placed the phone between them but Gilfeather didn't react, he just blew on his hot coffee.

"So, what are you saying, Davey?"

"I'm saying there's nothing. The investigation is over. His body may wash up, but it just as likely won't. That's it."

"And we all just move on, yeah?"

He shrugged.

She leaned over the table. "Still stinks, though. He didn't plan to kill himself that night. Not when he left the house, with the heating on and the wine ready."

"Yeah, but he left with a backpack that he fooled me into thinking was an IED. He wasn't popping out for a pint of milk, he was on a mission."

"Yes, he was. And you think that mission included walking off a bloody big bridge?"

He placed the coffee on the table and sat back, folding his arms. "I can't see any other ending."

"And you think he's dead?"

"Yes." He lifted his coffee.

Eilidh stood and looked out the window for a

moment, then turned and stared at him. "Ever get the feeling you're being watched? Snooped on?"

"Eh?"

She cocked her head back at the window. "Curtain twitchers. I can see into other people's flats."

"Most of Edinburgh is like that. Buy some net curtains, maybe?"

She examined him for a moment, then returned to the table. "Look, if there was evidence, you'd know, right?"

"There is evidence. Signed statements from boys. Pictures of him trying to break into the school."

"Have you seen it?"

"The evidence?"

She pushed her coffee aside and rested her arms on the table, leaning towards him. "Yes, have you actually seen the evidence?"

He sipped his coffee.

"I'll take that as a no. Is it under a D-Notice?"

He put the coffee down and looked straight at her. "What do you mean by that?"

"Well, I went to the website of the office where Hector worked and tried all the contact numbers for mobile phones. No answer."

"So they don't want to talk to you."

"Yeah, then they went from no answer to dead line. In minutes. And then it turns out the investigating officer, Inspector Davey Gilfeather, aka Roo-Ree the Red-Haired King, hasn't actually seen the evidence against my dad."

"I talked to him. It's real. He knew it."

"But that's not the same, is it? And then all the people who work with him can't be contacted."

"Coincidence. They might all share the same phone supplier."

She pushed both hands flat on the table, then tapped one finger as she spoke. "You're a cop. I'm a reporter. We both know there is no such thing as coincidence. And then the guy he works for suddenly tops himself. And everybody says, oh, what a shame. And I say, 'how is this connected?' Did he leave a suicide note?"

"Maybe there isn't one."

She shook her head. "Ah, Davey. You didn't say there wasn't one, you said maybe there isn't one. That's a big difference. You met Campbell. And since you were investigating Hector, you'd go around and check Campbell too, to see if it was connected. I know you would. So, is there a suicide note? And before you ask, Campbell's demise is common knowledge on the kind of sites operated by men who wear tin foil hats."

Gilfeather stared into his coffee. "I don't know."

Eilidh stood and picked up her phone. "Excuse me for a moment."

She walked out of the kitchen and into the bathroom. She leaned against the wall, phone in her hand, taking several deep breaths, then placed the phone on top of the cistern and pressed the flush. She looked at the phone, and then turned away, back into the kitchen.

He finished his coffee. "I'd better go."

She stood beside him. "Hector is framed for child abuse and tells you he's innocent. He walks off a bridge and then his boss tops himself. You haven't seen the evidence, you haven't seen the suicide note, the phones are down for anyone who worked with both of them and you wonder about a D-Notice?"

"Ellie..." He looked down at his shoes. "There's

nothing here. Hector killed himself rather than face charges. He threatened me with an IED. As for Campbell, he was an arsehole and I couldn't give a shit if he's dead. But I'm sorry Hector's dead. He should have taken his chances in court."

"So why didn't he?"

"I don't know."

She shook her head. "They're pulling your plonker, Davey. They're hiding the evidence that you need." She moved closer. "Hector might be dead, but this isn't over. This stinks. The note, the evidence and two suicides under a D-Notice? Is your spidey-sense tingling, Davey? 'Cos mine sure as fuck is."

She lifted a hand towards him and pulled back a strand of hair that had fallen over his ear. "If I hear anything," she said, "you'll be the first to know. I promise." He shook his head and she stepped back. "You better go."

He turned towards the door, then stood in the hall. "I'm sorry, Ellie."

She walked past him into the bathroom and picked up her phone. "Yeah, me too." She waggled the phone at him. "Maybe I'm just gonna go back to London and forget all this shit. There's nothing here but heartache." Then she raised an eyebrow.

He looked at the phone and then her, his eyes narrowing, then nodded. He made to say something then stopped.

"What were you about to say?" She smiled. "Next time you're in Edinburgh, look me up?"

He managed a thin smile and looked at the floor. "Yeah, but that would be in bad taste."

"That's why I like you, Roo-Ree." She nodded at the door. "On your way. Be good."

Gilfeather didn't look back. On the monitor, he emerged onto the street and walked to the corner, then turned up the road towards the town. Ellie stood at the window looking down at him, then stuffed her phone in the pocket of the overcoat. She knew she was bugged, at least with the phone, and now he did too. She pulled the folded pages from her jeans and threw them on the table, then she lifted the overcoat and searched another pocket, pulling out a different phone and switched it on.

I peered at the monitor and focused in with the cameras as she punched the buttons to set up the phone. A burner phone, just like those in my rucksack. Use once and discard. But if they were monitoring her signal and location and she switched it on in close proximity to her own phone, they might detect it and bug it too. No, there was no doubt. That is exactly what they would do.

I recognised the website for Google Flights and sat back in my chair and felt my whole body slacken. She was going, I thought. They think she has nothing. And she was going now. To safety.

She thumbed the buttons then pulled a credit card from her back pocket and keyed in the number. My chest shuddered as she waited, then she dropped the phone on the table and ran to the fire and grabbed some kindling and threw it in the fireplace. She looked left and right, then opened the Edinburgh press and found the firelighters and matches.

Tears slipped down my cheeks. All they would see is her booking a flight out of the UK, it didn't matter where. They'd be glad to see the back of her, no doubt, but she would be safe. She knelt beside the fire and lit the firelighters and the kindling caught, burning in a high yellow flame.

She stepped back and watched it for a moment, and then ran from the room. I could barely see through the tears as she pulled t-shirts, knickers and socks from the bedroom and carried them through and stacked them on the table.

The fire was burning and spitting with the dry kindling and she picked up the pages from the table beside the t-shirts. She was going to burn the evidence. It was over. They would find nothing. And when she was safe, I had no doubt that she would…

The breath caught in my throat as she unfolded the papers and spread them over the table. No, please, the cameras…

She lifted the burner phone and took photos of each one in turn, then grabbed the papers and threw them on the fire and watched them burn.

I stood up. They would have seen the papers. I covered my mouth to muffle the sound of my cries.

She phoned a taxi and put on the overcoat, then sat in the armchair, staring into the dying fire.

Chapter XXXIV

"Thank you for coming so quickly, Inspector."

Gilfeather followed Sussex across the stone-vaulted room, past the techs at their desk and through to Hastings' room. He wasn't sure if Sussex was being sarcastic, but decided he didn't give a shit either way.

"Nah, no problem. I got your message as soon as I left the place and stuck on the blues and twos." Hastings' desk was empty. "Where's your Lord and Master?"

Sussex ignored him as he gathered papers on Hastings' desk and shoved them into a file. "May I say, Inspector, that was hardly a taxing interrogation on the whereabouts of Hector Lawless."

"Ah, of course, you were listening. What do you suggest, electric nipple clamps and spikey baseball bats?" For once, Sussex looked annoyed. "Look, you do it the spook way, I do it the copper's way. We rely on more subtle methods. Soft skills. A copper's skills. Empathy, sympathy and listening. Just leave a gap in the conversation and the other person will fill it. They can't help themselves, especially if they have something to hide. Anyway, I am absolutely sure she doesn't know where he is, and she gives no indication that Hector Lawless is alive."

"Really? Well, I beg to differ."

A tech opened the door and stuck his head in. "As you requested, Mr Sussex, her phone pictures are up on the screen." He closed the door behind him.

The wide screen on the wall flashed into life showing three pictures in close up. Sussex scrambled for a remote control on the desk then switched it off. Gilfeather caught the words Hastings, Campbell and a phrase that chilled his skin, 'killed using officers of the state'. He cleared his throat. "Mr Sussex, was that Lord Campbell's suicide note? The one I asked about at the post mortem and was told didn't exist? Because when I got to Campbell's address, your men were cutting him down, not mine."

"Fabricated tittle-tattle, Inspector. Hector Lawless is a very disturbed man."

"I can keep a secret. Bring it up, let's have a look. Professional curiosity. You might even convince me that Hector Lawless doesn't sleep with the fishes after all."

"Well, he has already escaped you once, Inspector, which I thought was rather careless. Are you going to let it happen again? That's not a good look for your career."

"Mr Sussex, if I meet him again and he's as armed and dangerous as I think he is, I'd book him a taxi and give him the fare to bugger off far away from me, so let's not pretend I'm a TV detective willing to lay his life on the line. That's for cheap cop shows. But I have a question for you. After I so carelessly let Hector Lawless escape from the garage so he didn't blow me to burnt mince, I asked a copper to retrieve files from the boot of Campbell's car. Files which Hector Lawless told me in person contained evidence of his innocence. He also called Campbell a liar and a murderer. But Campbell blocked the copper from searching the car, stating that

252

it was, and wait for it, this will really surprise you, an issue of national security that required a search warrant. Then when I go to Campbell's house after he took a long drop on a short rope, I find all his papers are gone, including those in the car. Everything."

"Inspector, I'm sure as a policeman you concentrate on evidence, not weave conspiracy theories that…"

"And then when Hector Lawless jumped off the Forth Bridge and I go around to his flat, I was told that all his papers must be taken away to be examined by MI5. So, where are all the papers?"

Sussex cleared his throat and shuffled a few folders around on the desk. "Relevance is crucial in an investigation, Inspector, and none of Lawless' utility bills and bank statements are…"

"When I first went the flat of Hector Lawless, the fireplace was full of ashes from burned paper. And when I went to Campbell's flat? The same. Grey ashes from burned paper. Lots of paper. What is so important that it must be destroyed by fire?"

Sussex placed the remote control on the folder of papers and tried to make himself comfortable on the edge of the desk. "Did you know, Inspector, that Eilidh Lawless photographed hard copies of this fabricated nonsense on a new burner phone as soon as you had left."

"A burner phone? Did she now?"

"Yes, and I wonder why. And, more importantly, where she obtained these copies?"

"All fair questions. You're listening in on her conversations, did you intercept her mail too?" Sussex shrugged. "I'll take that as a no, Mr Sussex."

"Someone is quite evidently feeding her information."

"I would agree. And very successfully, too. Shame about the mail, or she'd have nothing and you'd have it all. Still, we live and learn. And this burner phone, you got to that too?"

"It's a new and unregistered phone but was switched on right beside her existing number. It accessed the mobile phone towers from exactly the same location. It's rather easily triangulated. Not the first time we've seen this, our systems are very adept at tracking such behaviour."

"I'm impressed. Just as well I gave you her number. So, if it's on her burner phone, is she going to send it to someone? She knows about the D-Notice."

Sussex gave him a thin smile. "Signal strength is reduced in that area, as of a few minutes ago. She won't be sending it to anyone. And if she tries, we'll know."

"Wifi?"

"I wouldn't be too concerned, we do have our own methods of…"

The door burst open and Hastings marched in. "Arrest her!"

Gilfeather puffed out his cheeks and shrugged. "On what charge?"

The purple veins pulsed on Hastings' nose. "She has possession of… State secrets."

"Secrets? Mr Sussex told me it was just fabricated tittle-tattle. You lads have got to get your story straight. You wouldn't last ten minutes in a cop shop interrogation room."

Hastings seemed to choke on his words, and he strode off to stand behind his desk. "It is slanderous fake news, but must remain a secret."

Gilfeather nodded his head, looked at Sussex then

back to Hastings. "I retract my previous statement. You wouldn't last five minutes." Hastings began to splutter, and Gilfeather crossed his hands behind his back and looked up to the vault of stones above him as he walked slowly around the room. "I'm a wee bit annoyed that she gets to see this evidence, no, sorry, title tattle, and I don't. I'm not feeling part of the team, eh? Anyway, let's assume this was sent by actor or actors unknown. And you think the most likely is Hector Lawless."

"Of course it was him," said Hastings. "Who else could do this?"

"Well, someone who has access to the evidence, and let's call it that, whatever it is, plus access to a printer and the Royal Mail. Not too tricky, especially when no-one is checking her mail. You might be wanting to look closer to home. Any enemies, Mr Hastings, who would benefit from your downfall? No, don't answer that, we'll be here all day. And you're sure this is Hector Lawless, rather than someone from Campbell's office, which you shut down with the D-Notice and perhaps an injunction? A photo of a phone screen, I assume, looking at the printout that flashed up on the screen before Mr Sussex found the remote control to stop my fun."

Hastings glared at Sussex. "Look, Gilfeather, she has to be stopped. If this... these lies get out we'll never be able to contain it. It will have dreadful consequences."

Gilfeather nodded slowly, but said nothing until Hastings took a deep breath and was about to speak, then interrupted him. "Consequences, Mr Hastings. They can be inconvenient. Okay. I'll arrest her on instruction from MI5 on suspicion of handling state secrets. I assume you'll supress the evidence, so what will be left is conjecture. Given the D-Notice and injunction, the press won't touch it. And if she wants to talk about it, she'll be portrayed as disturbed, like her father."

Sussex stared at him for a moment, then nodded, his chin bouncing up and down. "Oh, absolutely."

"Then you're still in the shit. Because if Hector Lawless is out there, he'll just release it to the public. Social media. It'll spread like wildfire."

The room was silent, save for the tapping of keyboards behind the door.

"So," said Sussex, "we find him."

Gilfeather smiled. "So, we set a trap."

Hastings threw his arms in the air. "No, Sussex, just close her down and you, Gilfeather, find that bastard Lawless."

"What do you mean close her down? Arrest her under terrorism laws? It'll buy you some time, but Hector will still be out there. You better be good pals with the judge that keeps her in without charge. Well, you probably went to school with them, but at some point you'll have to let her go. You can't present this evidence in court against her, I assume?"

The room was silent once more.

"I said you'll have to let her…"

"Not something to be concerned about, Inspector," said Sussex, "leave these tricky legal issues to me."

Hastings leaned on the table. "Gilfeather, you must understand, this is not the first time we have had this dreadful problem. You remember the press hounding the former Head of the Army over completely false allegations of abuse by a psychologically deranged man. It took three years to clear him. We can never let that happen again."

"Agreed, but you used a gagging order or D-Notice

for this one. You shut down the press for some bloody gossip?"

Hastings shuddered as if he had been electrocuted and Sussex stepped between them. "Inspector, this evidence has very serious implications. We cannot…"

The table legs squeaked as Hastings came out from behind his desk and shoved Sussex to the side. He stood in front of Gilfeather who didn't move. "We cannot take the risk. Bring her in. Then we'll…"

Gilfeather edged forward. "But she hasn't sent the evidence anywhere, and she can't, so Mr Sussex tells me. And you'll leave Hector Lawless like a loose cannon."

The room was silent for a moment. Then Hastings swallowed hard. "Sussex, shut everything down. Internet, phones, wifi."

"Sir, we can control data on the wifi, although we may lose the cameras if we shut down…"

"Cameras?" said Gilfeather. "Were you watching me in there? Guys, you got to learn to share if we're going to make this relationship work." He looked up at the stones. "Listen, if Hector is alive and out there, and she disappears, he'll send the evidence to the world. He won't give a shit about a D-Notice. I'll bet the Irish Times will give it a whole-colour supplement. Followed by a pop-up version for the Christmas market."

Hastings shook his head. "She is too much of a …"

"You know why?" Gilfeather looked first at Hastings and then to Sussex. "If this is Hector Lawless, you know why he gave it to her? Because she's a reporter. He was going to do this himself, using Campbell's pals at the office, but you got to Campbell before me, so you shut it all down. Then little Miss Ellie rocks up out of the blue.

I'll bet she was a big surprise for old Hector. She wasn't supposed to turn up for months."

Hastings and Sussex glanced at one another.

"I can tell this is news to you. You see, he thinks he's doing her a favour. Giving his kid the big break. Seems he was wrong. He still thinks she's going to release the evidence and win Journalist of the Year. And he can't, because he's dead, right? And it looks like he doesn't know about the D-Notice or he'd just pump that shit right into the veins of all the social media nutjobs on Twitter, slavering at the thought of kicking the establishment right in the plums."

Sussex looked down at the floor.

Gilfeather scratched his nose and stepped back. "So, you're safe, for now. But if you bring her in and he finds out, Hector's going to go fucking tonto. And if you want to really supress the evidence, you'll need them both. And it's your last chance, because if she was going to send this to the press, she would have done so already. And if you spook her, she might just do it anyway. She'll find a way. So, don't have any of your goons kicking down doors and throwing her in a Dartmoor Gitmo. She might just nip out right now with her phone and send it from a pub wifi. I'm sure she has no idea where the evidence came from, and she could send it to the world anytime, but she's hasn't. And she won't until she's safely out of the country. I'll bet she knows fine what happens when you cross a D-Notice. So she might not be nipping down the pub for a pie, a pint and a chaser of treason. She'll be thrown in jail, and no one wants that. Right, Mr Hastings?"

"Inspector," said Sussex, "we understand, but she's booked a flight."

"Then cancel it."

"But then..."

"But then she'll know we're on to her. And with the slim possibility that she knows Hector is alive and where he is, she'll try to contact him. And if she doesn't, he'll contact her and she'll find out the net is closing. Then you can throw a weasel up his kilt."

Hastings stood blinking, trying to take it all in.

"So," said Sussex, "she'll know she's being trapped."

"Exactly. Then wipe her burner phone with the photos and evidence."

"What?"

"You've hacked it, so wipe it. That'll stop her sending anything. Then you've baited the trap. And it might wind up Hector Lawless so much he might come riding to the rescue to save his daughter with his copy of the evidence."

"What if she had transferred it to…"

"You've got cameras, why don't you look? Hack her laptop. Hack everything."

Sussex strode towards the door.

Gilfeather faced Hastings. "And when all the evidence is gone, you can let her go."

Hastings' eyes flitted from one side to the other.

"I said you can let her go. Set her running. She's harmless without evidence, so follow her wherever she goes, you know, like maybe straight to Hector?"

Sussex came back into the room. "The procedures are in progress. We can close her wifi down but still retain video feed. It'll take a few minutes."

"I was just saying to Mr Hastings," said Gilfeather, "once she has no evidence, you can let her go. See where she goes. I'll send policemen, we can follow and arrest them both. Possession of state secrets, wasn't it?"

Sussex waved a hand. "No need, Inspector, we'll take care of that."

"But you'll have to arrest them. You'll need a cop."

"Perhaps."

The door opened and a tech stuck his head through. "Ticket cancelled."

Gilfeather stared at Sussex. "You can't make her disappear like the evidence."

"Thank you, Inspector, this is a security matter, we'll deal with her."

"Yeah. I'll bet you will. You know, I'd love to see that suicide note, and see what makes you two react in this way. Never mind Hector, you both look like you've got a weasel up your kilt on MDMA doing the Dashing White Sergeant."

"It's merely the most base form of allegations that..."

"I mean considering you may be committing a crime to supress it."

"Inspector, the law allows us much more leeway than you think."

"Yeah." Gilfeather stood directly in front of Hastings. "Still like to see that suicide note, though. I'll bet it's fucking dynamite."

Hastings tried to speak but only a guttural sound emerged as saliva sprayed from his lips.

Chapter XXXV

My eyes strained to focus and I pulled my face back from the monitor and dropped to the chair. Her voice pierced through my earphones.

"How can they cancel my ticket? What the hell?" She punched the buttons on her phone. *"Work, you bastard! Jesus, only 3G?"* She flicked off the phone signal and ran out the room to the wifi router in the hall. *"C'mon, I've got five bars. What the hell is wrong with this site?"*

She ran back and sat before her laptop. In a moment, the sleepy face of her boss appeared on the screen.

"Hey, Ellie, what..."

She leaned into the screen. *"There's more weird shit going. My ticket to fly out was cancelled. And not by me. The flight is still there but I can't book anything. I tried another and my credit card is..."*

The laptop screen flashed, then dropped and began scrolling digital text.

"No!" She hammered the keyboard with her fist.

I jumped up. On the camera outside, two black cabs passed the alleyway to the garage then stopped. One driver got out and the side of his waterproof jacket hung down with the pocket pointing to the ground. A gun.

He got into the other cab and settled back in the seat.

This is not an arrest, I thought. This is an assassination.

They can't... The backpack bomb in the garage. Gilfeather had grounds for treating this as domestic terrorism. No, not Gilfeather, he knew it was a bluff. But Hastings would seize upon it to kill anything that threatened him. Like the boys. One more death would mean nothing to him. No, it would. It would bring him satisfaction and joy.

On the monitor, Ellie paced the room, then threw the burner phone to the ground and grabbed her other phone.

This was my fault. On the monitor, the taxi's lights shone down the street and then went out, leaving the interior in darkness. How long would they wait? There was no time.

I stuffed the burner phone into my pocket and turned and grabbed the rungs of the ladder and hauled myself up, throwing the planks aside and scrambling into the attic.

This was the price for Campbell's murder. Her death. My penitence.

The cold wind froze my eyes as I tumbled out of the skylight into the dark, then turned on the burner phone in my pocket and ran between the roofs, around the skylights and cupolas, slipping on the wet lead and tiles. One boot shot out from under me and I slammed into the chimney stack, my head bouncing off the sooty stone.

My vision swam, but I had to move. Nothing else mattered at this moment, speed was everything.

I heard cries with each of my breaths exploding out my lungs. At the corner I slid to another high chimney stack and pushed myself sideways, sprinting to the next block, weaving past the scaffolding that led over the edge and to the next corner, then crouched between two peaks of tiles in the leaf-choked gutter. I pulled the phone from my pocket, my fingers so cold they did not register on the screen as I typed.

Hastings' eyes were fixed on the open door to the tech room, where Sussex stood in the doorway. Gilfeather leaned against the wall, his eyes drifting towards the screen where he had seen a glimpse of the suicide note.

Sussex turned to them. "Her flight ticket is cancelled, and her laptop wiped. She was trying to talk to her editor in Australia."

Hastings stood up. "Is the wifi…?"

Sussex nodded. "It's down and her burner phone is wiped. She cannot send text messages from any phone or connect to the internet to transmit data, and all the phone signals in that area are too weak to make a call, transmit data, send a text or load a website."

"Okay," said Gilfeather, pushing himself up from the wall. "So, she has nothing. She is no longer a threat. Remember that."

"What now?" said Hastings.

"Now, we wait." Gilfeather nodded to the open door where Sussex stood. "Are you tracking her original phone?"

"Yes. That phone is clean, we've accessed the photos." Sussex twisted his head to hear the voice of one of the techs then turned back to Gilfeather. "The wifi is split so only we can use it for the camera feed. It'll look like it's working, but she won't be able to connect, and we can monitor what she does on her phone."

"Then bring up the cameras," said Gilfeather, and nodded to the wide screen.

"Inspector, that's strictly…"

"You've wiped your evidence, just bring them up. I need to see what happens next. Does she run? What is she going to do? I need to know."

Sussex looked at the ground for a moment, then gave the command. The picture on the screen opened to a grey light, then focused to a sharp image of Eilidh in the flat, holding her phone. "She's trying to book a ticket on a different site on her personal phone. We can wipe that at any moment."

Gilfeather held up a hand. "No, don't do that. Timing is everything. It's clean, right? And she can't call anyone?"

"Yes. If she runs, our men are in position."

On the monitor, Eilidh ran to the window and looked down to the street.

Gilfeather jumped as the phone in his pocket let out a loud ping. He pulled it out and read the message, staring at the screen, his mouth open.

Sussex walked towards him. "What does it say, Inspector?"

Gilfeather held it in his palm for a moment, then lifted it up to show Sussex.

Let her go. I'll give you what you want.

Gilfeather held the phone tight in his fist. "Hector Lawless. Hook, line and bloody sinker. I'll show this to the boys next door and get them to track the number."

Hastings dropped onto his chair, his mouth open.

Sussex followed Gilfeather through to the tech room. "Do we respond?"

"No. We wait."

"Inspector, remember Hector Lawless threatened you with an IED in the garage of the High Court. We

264

are treating this as a domestic terrorism incident. This is no time for games."

"Terrorism?" He swallowed, his throat dry. "Are you even going to attempt an arrest?"

"Bring him in now, Inspector. Reply to Hector Lawless. Send him to her. We will deal with this."

"No." Gilfeather held out the phone to the techs to copy the number. "To quote Napoleon Bonaparte, *'Never interrupt your enemy when he is making a mistake.'*" He returned the phone to his pocket. His thumb found the 'silent' switch and he pressed it.

Chapter XXXVI

I had to turn my face away from the cold as I crouched over the gutter of rotting leaves, staring at the phone. Gilfeather would be waiting for her to move. The wind changed direction, freezing the tears in my eyes and I had to turn away once more. He would be tracking the phone before he replied. He'd know the phone was nearby. The scaffolding to the ground at the rear of the adjacent block was not far. I could be down on the street, but he would know. And they would be waiting.

The wind changed again and brought the sound of diesel engines from below. They were looking for me. They might work it out after a while. Or send a helicopter. I had to trust him.

The reek of the decaying leaves and drainpipes drifted up at me. I am no better than the rest, I thought. The stench of rotting Edinburgh was part of me too. I have been dragged down to the filth and blood that seeps into every stone.

The scream came from my gut. "Answer me!"

She was alone. I pulled out the phone and typed.

She has no evidence, only hearsay. Once she is out of the country, I will deliver the evidence to you. I have a copy of the suicide note by Campbell, the confession to his crimes that was sent to his office, WhatsApp and the video of James Torridon stating that Hastings and Campbell are abusers who have murdered boys, before Hastings and MI5 had him murdered. They are going to kill her if you do not let her go. Are you a murderer, Inspector?

I stared at the screen, then stood up, the wind filling my mouth. Over the roofs lay my skylight, where below she was trapped. They might take her anytime. Perhaps he would do that before he answered. Then it hit home.

They weren't waiting for her. They were waiting for me. He didn't have to respond. They had set her up as bait in the trap. And I had walked straight into it.

I stared at the phone in my hand. There would be no answer. I set the phone to airplane mode and my boots slipped on the rotting leaves as I scrambled for the corner chimney stack.

The phone vibrated in Gilfeather's pocket, but Sussex didn't look his way. Gilfeather walked over to Hastings desk. "You need coppers. You can't perform a summary execution."

Sussex waved a hand in the air. "There's no need to be so dramatic, Inspector. If it's possible to take them in for questioning, that's exactly what we'll do. After all, there is the murder of Lord Campbell to investigate. We want to get to the bottom of this. There's no need for unnecessary bloodshed."

"Can you guarantee it?" The phone vibrated in his pocket again. He didn't move.

"Since Hector Lawless threatened you with a terrorist weapon, an IED, Inspector, we can't guarantee anything. Lawless is a very disturbed man. Who knows what he has prepared for us? I'm not prepared to put the

lives of my men at risk, but we will do our very best."
Sussex moved closer. "Any more messages, Inspector?"

Gilfeather shrugged, then took out the phone and glanced at the screen. "No."

The door opened and a tech stuck his head in. "The phone that texted the Inspector is about two hundred yards from her."

The room was silent for a moment then Hastings spluttered while trying to form a word.

"Can you hack it?" asked Sussex.

"It's gone. He may have turned it off. We'll keep looking. Next time it's online we'll hack it."

Gilfeather turned away from them and glanced at his phone, keeping it turned away from the room. "Okay." He spun around. "Time to end this fucking charade. Keep your men ready for him to arrive. He could be sat in a car on the street or in a garden. I can order the police helicopter to…"

"No," said Sussex. "We'll find him." He lifted a phone to his ear and walked across the room, whispering commands.

"How did he do it?" said Hastings.

Gilfeather stared up at the stones. "He was heading for the Kingdom of Fife in his car and then the roads north to God knows where. The Highlands, probably. And when that route was blocked, he had a backup plan. He walked over the bridge and didn't come back. Cameras show he didn't make it to the other side. That means he must have gone in the water."

"That's impossible. How could he plan such a thing in so short…?"

"I've been in his flat. Above the fireplace is a painting showing the school that he attended and the Forth

268

Bridge in the background. King George's, the school that Campbell also attended after he was expelled from Heriot's. Hector Lawless would be very familiar with that bridge and the countryside around it. And the tides and currents, the deep channels and shallows.

"I don't think he jumped, it's too risky. It could be done, but... he found another way down to the water. Maybe climbed down the steel web of the bridge. And he was prepared. Without a wet suit or some other method he wouldn't last long enough to reach the shore, it's too cold. But he did. Then he disappeared."

He turned to face Hastings. "He spent six years at that school. It's surrounded by acres of thick woods. He'll know that place like the back of his hand. I think that's where he went."

Sussex turned back towards them and cut the call. "Everyone is in place. We're ready."

Chapter XXXVII

Islid down the ladder into my cell. On the monitor she was standing before the wifi router in the hall. She threw a phone to the floor. Her burner phone. She grabbed another from the table and thumbed the screen, glancing at the router. The activity light was dead. They had cut the internet connection and the wifi.

Their plan was perfect. Gilfeather would assume the evidence had come from me. And then they'd begin to close every door to draw me in. As soon as I arrived or was close enough, they would kill us both. And she was trapped. They could take her any time. In the cameras, the two taxis stood outside the door, but the men inside didn't move. Others might be checking the streets. I looked down at my phone, on airplane mode. They were waiting for me. And it was only a matter of time before they worked it out.

On the monitor she lifted her phone to hurl it across the room then stopped and turned into the sitting room. She pulled on my old overcoat, then stuffed the knickers and socks from the table into the pockets. She looked at the phone once more, then outside the window, to where the two black cabs were waiting.

No, please, don't go, they'll... I lifted the phone in

my hand and switched on the Bluetooth and typed the number, then texted STOP.

I heard the ping through the wall. She was about to open the front door but twisted her head to the sound from the sitting room. She looked down at her phone, then picked up the burner phone from the floor. It was dead. She walked back into the sitting room. I sent another message, and she looked towards the escritoire, then pulled down the lid. I typed once more. She pulled open the drawer and took out my burner phone.

Hastings stood close to the screen. "What is she doing?"

Gilfeather ignored him. "If it's any help, there's a helicopter in the air, returning from a different job."

"Send it away!" Sussex hurried in from the tech room. "Now."

"I don't get it," said Gilfeather, "why wouldn't you want a chopper? If he's close we can see him from miles away. Is this an execution?"

"For the last time, Inspector, a helicopter will scare him away. We cannot risk that. Get rid of it."

"Or they'll record what happens?"

Sussex threw his hands in the air. "Inspector, please, just…"

"Okay, will do." Gilfeather checked his phone. "No messages, he's gone quiet. He might be moving in."

"All exits are being monitored. The streets are being checked. And there is a back exit to the mews courtyard at the rear."

"Have you checked his garage? It's in the courtyard."

Sussex stared at him for a few moments then whispered into his phone. "Already on it, Inspector."

"Of course you were. Where's Hector's phone?"

"Still no signal."

Hastings spun around from the TV screen, his voice near a screech. "I said, what the hell is she doing? Which phone is that?" On the screen, Ellie held a phone in her hand.

"She took it from that drawer," said Hastings.

"In the escritoire?" said Gilfeather, peering at the screen.

"It seems so." Sussex ran out the room, returning a moment later. "There's no other phone in that vicinity."

"Well, there is," said Gilfeather, "she's holding it. But there's no signal from it."

Hastings jabbed a finger at the screen. "It has to be him. It's Hector Lawless."

"If there's no signal," said Sussex, "how is he going to communicate?"

"Where is he?" screamed Hastings. "Check all the cameras!"

Sussex edged towards the screen and lifted his phone. "All sections. Get ready to move on my command. Front and rear entrances. Use any force necessary."

Chapter XXXVIII

For a moment I froze, my chest shuddering. Then I choked on my dry throat and dragged in a breath. My fingers hovered over the phone, then jabbed the screen.

There are cameras everywhere. Go to the pantry. Put the kettle on so they think you are staying.

She bent over, staring at the phone.

I typed again.

Please, no time. Go to the pantry. They can't see you there.

Her eyes flicked left and right, then she stuffed the phone in her pocket and turned out into the hall then into the kitchen. She stopped, pulled off her coat and filled the kettle, then opened the pantry.

I typed again.

Be ready to move quickly. I will guide you.

She looked around the pantry. She opened her mouth to speak, then typed on the screen. *Can you see me?*

Yes.

Can you hear me?

No. But they can.

Her hands were shaking.

Where are you?

Eilidh, they know you've seen the evidence. If you leave they'll take you.

My taxi is outside.

They're in the taxi.

She threw her head back. *This isn't real. I have no evidence, it's all gone.*

You read the evidence. They saw you take photo of it on camera in room. They have killed to stop the story, they will kill again.

Why? Why me?

If Hastings falls, then so does the Government in Westminster.

She stamped her feet and bared her teeth. *WTF?*

15 yr ago, man accused of sex assault on boy. Hastings gave false alibi. Abused boy killed himself. Man is now PM.

She jabbed the screen. *Fuck them. A D-Notice doesn't work in Oz. They can't shut me up.*

Correct. So they kill you. Your death means nothing. Mine too.

She leaned against a shelf for support, then dropped to her knees, the tears shining on her face. *Are you my father?*

Yes.

I can't leave here.

You can. I show you. I know Edin.

How the hell - this is Bluetooth?

Yes or they see this msg. They hack this soon. Must move fast.

Where are you?

Go into hall and pull out ALL cables on router. Then they r blind.

How do we get out the door?

We don't. Listen. Rip out ALL cables then open front door. Beside main staircase is another door. Open it come back coat on. DO NOT stand in the hall. Do it now. Go.

She ran out to the kitchen and threw herself at the router, tearing out all the cables and launching the router down the hall. She tore open the front door.

I grabbed my rucksack and scrambled up the ladder.

Hastings stood so close to the screen he blocked Gilfeather's view. "What is she doing now? I can't see her. Where is she?"

"I've no idea, you're in the way." Hastings stepped to the side, and on the screen the kitchen was empty. "She's in the pantry. You don't have a camera in there." He turned to Sussex and raised an eyebrow. "Old Edinburgh flats, they have a pantry big enough for a spare room. Too posh to keep the coal in the bath." He turned back to the screen. "She's taken her coat off and put the kettle on, so I assume she's looking for some coffee. Last time I was there, she couldn't..."

"The phone," said Hastings. "In the sitting room. Who was she texting? It must be Lawless. Where is he? Is she waiting for him?"

"All exits and entrances to the building are monitored," said Sussex, "If he..." He ran over and opened the door to the tech room.

Hastings face went from pink to red to purple in a few moments. "If the wifi and signals are down, how is she communicating? What the fuck is going on?"

Sussex stood in the doorway, facing the techs so they could hear him. "Does she have a signal? Well, how can she communicate? Bring down the phone towers, I'll get BT to…" He stopped as they heard the reply from the tech behind the door.

"Must be Bluetooth. He's right there. He's right there with her."

Hastings strode over and pulled open the door and it rattled on the hinges. "What do you mean he's right there? We have the cameras, he's not bloody there!"

Gilfeather joined him in the doorway and saw the tech turn in his chair. "I mean, he doesn't have to be standing right beside her, just under thirty feet away. As long as there's not a lot of stone or metal in the way, then…"

Hastings jabbed a finger in Sussex's face. "Find him!"

Sussex ignored him and ran back into the room. "I'll check the cameras, he could be…" He stood facing the screen.

Gilfeather hurried over. The screen was blank.

Chapter XXXIX

The light burst into the attic as the folding ladder slid down, metal screeching, and slammed into the hall floor below. I stuck my head through. Eilidh looked up from the bottom of the steps, her eyes wide. "Hurry," I said, "we have very little time."

She scrambled up the ladder and into the attic, and I hauled the ladder up behind her and shut the hatch.

"Hector?"

"I'll explain later. Follow me." I opened the skylight and pushed my rucksack out then pulled myself through. I turned to help her, but she was already halfway through the skylight. She fell forward and slid down the tiles. She had a tattoo of a compass on the back of her hand. I closed the skylight and pointed west. "We have to move."

She wiped her hands on her coat. "Let's go, Dad. Show me the way."

Tears blurred my vision as we hurried forward. "Keep low." My voice shook. "Avoid the cupolas." I glanced around as we passed the first, keeping away from the glass in case we were spotted from inside the neighbouring flats.

"I'm still here," she said.

I gritted my teeth and scurried over the roof, dragging

the rucksack behind me, and ignoring the impulse to look out from the chimney stack as we rounded the corner. "Over there," I said. "The scaffolding. We're going down."

It seemed to take forever to reach it, passing tiled peaks and cupolas, but we got to the edge where the wooden planks led down a short ladder to the windows below. "We're going to make some noise, just keep going. They'll work it out long before the residents call the police." I grabbed the freezing scaffolding, then stopped. "I have to know where they are." Scrambling back, I ran over to the far edge and looked down and could hear her right behind me. The black cabs at the garden had gone. There were no police cars. This wasn't an arrest. The streetlights shone dimly on a man walking his dog. "That private garden." I pointed across the road.

"I see it."

"There are cars behind the garden we can use. Let's go." I turned back and grabbed the scaffolding pole, then dropped down the ladder to the next level, kicking the rucksack before me, my boots thumping the wood crusted with powdered stone. I didn't have to look back, her boots thundered in my ear.

Down and down we went, the scaffolding rattling and the wood echoing until the last level, twelve feet above the garden. Voices came from above.

"We jump?" she said.

"Too high. Follow me." I threw the rucksack into the garden and sat on the edge of the wood, then turned, holding on to the edge and pushed away, my fingers barely holding me, then let go and dropped onto the grass and rolled forward. I scrambled to my feet as she rolled over the edge, her hands slipping and she dropped. I caught her and fell back, her weight blowing the air out my lungs.

"Sorry." She rolled off and pulled me to my feet.

"Over that wall," I said and began to run. "I'll show you the handholds."

"You've done this before."

"This was my childhood. Over the wall is a dark lane. If the road is clear, we run for the rear of that private garden. Look for two small white cars parked together." We reached the wall. "Check where I put my hands and feet." I grabbed the stone and jabbed my boots onto the edges of protruding rocks, then pulled myself up and turned to hang over the edge, but she had already reached the top and our faces touched.

"Just go," she said.

I dropped and hit the cobblestones, then looked up as she landed right beside me. In my hand I switched on a new phone.

"A burner?" she said.

"Yes." I edged to the corner and looked out into the darkness. "They must all be in the flat. Ready?"

"Go."

My old coat flapped as she ran beside me, across the wet road and over to the corner of the garden, then along the path to the rear and around to the dark street at the back of the garden, where a line of cars were parked. I stopped beside a small white car and brought up the Community Car app on the phone.

"Your car?"

"No, the council owns them. You can hire it by the hour." I thumbed the car licence number and waited while a sand timer spun on the screen.

"You were ready for this."

"I had made plans, Ellie."

She smiled.

I stared at the screen.

"What about the police?"

"No, they would be an inconvenient witness."

The smile vanished, just as the locks popped up.

"Hector, where are we going?"

I pulled the door open. "To the sea."

"Power is down on the cameras," shouted a tech. "Battery backup will be up in a minute. We have radio connection if the internet is down."

Sussex and Hastings were two feet from the wide screen. Gilfeather flicked his eyes from one to the other. The pictured remained black. Sussex was breathing steadily, but his lips were curled into a snarl. Hastings' face twitched, his jaw tight.

The screen flickered, then the bedroom camera came online. The bedroom was empty.

"Not that one!" screamed Hastings.

"They come up in sequence as they connect," said Sussex.

The sitting room camera came on next. She was not there.

Sussex spoke into his phone then looked up. "The teams are covering the exits. The targets have not left the building."

The kitchen camera came up, and steam rose in wisps from the kettle.

Gilfeather stepped back, and glanced at the message on his screen.

The hall camera flickered into life. The cables and wifi router were strewn across the hall. The front door was open, and beyond it, another door lay open on the wall by the staircase.

Hastings' spittle sprayed the screen. "Where is she!"

"That's an old servant's staircase," murmured Gilfeather.

Sussex looked around at him. "What?"

"Leads down to every level. Then to kitchens or storerooms in the basement. You've got the, er, tradesman's entrance covered?"

"Every entrance is covered," whispered Sussex.

Hastings' voice was tight through his clenched teeth. "Then where the fuck are they? Under the carpet?"

Sussex jammed his phone his face. "Targets missing. Go, go, go. Search every flat. Check the courtyard. Kick the doors in and use all the men."

"This is impossible!" Hastings screeched, turning as if to grab Sussex by the neck.

The sound of boots on the stairs came over the speakers and two men in balaclavas reached the top of the stair, pistols in hand. One pointed to the flat and the other man threw in a small cannister that bounced on the carpet. The detonation made everyone jump and one man rushed into the hall. The other disappeared into the servant's staircase.

Shouts came from the staircase and the wail of an outraged old woman.

Gilfeather leaned forward to Hastings. "Don't suppose you got a search warrant to cover all that?"

Hastings' reply choked in his throat.

Chapter XXXX

The streetlights were brighter as we turned onto the main road leading west out of Edinburgh. The breath shuddered in my throat when I spoke. "I'm sorry. I'm so sorry. You look so like your mother."

Ellie held her hands tight together. "If this all ends in shit, Hector, I want you to know. I asked her about you. She said you were the kindest man she had ever met. She never wanted to leave you that day."

Slowing for a red light, I held on to the steering wheel, my chest locked and almost unable to breathe, rocking back and forth as we stopped.

She leaned over and placed her hand on mine. "Hold it together, Dad. We'll get there."

I cleared my throat and the lights changed, and I pulled myself up in the seat. "Yes. This is not the time." My heart hammered against my ribs and I blinked away the tears. "First, we head west."

Ellie took a deep breath. "Sounds like you have a plan."

"Yes, yes, I do."

"But how did you know?"

I handed her the phone in my lap. "Please, turn this off, and any phone you have too."

She thumbed the power button. "Don't have a phone. Not anymore."

"That's for the best. We can assume they have every technical resource of GCHQ at their disposal." I wound down the window and could hear the first of the sirens.

"Yeah. But how did you know?"

At the end of the road the lights were green; they led to the arterial road leading out of Edinburgh to the bridges. A turnoff, a few miles in front, headed away from the bridges, towards the road west to Glasgow. "I had to adapt."

"Well, I've got to say it worked." She looked around her at the darkened suburban homes. "Are we heading for the bridge?"

"Not tonight." Above the traffic lights sat CCTV cameras as we passed. "Pull the sun visors down. Please."

She didn't hesitate. "Cameras?"

"Yes, but I know where every traffic camera in Edinburgh is situated. Plus all the CCTV."

She turned in her seat. "How the hell do you know that?"

"Planning. Details. It's what I do." I tried to relax my hands on the wheel, although I had to peel them off where the skin had stuck to the leather. I cleared my throat. "May I... May I call you Ellie?" In the corner of my eye, I watched her smile.

"Of course. You were listening! That's some sneaky shit. Sorry. Er, I've been calling you Dad. That might be a bit presumptuous."

For a moment I couldn't reply. I had been over this so many times in my life. One day, meeting them both. When they had come back, together, to see me. But they had been dreams I had always tried to supress. "I'd prefer Hector, please. This is very emotional. The other is… difficult. I am …" My voice cracked. "Very proud. I am very proud of you. Ellie."

She leaned back in her seat. "After what I've just seen and done, I'm very proud of you, Hector. How did you know? And where the bloody hell were you?"

For all the tears and hellishness, I began to laugh, in short bursts at first and then a long deep bellow that shocked me into silence for a moment. "I was close."

"Well, yeah, for Bluetooth, sure, but in the attic? All that time they were looking for you? Because Davey Gilfeather went up there and it was empty."

"The cupboard in the hall. Behind the shelves. It was a box room. I added shelves to make it appear it was just an Edinburgh press. A cupboard."

"Jeez. And you got in and out through the attic and the roof?"

"Yes. When I undertook investigations of child abuse for Lord Campbell…"

"Wait, you investigated for him?"

I nodded slowly. "It was a setup. Once I had gathered evidence implicating, er…"

"Mungo Hastings. You had the evidence. Secretary of State, member of the cabinet. I get it. But you were ready for them."

"Perhaps. But I wasn't ready for you."

She said nothing and stared straight ahead.

A black cab passed. The driver didn't look my way. "I thought you were in Australia. By the time Mr Shiresman had contacted you and taken care of the inheritance, I would have been far away, far across the sea, and it would all have been forgotten. Except by me."

"Yeah. And then I walked in the door. Literally."

I began to laugh again, the pitch high and strained, but she joined in. The signs for the bridges to the north appeared, directing cars into the correct lanes.

"Were they going to kill us? Hector?"

My breathing quickened. She was no fool. "Yes. And if they find us, that may still happen."

"Hector, you had no idea I was going to turn up and blow your plans out the water. If I'd missed my train from London, you'd be gone, right?"

"Yes, and you'd be safe. I'm so…"

"No. Don't apologise for something you didn't do. If I'd been a day late and you were gone, I'd still have done the same. And you wouldn't be here to protect me. I'd have got in the cab outside my front door and I'd be dead, right?"

"Possibly."

"They used me as bait to lure you in. But if you didn't appear, then you were dead. And a reporter with that kind of scoop wasn't going to get off this island alive, were they?"

The road became wider as it headed out of town, and the speed of the traffic increased. "No." A police car flashed past in the opposite direction. "How did you get copies of the evidence?"

Eilidh pulled her coat closer and turned up the heating. "Your mate, AJ, is my best guess. I think someone gave him the nod."

"Shiresman? Yes, he has many confidantes. Someday I hope to see him again. He is a great man."

"Maybe, but I'd be deep in the shit if you weren't

here, Hector. Thanks." She peered under the sun visor. "Are we going to the bridges?"

"No, too much of a risk. Once on or near the bridge, you're too easily trapped."

"There's a camera," she said, as we passed a traffic light. "Will they track this car?"

"No, it's a community car, quite anonymous. They'll find out, but too late."

"Where are we going?"

"Grangemouth. And a ship out of here."

"A ship? You said the sea, we're going to a port?"

A helicopter appeared in the sky, heading towards the centre of Edinburgh. "Yes. This was my original plan to leave Scotland, once they were convinced of my death."

"The ferry, where does it go?"

"There's no ferry, It's a container ship port."

"Really? How do we…?"

"We buy a ticket for passage. There are more burner phones in my rucksack. Use the red one. Right hand side pocket. We need to make a booking."

She pulled out several phones, then chose one and switched it on. "A cargo ship? I didn't know you could do that. Just like a passenger?"

"Yes. On the red phone there is one website bookmarked. Book a ticket on the next ship to Rotterdam. Don't use the card you used in the flat for the flights. If you can, use an Australian card. You'll need your passport number."

She began to enter the details.

"On the back of the phones is taped a new gmail address and password. Use it to register for the ticket."

She looked up as she typed. "Is it far? What if they blocked the roads?"

I took the exit for Glasgow, then turned off onto a narrow road between houses. "We'll skip the main junctions, there are always side roads that bypass them."

"Yeah, you've been here before."

"It's just planning."

She let the phone rest on her lap as it processed the ticket request. "Hector? The bridge. How did you do it?'

The road wound through the streetlights and suburban houses, then became narrower, leaving the streetlights behind. In front was the dark, rolling countryside that led down to the forest on the shore.

"I was prepared in case of eventualities. If the road bridge was blocked then I'd be trapped. But I was ready. I walked out on the bridge."

"You jumped?"

"No, that was the original plan. I had a method of slowing my fall, but in the thick haar, the sea mist, I realised no one would see me fall. The cameras were blocked. Then I saw maintenance ladders that led down to the sea. A detail I had not foreseen. I climbed down and swam ashore, where I had made preparations."

She nodded slowly. "Helluva plan. You know, Inspector Davey Gilfeather thinks you're dead."

"I know. But I was prepared for the eventuality of being trapped by the Security Services who might try to stop me. I wasn't prepared for being framed for the murder and child abuse by Campbell."

"Campbell. I heard. How did he die?"

The road ahead was dark. "Not well." I pulled myself up in the seat and peered forward as the darkness dissipated where the road joined a well-lit road heading to Glasgow. "Ellie, I am sorry, if I knew you would be involved this would never have happened. I would have disappeared. I would never have put you in danger. But I had to stop the abuse of the children."

"I understand." She looked down at the phone. "Got my ticket. We're going to the sea. Okay, shall I book yours?"

"No. You'll receive a QR ticket on that email address. Once you do, switch off the mobile phone signal. There's cash in the other pocket of the rucksack. Take it, and don't use your cards. Go to the security gate at Grangemouth, show him your passport and the QR code, and say you are on the boat to Rotterdam. I'll give you my phone with the evidence, but do not switch it on. Not even Bluetooth. Then, when you reach Rotterdam, you know what to do. Next stop will be in twenty minutes."

"I got it, Hector, but what are you gonna do? You have to come with me."

The lights of the motorway appeared. "I have other plans."

The man in the balaclava stood in the hall, looking up at the screen. Sussex and Hastings edged forward. "All the flats have been checked, there's no sign of them. We're checking the attic and roof."

Gilfeather shook his head. "Ah, where was that copper-chopper when we needed it?"

Behind the man in the balaclava, another came down the folding ladder from the attic and stood in front of the camera. "The skylight was unlocked. That's the most likely exit."

Hastings turned to Sussex. "How the hell did they get down four storeys? And why didn't anyone stop them on the street?"

"Because you didn't want any coppers on the scene," said Gilfeather.

Hastings spun around, his face puce, but Gilfeather looked up at the old stones and Hastings turned back to the screen. "I asked how? What the hell is going on?"

The man didn't reply.

"Captain,' said Sussex, "your assessment of the situation, please."

"Teams were called in off the street, sir, so we couldn't cover a street exit around the block. There is scaffolding on the other side of the block that leads down to the street."

"Scaffolding?" said Sussex.

"Yeah," said Gilfeather, holding his phone to his ear, "and my men tell me of complaints of people running down the scaffolding right outside their windows three floors up. But this is Edinburgh. There's always scaffolding. The New Town is around two hundred and fifty years old, built with soft stone, it's a constant battle against the weather."

Both Hastings and Sussex stared at him.

Gilfeather shrugged. "So I'm told. Hope that helps. Anyway, do you want me to get a chopper in the air? I have three cars in the area I can bring in right now."

Sussex walked over to Gilfeather, his face tight. "I want access to all the CCTV and traffic cameras."

Gilfeather shook his head. "No. You can't get over a hundred cameras up on your wide screen here in the Secret Squirrel dungeon and think you'll spot them. What you need are the people who are trained to do this in Police Scotland Headquarters. Give them a description and last location, and they will monitor all the cameras, which is what they do every night."

Sussex's lips were shut so tight they turned nearly white.

"And," said Gilfeather, "get on to the Chief Constable for permission, and get the chopper in the air, so that they can see everyone on the streets in the New Town with infra-red. Even if they are hiding under bushes, they'll see them."

Sussex lifted his phone. "Get me the Chief Constable."

"Oh, and Mr Sussex, the police reports of the people on the scaffolding says two persons. One male, one female. This confirms your man Hector Lawless has risen from the dead, and it's not even Easter. Seems miracles do happen." Hastings' face was creased red with fury.

Gilfeather lifted his phone. "Description of targets. One IC male, Scottish, one IC female, Aussie accent, I'll get more later. Check the residents with the scaffolding for a better description. And I want a car with blues and twos outside the City Chambers to take me to HQ right now." He cut the call and turned to Sussex. "Fancy a ride?"

Chapter XXXXI

Collar up and head down, I turned my back on the ticket booth and weaved between the early evening revellers, all young and dressed in bright colours with little to protect them from the bitter wind that would blow. They hurried towards the trains leaving east for Edinburgh or west for Glasgow. The plastic-coated tickets were slippy in my hand and I'd said enough to at last make the grey-faced, recalcitrant wraith behind the glass look me in the eye.

Once outside, the wind picked up and I leaned forward into the welcoming darkness and crossed the road, looking left and right for police cars, or interested bystanders.

There was no one, just tired commuters heading home and irrepressible youth heading in the opposite direction. The urge to run was almost overwhelming but they could be watching. I turned down a side street. She was still there.

I opened the door to the car, and Ellie jumped, grabbing the phone in her lap. "Sorry," I said and dropped into the seat, pulling the door closed. It was warm out of the wind.

She looked at her watch. "I couldn't leave you."

I sighed. "That's very much appreciated, but next

time, you should go if I'm not back in five minutes. If they find me, they'll know you are close."

She looked down at the tickets. "What's that for?"

"Two single tickets for Glasgow then onto Oban on the west coast, and the road north through the West Highlands."

"From here? And where is here?"

"This is Falkirk. It's a town on the road and train line to Glasgow, or east back to Edinburgh. A halfway house, you might say. But that's not why we're here."

"The cargo port? Grangemouth?"

"Yes, it's ten minutes north of here in a taxi."

"Hector, you have to come with me. If it works for me, it'll work for you."

"No, there has to be more. I'll ensure they look elsewhere. That is crucial. I can't do that with you. I must pull them away."

"They'll kill you. Maybe we could…"

"Yes, my plan has risks, although you now understand I am more than capable of executing it with skill and determination." I started the engine.

"But it's dangerous, Hector…"

"I can do it."

"I can't leave you, please, I…"

It was the first time I heard her weaken and in that moment, I saw her pain and the blood that had carried it to her, where her own terror grew. I held her hand. It was cold.

"I can do it. And I will."

"Yes, yes, you can. I believe you but I want you to come with me, we have to…"

"There's no time for this, Ellie. Go. The ship is

leaving in twenty minutes. My leaving will be later. At the end of the road is a taxi rank – see it?"

Her voice was a whisper. "Yes." She tightened her grip on my hand.

"The station taxis are covered by CCTV, and they'll be looking for us at every station." From the rucksack I took out another burner phone. "Use the red phone and enter this number into the contacts."

"But…"

"Please, there isn't much time."

She entered the number into the phone, then dropped it on her lap and pulled my hand towards her. "Where are you going to go?"

It was difficult to smile, but I knew she would hear it in my voice. I lifted the tickets in my hand then flicked them behind my head onto the back seat. "Well, it won't be Oban. When you have pulled away from the quay and the ship is heading east, text me. No names, just say… Say, I'll see you on the beach."

"The beach?"

I squeezed her hand. "I'll tell you later."

She looked down. "You have such warm hands." She lifted her head. "The ticket for the ship. Won't they search for my passport number?"

"From a Romanian website? Quite unlikely, and you credit the Home Office with skills and intelligence they do not possess."

"Look, behind the taxis, there's a shop. I could buy a new burner phone. I can Bluetooth the evidence over and send it right now. Straight to my boss. Or CNN and the Guardian."

"No, Five Eyes. And you'll give away your position.

Then they will kill you and tell CNN it's a hoax. And you won't be around to disagree."

"Five who?"

"Australian Intelligence works with MI6, part of the Five Eyes of Intelligence. The US, UK, Canada, New Zealand and Australia. They're all linked. They're probably bugging your Australian office, your boss, your boss' family, etc. They will be arrested. Technology is a wonderful thing. Except when it isn't. They'll be set up and ready to go."

"Jesus. We have to go back to the Stone Age just to stay safe."

I reached around to the rucksack and pulled out a yellow burner phone. "This phone holds all the evidence. You only have to wait until Rotterdam tomorrow morning. You can email CNN from there and disappear. I'll be ensuring that they focus on the rail and roads in Scotland. I have no idea how helpful the Netherlands would be to MI5, but let's not put it to the test. Get ashore and lose yourself in the city. Take the local trains to Amsterdam or east to Germany. Send the evidence to CNN, the Guardian and German Süddeutsche Zeitung. Oh, and especially the Irish Times."

"How will I find you?"

"You have social media. When I am safe, I'll find you."

"But you don't…"

Her hands were no longer cold. My blood had warmed hers. I shivered with pleasure and pride. "Believe me, I'll find you."

"Hector, you have made too many enemies, even if I get this story out, you can never go online again."

I shrugged. "You say that as if it's a bad thing."

She laughed and closed her eyes, holding tight to my hand.

"When it's over, get to India. If you have a tail, lose it."

"I can lose anyone in Kolkata. I have friends there." She sat up in the seat.

"Do that, then west to Goa. By the sea. There's a beach that runs north of a fort that sticks out into the sea. I'll find you."

She turned towards me, her face only inches away and laughed again. "The beach." She squeezed my hand, then let go, and our skin peeled apart. "Yeah, I'll see you on the beach."

I tapped the watch on her wrist. "Go."

She grabbed the handle and pushed open the door. "Bring me a cold brew."

Then she was gone. Her head bowed against the wind, and only the dark shape of my overcoat as she ran for the taxi rank.

Whatever happened now, I had met her, and she would remember me.

In the windowless room the lights were low. Gilfeather stood before the bank of screens, five high and ten wide, stretched across the wall. Below them a line of police officers had three screens each on desks, their faces lit by the glow.

On each desk, one screen showed a video rolling slowly backwards in time, and beside each policeman, a printed copy of the passport photos of Eilidh Strathmartin and Hector Lawless.

Sussex pointed at the screens on the wall and the

motionless figure of a sergeant in the middle of the room. "What are they doing?"

Gilfeather pointed to the desks. "Trawling the cameras around the New Town from when they escaped."

"But the screens are above them. For God's sake we should be seeing where they are now, not where they have been!"

"Those screens on the wall are for your benefit and whoever pays for all this. Also lets the sergeant see what's going on." He jabbed a thumb behind him and Sussex turned to the darkened office and rows of desks where officers scanned three screens on each desk. "Every officer is allocated a bank of cameras in a certain location. While scanning through previous footage around the time of their escape, they are also looking at the live feed. If you know where they were, you get a better idea of where they are going."

"What if Lawless and his daughter see the cameras?"

"Then it's too late."

"How many cameras?"

"On the street? Around two hundred. Not counting the ANPR number plate recognition cameras that record the number plate of every car that passes."

Sussex rubbed his face. "We have to find him. He can't know how many cameras are out there."

Gilfeather stared straight ahead. "You know, after what he's done, I wouldn't underestimate Hector bloody Lawless."

Chapter XXXXII

Through the windscreen, the lights of Edinburgh shone in the distance under the winter-black evening sky. And above them all, Edinburgh Castle was lit in cardinal red, as if the pinnacle of power and control, looking down and casting its red cloak around its bairns to guard them against the night. But only a mile behind it, unseen in the darkness, unsullied by any lamps or lights, lay the highest point of Edinburgh.

Arthur's Seat, a colossal, tumultuous mass of rock, shattered and carved by ice, rose over eight hundred feet at the foot of the Royal Mile, the remains of an ancient volcano.

The lights of Edinburgh reflected off low, flitting clouds, but the void on the horizon, where no lights shone, rose up and blocked the clouds in the east, where the outline of the rock sat like a monstrous black dog.

Few trees grew on the thin soil. Those that did, huddled in a bog-filled valley that lay like a great wound on the hill's flank. In the past, this ground was outside the walls of Edinburgh and its law, and in the impenetrable gorse bush, high grass, rocky cliffs and crags lived the outlaws, looking down on the smoke of Edinburgh from their fires in the night.

But now, there was no one. Arthur's Seat was a

hellish place to be on a winter's night, stripped raw by the wind from every direction. From the summit, when the weather was clear, you could see out to the east towards Denmark and Norway, and the beaches on the fringes of the sea and far along the coast.

"Another beach," I muttered, and then louder, "warm and golden." Not lined by the frozen sand that cracked under your feet on the shores of the North Sea.

The lights on the road became brighter as I neared the junctions for the wide bypass around the town and the cameras looked down from the signs over the road. It was time to leave them behind until I needed them for my own purpose.

The phone on the seat beside me lit up.

See you on the beach!

I let out a cry and the car weaved from side to side as the power coursed through my body.

She was still an hour down the coast. The big boats take time to manoeuvre into deeper water and wait for the pilots to guide them into the sea channels. Once under the three bridges and past the headlands into the Firth of Forth, the boats enter the North Sea where they can gather pace. But I would see her go, in the darkness. From where the outlaws once lived, I would see her light shining on the dark sea.

The lights became brighter still and the lanes on the road separated for north and south around the town, with cameras tracking in all directions. I turned off down a narrow slip road that soon left the lights behind and led deeper into the countryside, through villages of unlit houses and past black fields. I would return on the old roads.

*

The blackness was above me now, and out the car windows the deep red rocks of Arthur's Seat rose unseen in darkness to the night sky. The dimly lit road around the base, sunken in a deep valley, led to the foot of the Royal Mile and the lights on the road between Holyrood Palace and the Scottish Parliament.

The cameras would soon find me, but the car was only required for another mile at most. The rucksack on the rear seats was covered by my jacket. They would see what they wanted to see.

I turned left, to the road that ran close between the Palace, the stone carved, graceful and softly lit, and the Scottish Parliament, all incongruous, ugly concrete angles without one graceful line to please the eye.

The road narrowed where it turned past the gates of the Palace, only a few feet away, and the dark entrance to the Parliament. To the side was an unlit police car.

The urge to stop and turn back rose but I was hemmed in on each side by the old and the new, each a power that showed no mercy.

Though if they were expecting me, then the police car would not be unlit, and it would not be the only one.

I slowed, to give the security cameras a good look, then drove on, past the turning into the Royal Mile that led straight to the Castle, then up a side road that skirted the Old Town. The road was well lit, but only one person walked towards me, the light from his phone illuminating his face, rather than his direction. As the road neared the valley that lay between the Old Town and the New, where Waverley Railway station lay, I pulled into the side, beside a dark, narrow lane that bordered the Royal Mile.

Lifting the rucksack from the back seat, I weaved

my way towards Waverley railway station, where every entrance would be covered by cameras watching passengers entering and leaving the station.

The Royal Mile would be hazardous, for both cameras and police. Keeping to the side, I hurried past the station and up the Fleshmarket Steps, then turned right and uphill again, into a narrow close that rose steeply to the cramped, stinking entrance to the Royal Mile and to the late Lord Campbell's chambers.

The reek of urine had dissipated, but would be back the next morning. I checked behind me and took out my office keys, unlocked the heavy wooden door and pulled it behind me. Once through the glass door, I hurried into the secretaries' office and opened a cabinet door.

The alarm panel flashed red and I entered the numbers. The light flashed green, then died.

All the rooms were in darkness. In my office I turned on my desk lamp. My papers had been cleared. I pulled open the drawers, but they had been emptied. It was of no concern.

At the end of the corridor, Campbell's door was locked. Leaning the rucksack against the door, I took from my pockets a wallet of picks that had arrived from Amazon and pulled out a bar with a flat hook on the end and a rod resembling a thin corkscrew. I had yet to put my skills to the test, but after studying the videos, the technique seemed remarkably straightforward. I inserted the first into the lock, applied light pressure, then inserted the second and slowly turned, moving it back each time the pin dropped into place.

After several attempts, I closed my eyes and could feel the pins dropping. The last pin dropped, the lock turned and the door opened.

I returned the picks to the wallet. It may not be last time they would be used, and I placed them on Campbell's desk with the two long spanners from the rucksack.

Sitting in his chair, I switched on his laptop and searched for the map of CCTV cameras in Edinburgh, then picked the link where the council website showed the location of those nearest to me. I tracked my finger over the screen. I would be caught by at least three cameras. That would suffice. The route to the start point was crucial, and I traced my finger back from the door of the office, then checked my watch. It was too long. The quickest way was out the office and across the Royal Mile to the lane on the other side of the street, but I could walk straight into the police. And the cameras to the left and right held too much risk. There was only one other way.

Back in the corridor, I opened a cupboard where my colleagues had left warm coats for walking the short distance to the High Court in their robes. I grabbed one plus a tweed hat. An old cane completed the disguise and I carried them to Campbell's desk.

I took a ring of keys from his drawer, then placed the spanners in my pocket. In the corner of his office was a door to a small anteroom he used to keep his robes, and on one wall was a low wooden door to the cellars. Using his keys and a torch, I opened the door and descended a dark, narrow stone staircase to the cellar and flicked on the light.

Around me lay plastic boxes of papers, airtight against the damp. I was now just below street level, and I pulled the boxes aside to reveal a metal-barred gate, locked with two padlocks. I tried the keys from the ring and opened the first, but none fitted the second. I took the long spanners from my pocket and jammed the claws into the u-bar of the padlock. I used one spanner to hold the padlock tight against the bars, and the other I pushed down hard to lever it up and break the lock.

It wouldn't budge. Moving my hands to the end of the spanners to apply more leverage, I held them in place then took a deep breath and pushed with all my weight.

The padlock cracked, but did not open. I tried again, and it burst apart in three pieces. It had looked easier when demonstrated on the internet. I opened the gate and climbed down once more. There was no light in the room. I shone the torch around the bare, dark walls. Dust and fragments of stone lay all around, and the wall was pitted with holes where equipment had once been secured.

Now I was in the town under the city, where the medieval residents, hemmed in by high walls to stop the English armies, had dug down under the buildings and streets for more rooms, then built up to create Europe's first skyscrapers. From the entrance to the Royal Mile there may be six or eight storeys above, but behind, from the bottom of the slope that led to the Nor' Loch and now the railway station, there might be up to fourteen. Many had collapsed over the years, or had been torn down when the rich on the lower floors had moved to the New Town, then rebuilt in a grander, Gothic style.

But the Old Town still remained, buried under the later buildings. Records showed that the last occupant had been a shoemaker, and below his workshop lay rooms where his workers and family had slept. In the corner was another iron gate. I tried the keys, searching for the oldest and found the right one, then shone the torch through. There was no ladder, only a five foot drop to the floor below. I lowered myself down and found the soft, earthen floor.

I could feel the damp in my throat, and the walls were blackened from candle smoke. In the corner lay a fireplace, and to the right, a low wooden door, with another padlock. This would be the last of Campbell's keys.

Once through the door, the corridor was low with rough-edged stone where it had been hacked through the rock. The reason was lost over time, but smuggling and a quick escape from the law or the Church were most likely. It was quicker to crawl, the torch between my teeth, until at last, I came to another iron grate. The ancient padlock was welded to the grate by rust. No picks would open it. I lay down on my chest and grabbed the grate with both hands and pushed. A shower of rotten mortar fell like dust in front of me. It moved a fraction.

My knees and head scraped the roof and sides as I turned around then lay on my back, took a deep breath, lifted my knees then booted the grate hard. It burst out and clattered to the ground below.

I lowered myself to the ground, then shone the torch around. There were boxes of papers and old furniture, and in the corner, another low door. This padlock was new, and I was through it in a moment with the spanners, and down stone steps to another room.

This room was empty and the walls were vaulted into close-fitting stone hung with dark stalactites. I had found it. The Vaults.

In front of me was another door, this time of thick

wood and six feet high. Behind it would be endless other vaults and narrow lanes that once held gas streetlamps and a thriving community, all under the grand streets of Edinburgh. When they built a bridge over the valleys between the low hills, either side of the Royal Mile, they built over the existing streets, with vaulted arches built on top, rising at each level, and passageways to a warren of underground workshops, often joining up the old medieval cellars. But after the damp and cold had penetrated through the stones, and the town had expanded to more pleasant buildings outside the old walls, the vaults had been abandoned to the poor and homeless. Now, some of the streets were lit again, to hold nightclubs and tours for the tourists.

I unlocked the door and listened, then looked out. From one side came the thumping of music, and from the other, the chatter of a restaurant. I pulled my head in and closed the door, left it unlocked, then turned back to the steps.

Once back in Campbell's office, I wiped the dust and damp earth from my clothes and pulled on the hat and coat, then hurried along the corridor and unlocked the door to the close. The heavy wooden door swung shut behind me. To the right was the Royal Mile and the sound of nightlife. I pulled down the hat, fixed on a face mask and headed towards the lights.

The Chief Constable stood in the middle of the room, slowly scanning the bank of screens on the wall. "We've checked all the taxis, including private hires. His car is in his garage. Every camera in Edinburgh is being searched. He can't just jump in a cab. If he does, we'll know."

Gilfeather stood behind him. "Community cars?"

The Chief jumped and spun around. "What?"

"Community cars. They're run by the council. Or used to be. They're parked around the town. You can hire them by the hour." Gilfeather walked over to a police officer behind a desk. "Get me the community cars around this address. I want their licence plates. And I want to know if Hector Lawless is registered to use them."

Sussex hurried over. "What cars?"

"Hire cars. Parked in special locations around the town. You just need an app to use them. Saves people buying a car. Very popular."

Voices came from behind and they turned to where a constable stood up from his desk. "Sir? We've found him!"

"Where?"

"Transport Police. He was seen at Falkirk railway station."

Sussex threw out a hand towards all the screens. "He's on a bloody train?" He followed Gilfeather over to the officer's desk.

"Mibees aye," said Gilfeather, "mibees naw."

"What?"

"Probably a ruse. They could take a taxi anywhere from there. Or a private hire, off the books."

"They can do that?"

"Cash works wonders. And we'd never know. Constable, is it just Lawless?"

"Yes, here's the photo from the ticket booth. The tickets say he's going to Oban."

"Bet he's not."

The constable pointed to the screen. "And this is him leaving the station."

"Thought so. Any sign of her?"

"No."

"Okay, they're in a car."

Sussex leaned over the desk. "Are the bridges are closed?"

"Not entirely. We've slowed down the north side to one lane, so they back up and we can check every car that passes."

"Close the bridge!"

"No, we keep it moving, so he's drawn into a trap. If we close it, he'll go elsewhere." Gilfeather turned to the room and gave the orders. "Listen up. Concentrate on the roads to and from Edinburgh and Glasgow. Get the number plate recognition cameras to build a database of all the cars on those numbers on those roads since the time of the alert." He turned to Sussex. "Once we know his licence plate, we'll know where he's been and where he's going."

"And what if he turns off?"

"Then we'll know what junction he turned off at and close the net."

"Sir, we have the number of two Community cars very close to his address. One is still there. We're tracking the other."

"Received," said another policeman, "running it against the database now." He stared at the screen for a moment as Gilfeather and Hastings hurried to his desk. "We have a match."

On the screen was a list of locations and times.

"He first left Edinburgh, heading west towards Glasgow, then he disappears from the cameras, so must have taken a back road. Then he turns up in Falkirk, and ten minutes later he's going east on the road and returning to Edinburgh."

"When?" Gilfeather leaned over the desk and peered at the list of figures on the screen.

"Twenty minutes ago. He kept on the motorways, cameras got him all the way, then he turned off before the bypass. Probably entered Edinburgh by the back roads. Swanston, Oxgangs, Morningside. Then the next is the security cameras outside Holyrood. Right outside the Scottish Parliament."

"Shit." Gilfeather stood up. "Who's got Holyrood ANPR?"

A police officer waved them over. "I have him."

Gilfeather weaved between the desks. "Play it."

On the screen, a small car drove past the gates of Holyrood Palace, then turned off. "Sir, he's heading for the back of Calton Graveyard. It goes all the way to Waverley Station."

"Got him."

"Find that car," shouted Sussex.

"Already on it," said the police officer.

"We'll find it," said Gilfeather, "but it'll be empty. He's not daft."

"And not that clever either," said Sussex. "We have him all the way."

Gilfeather didn't reply, then leaned into the screen. "So where is she? Eilidh Lawless."

The police officer pointed to the screen. "The car's too small for someone to hide in the boot, but there's something covered on the back seat. Big enough for a person."

Sussex's voice lowered to a growl. "Then we have them both."

Hastings said nothing, but grabbed his coat and hurried from the room.

Sussex leaned in towards Gilfeather. "Get every fucking copper you can down there. You know, use all your police skills. Remember, he is armed and dangerous. When you find him, leave this to the professionals. We'll take care of them."

Chapter XXXXIII

Keeping my head low, I stopped at the junction of the Royal Mile and the North and South Bridges. On the corner was a camera, around fifteen feet above the pavement. It moved slowly from side to side. There were sirens in the distance.

Not far now. I kept close behind people waiting to cross the road, then crossed over, keeping to the side, waiting for the turning on my left and another dark, narrow lane, then turned into the shadows. Past a line of plastic bins, I peeled off the coat, mask and hat then pulled a phone from my pocket, checking it was the one I had used to text Gilfeather from the roof opposite my flat.

Time to let the dog see the rabbit.

Striding up the hill, I glanced at the camera and stood against the wall with my face visible. From the corner of my eye, I watched the camera turn towards me, then stop.

Would it move? I tried to avoid looking at it, but it didn't move. Then I looked up and stared directly at the lenses. I couldn't make it any easier for them without waving. I strode forward once more, caught the camera moving with me, and turned at the corner towards Waverley Station, down the North Bridge.

I stopped and glanced over my shoulder and the camera was looking directly at me. I ran towards the station, then slid to a halt, turned and ran back under the camera, across the road and towards the South Bridge.

The next camera was across the road and I ducked into a doorway for a moment, then under the camera and down a side street. It followed me as I ran.

At the end of the street was the final camera. I was trapped.

"Sir! We have him." The policeman pointed to the bank of screens across the wall then hit a key.

The screens blended to one picture and showed a man with a phone by the side of the road, half hidden behind an alley. The man looked up at the camera, then ducked out of sight.

Sussex held up his phone. "It's Lawless. He's using a phone we tracked before."

On the screen, the man came into sight of the camera, head down, and crossed the road towards the station.

Gilfeather nodded to the Sergeant. "Alert Waverley, he's…"

"Wait!"

The man stopped and looked back, then directly at the camera, and began to run back along the South Bridge.

"Forget Waverley Station," said Sussex, "he's on to us. Where's he going?"

Another camera came up onto the screen, with the same figure running towards it. The man stopped when he spotted the camera, and the operator zoomed in on him just as he turned and ran down a side street.

"Police are in the area and on the way," said Gilfeather. "He's going nowhere."

Sussex lifted his hands into the air. "Come into the web, little fly."

The screen camera switched to another with the same man again running towards it. Then he stopped in the middle of the street and looked up. The camera focused in on the startled face of Hector Lawless.

"Well," said Gilfeather, "that was an entertaining first half. Have we forgotten something?"

A policeman raised a hand. "We've found the car. She's not in it. But it's near Waverley."

"He's a decoy," said Gilfeather, "he's leading us away from Waverley." He nodded to the Sergeant. "We have her photo on the phones of every copper in Waverley. Let's see how far she gets."

"Transport Police are ready to seal off the station. All camera operators have her photo and are looking right now."

Sussex smiled at Gilfeather and spoke into his phone. "Mr Hastings? We have them cornered."

I slid to a halt on the cobbles in the middle of the street. The camera at the end pointed straight at my face.

The choice was a night club, restaurant or a ghost tour. They all had access. The ghost tour was nearest and I opened the door into a room with a counter like an old bank. A young woman dressed as a Plague Doctor removed her leather face mask and smiled. "Can I help you?"

"The tour, have I missed it?"

"Started five mins ago, I'm afraid."

"Damn it. Can I join them? It's my last night in

Edinburgh. I was so looking forward to it. Happy to pay double, and a decent tip if I can run and catch them up."
I pulled cash from my pocket and pushed it towards her.

"Well, er, through that door, straight down the steps, follow the line of blood splashed on the floor and make for the screaming. You'll find them."

"Thanks!" I rushed through the doors marked with a red cross and PLAGUE! KEEP OUT.

On the floor were blood splashes and I followed them to the sound of voices, past iron-barred rooms with dummies of plague patients, through a red-painted door and then down again until the stone on the wall became rough and damp.

The voices were closer and I slowed, edging around the corner. In one direction, I saw a gaggle of people heading deeper into the vaults, descending steep steps. I followed them to the top of the steps where they turned a corner at the bottom and out of sight. Facing the bottom of the steps lay an iron gate, padlocked shut against a dark passageway into the rock.

Not all of the vaults were safe for tourists. Once down the stairs, I peeked around the corner, but the voices had faded. I pulled out the two spanners, levered one against the other under the shackle and burst the padlock at the first attempt, the two pieces flying past me. Adrenalin was my friend. I grabbed the pieces of the padlock then kicked open the iron gate and closed it behind me, pushing the padlock together through the holes in the gate. It held then dropped off, and I jammed it together hard and rested it on the grate.

It wouldn't stop anyone kicking the gate, but it was better than nothing. It looked locked and might buy me a few seconds.

Hurrying into the darkness, I pulled out the phone and lit the torch app. The signal was dead. They couldn't track me. I kept going, the dark and dampness almost palpable until I came to a junction. The tunnels turned left and right. I ducked into one side, and tried to think.

I had entered the tour office pointing east, then turned north through the doors, then down steps, east, then north, then east though the grate to this junction. I turned around and headed west. At the end was another locked grate, oddly fitted with a yale lock rather than a padlock. I placed the phone on the wall where an oil lamp would once sit, and took out my lock picks. My hands shook, but I closed my eyes, and slipped in the picks, varying the pressure, and turned the corkscrew gently until I felt the pins drop one after the other. The lock popped open.

I grabbed the phone then locked the grate behind me, trying to picture the distance above me along the Royal Mile.

The darkness softened and I could hear music. Was it the same as before? The tunnel widened into a covered street with dark vaults either side of me. Some were blocked off with doors and I moved from side to side, pushing at the doors until one opened.

The rush of adrenalin nearly threw me forward into the stone as I ran inside, felt for the snib and locked the door behind me.

I stood and lifted the torch to the steps up towards the cellars and the low tunnel under the road.

Now Edinburgh was protecting me, here in the darkness, as I scurried around under her filthy petticoats.

*

The policeman waved the car through and Gilfeather and Sussex got out. Several cars lined the streets, blue lights flashing up and across the old stone.

A sergeant ran over. "He's in the Vaults. Went down with the tourists. We've got all the exits covered."

"Really?" said Gilfeather. "All of them?"

"All the known exits. We'll flush him out."

Sussex nodded to three men in black wearing police baseball caps over black balaclavas then walked over to Gilfeather.

"Mr Sussex," said Gilfeather, "they are not police. Tell them to remove those hats."

"Inspector Gilfeather, just mere detail. Anyway, they're carrying automatic weapons, so best for all if everyone thinks we're on the same side. When we find him, we'll send my men in."

"And, sir," said the sergeant, "we've men stationed on all the streets above. He's got nowhere to run. As soon as he comes out, his phone will give him away."

Sussex looked at the sergeant then at Gilfeather. "What do you mean, all the known exits ?"

Gilfeather sighed. "Mr Sussex, you're standing above thousands of years of human occupation. The Vaults are mostly mapped, but underground Edinburgh remains, shall we say, something of a mystery. Cellars over cellars, streets over streets, all dug down into the rock."

"Sergeant, tell your Chief Constable I want all his men to scour this place and…"

"Look, you're standing on a bridge you can't see," said Gilfeather. "Edinburgh is built on hills, just like Rome. But here, they're covered over. At the bottom are the original houses, cellars and streets, then above them layers of brick vaults that have alleyways where some are wide enough for a horse and cart. They had it all – shops, pubs, Hellfire clubs, distilleries and factories, until it went to shit and the poor moved in. All those levels, just under your feet. Trapped he might be, but finding him will be a different matter."

The Chief Constable strode towards them. "Well done, Gilfeather. Inspector Broadfoot will take over from here. Your shift is over, and I'll be paying enough overtime tonight already. Also, report to the Divisional Office in Inverness first thing tomorrow, I need you…"

"The Highlands?"

"Yes, the Press are gathering like locusts and they'll only find one policeman close to the case to talk to, and that's me. "

Gilfeather stood open-mouthed. "Chief, you can't…"

"Yes, I can. I'll send for you when things have quietened down. Ah, Inspector Broadfoot." A tall man walked over to the Chief Constable. "Has Mr Sussex briefed you?"

The man stared at Gilfeather. "He has."

"Who the hell…? I've never heard of you, where the…?"

Broadfoot lifted his chin into the air. "I'm the new liaison with Mr Sussex. Been nice to meet you. Bye."

"Piss off." Gilfeather turned to the Chief Constable. "This is an assassination not an arrest. You can't…"

"Go home," said the Chief Constable. "Inspector Broadfoot is trained in domestic terrorist threats and CQB. Close Quarter Battle. And you are not. I want a full report tomorrow, so leave tonight. And I need you away from the press. We have Lawless trapped so you're surplus to requirements. We'll find him, or as soon as his phone signal emerges, we'll spot him."

"You think this is going well? Are you not even slightly concerned that Lawless or his daughter are not in custody?"

Broadfoot smirked. "Looks like I'll have to accelerate progress."

"Chief, Hector Lawless has been one step ahead the entire…"

"Gilfeather! Walk away. I'll speak to you in the morning. Get some sleep. You found him, so well done, this is all good on your record."

"Oh, this is…"

At the end of the street in an unmarked car, the face of Mungo Hastings was staring out at him. The Chief turned away.

Broadfoot walked over. "I'll have to clean up your shite. I'll remember that. All that effort and you couldn't win the wee silver 'Top Policeman' cup to put on your mantelpiece. Shame. My wee lamb. Now, piss off, and I'll go and find Hector Lawless."

"Find him? You couldn't find your arse with a map and a mirror. You know why you got the job? Cos they want a good little doggy who will turn tricks for them. Bet you lay on your back to get your tummy tickled at the end, eh? I know coppers like you. You'll end up like the Chief. Because there is not an arse in this world that you would not kiss. Now, go and be a good doggy. And if you win the wee silver cup, you can ram it up your rusty sheriff's badge."

Broadfoot made to grab Gilfeather when the Chief Constable pushed his way between them. "Gilfeather! Don't fuck up your career. Your shift is over and sometimes you just have to walk away." He turned his back. "Inspector Broadfoot, come with me, I'll brief you on the maps."

"Walk away?" Gilfeather watched them move towards the entrance to the Ghost Tour. Outside, in the back of a van sat the Plague Doctor. She was wearing her mask and waving at policemen and the crowd behind the tape taking photos. "Maps? Good fucking luck with that."

Fairbairn stood at his side. "Need a lift home, Inspector?" she said.

Gilfeather said nothing.

"Inspector," she whispered, "every copper here is giving the Chief the side-eye. You see, the Chief is from Aberdeen."

Gilfeather turned to her. "Really? I though he was born in Inverbellend."

"He's never had a beat here. He thinks that below our feet there's a few dingy cellars jazzed up to frighten the tourists. So, whatever happens, we're about to witness one total clusterbourach. With fireworks and a marching fucking pipe band. The further away from this you are, the better."

Gilfeather said nothing.

"I heard about the smoke bomb. And what he said. To be fair, he's brought it on himself."

Gilfeather closed his eyes for a moment, then nodded. "Aye. That's true. Not fair, but true. If he'd done that to one of my coppers I'd send those Army bastards in." He turned towards her. "Fuck this. Fuck everything."

"You needing a lift?"

"Nah. I think I'll walk home."

"Right, sir. Stay out of trouble, eh?" She placed a hand on his arm.

"Aye." He nodded to her and turned back to the Royal Mile then stopped. "He turned his phone on. Why did he do that?"

Fairbairn shrugged. "Draw them away from the station? Or wherever his daughter has gone?"

"Maybe. And why Falkirk? He could have chosen any other station on the line to Glasgow. Why go that far? All that way?"

"If his plan was to feint using the train, it's near enough and far enough away."

"Yeah. But why come back? He could have been past Grangemouth then over the river at Kincardine in five minutes, then he'd be lost in all the wee roads to the Highlands. Why the hell would he come back here?"

"Well, we'll know when he's in the nick. If he talks."

"If they let him talk."

Fairbairn gave him a look. "Eh?"

"Never mind." He looked down at his phone.

"Switch off, Boss. We're coppers. It's never good news." Fairbairn turned away. "I think I'll go over and close the doors of that van before that wee Plague Doctor wins the internet."

"Aye."

He turned back to the Royal Mile, ducking under the blue police tape and joined the tourists being ushered away from the scene, then down the hill past a hotel and bars, towards Easter Road and home.

He stopped at a junction waiting for the lights, and turned to the pub on the corner. The World's End. That marked the border of old Edinburgh and where the high stone walls against the English had forced the builders down into the ground and into the skies to stay within the protection of the city. And outwith, he thought, lay the outlaws. Not anymore.

A pint would help him sleep. Maybe.

Once inside, the crowded warmth made the blood flush to his face and he ordered his beer, then stood to the side with the cool, sweet beer in his hand.

In the window outside, blue lights flashed and policemen hurried past. They might empty the pub, they might not. They would be better going down in the cellars. Old pubs had their secrets and their ghosts. Maybe they would. This pub had an entry to the Vaults, just like most cellars around him.

He turned away from the window, and there on the wall was an array of prints to please the tourists. Stags, mountains and kilted rebels, and an old map of Scotland, before the existence of bridges, wide roads and railways. Edinburgh was there, and Glasgow. And so was Falkirk, on the line of one of the old Roman walls that stretched across the country to keep out the Caledonians and Picts.

He traced the line to where it ended on the banks of the Forth. The scattered Roman rocks near the town where he had been born, the mining village of low houses in the shadow of the mill, close to where the huge coaling ships had berthed, then down the river to Edinburgh, marked by the Castle, the Palace and then Arthur's Seat, standing high above them all.

His phone buzzed. He pulled it out, but the screen was blank. He remembered his personal phone in his jacket.

On the screen was a friend request.

Chapter XXXXIV

The sirens and blue lights cut through the night far below me, but I didn't turn to look. That life had gone. I had left them behind at the foot of the hill. The Parliament and the Palace, the State and the stink, and had climbed towards where the outlaws once lived. By the time they had searched every possible close, vault or cellar, I would be over the hills to the south, and be ten miles away on the old drover roads to the Borders, then on to Northumbria and England.

Perhaps they would assume I had slipped away and was now hiding somewhere in the dark closes and arches of the Old Town, and the search would continue until the morning. And in the morning, my name would not be on the lips of murderers for the State, but on newsreaders and websites. The rucksack no longer felt heavy as I climbed, and I picked up the pace through the darkness and out of the valley, up the steep slope, keeping my eye on the narrow path as I climbed, until the stars over the Pentland Hills appeared to the south.

A flat rock jutted out to my left, sheltered by the peak of Arthur's Seat fifty feet above me. I let the rucksack drop then turned to the North and saw the wide darkness of the Firth of Forth and out to the North Sea.

And in the distance, hemmed in by nothing other than the comforting darkness, the lights of a container ship sparkled in the water.

In front, the arc lights of a small pilot boat turned and sped back towards Grangemouth, and the ship was free to sail into the North Sea.

At first, I didn't hear the squawk of the radio because of the wind, but then the wind changed. A head appeared, stamping his feet into the thin earth and climbed towards me until he reached the flat rock, and pausing for a breath, he sat down and looked out over the lights of Edinburgh.

The wind dropped and flakes of snow drifted past my face.

"Good evening, Mr Lawless."

"Good evening, Inspector Gilfeather."

He took a few deep breaths then pulled the police radio from his jacket. "It's all going on down there, I can tell you."

I didn't reply.

"And I forgot what a bastard climb this is, never mind in the dark."

The container ship was lit from bow to stern and tendrils of mist danced over her lights. My voice seemed to ache in my chest. "I sometimes came here as a young man in the summer, to watch the sea at night when it was never really dark, and wait the short hours for the sun to rise again. I was home before my parents awoke. I saw the milk trains coming into Waverley."

Gilfeather pulled up his collar as the snow blew around him. "It was the harbour for me. No great hills around my village, just big ships, the last of the old coalers sailing east down the river, under the old rail bridge, past Edinburgh and out to the sea." Gilfeather jabbed a finger out to the north then shoved his hands in his pockets. "Like that container ship. When the mines were shut down and the old coalers never returned, the cargo ships took their place. They're bigger than the coalers. They had to dredge the harbour."

The old coal fields spanned out from Arthur's Seat, down the coast in all directions, under the river and out to the sea floor for miles. I watched the ship turn south on a course for Rotterdam.

Gilfeather hunched his shoulders against the wind. "It was Falkirk that reminded me. I grew up in a wee mining village not far away from there, but I'd walk the mile to Grangemouth docks, just to see the ships and the coalers, when we dug coal, that is. My father was a miner. The work of his hands and his mates filled the ships. He sometimes said if he hadn't met my mum, he'd have sailed away on the boats. As a bairn, I always thought I could just jump on the boat and leave. Just be away."

My eyes streamed as the wind changed direction. "Yes, I had that dream too."

"That's when the penny dropped. You could have gone to any other station on the line to Glasgow, yet you chose Falkirk. And rather than drive over the Kincardine Bridge and be away up the roads to the Highlands, you turned back. And I asked myself, why?"

I couldn't feel the snow landing on my hands. "Reasons, Inspector."

"Aye, reasons. Then you turn up on your own. And you switch on your phone. Then all hell breaks loose."

I let the wind blow over my eyes, and I was crying.

"The Vaults, though. That was quite a move. They could be looking for days down there. But it was Grangemouth, you see. The ships, that I once dreamed would take me away. And if you had to find the highest, darkest place in Edinburgh to watch the ships, you'd come here."

My voice was half drowned in the wind. "They'll kill her. Then they will kill me. But I do not care if…"

"I'm not here for your protection. Or hers. I'm a policeman. I'm here for a career-defining moment, so they said. Well, that moment's been going on for quite a while, so time to bring it to an end." Gilfeather got to his feet and looked out over the town, the sound of the sirens faint then louder as the wind changed. "Your text message. I thought what you said about the evidence was just another ruse. Another feint. Then tonight, I get a new internet friend. No idea who it could be, but they sent me some very disturbing things."

The lights of the ship were diffused in the mist. There had to come a point when I would die for my sins, take my penance. *When she is safe, then they can kill me.*

"Inspector, please, let her leave. I will stay. I'll admit to the murder of…"

"I'm not interested in confessions. I've seen what I need to see. Even though it'll haunt me the rest of my days. But I learned an important lesson tonight."

"I understand. And so evil wins."

"Not tonight. Otherwise I wouldn't be doing my job. Tomorrow, though. Oh, that's going to be some day."

Gilfeather stood in front of me, the lights of the ship over his shoulder.

"Sometimes, Hector, despite the tears, the shit and blood flying in all directions, you just have to walk away."

He pointed to the hills behind me. "Walk away."

He headed down the hill.

Acknowledgements

With thanks to editors extraordinaire, Georgie McNamara and Izzy Toner for making all the difference, Clare C. and writer buddies Neil B. and Tom W. for the craic.

Previous titles by Mark Leggatt

The Connor Montrose series

Names of the Dead
The London Cage
The Silk Road